THE PERFECT DEBUTANTE

THE PERFECT REGENCY SERIES, BOOK 1

ANNABELLE ANDERS

ANNABELLE
ANDERS

The Perfect Debutante

Annabelle Anders

Copyright © 2019, 2020 Annabelle Anders

❀ Created with Vellum

ACKNOWLEDGMENTS

A special thank you to those who've shared their experiences with me so that I could better understand the phenomenon of cutting. You know who you are.

To Tracy Seybold, Kay Springsteen and Mary Ellen Blackwood for helping me bring this book to life. To Rebecca Jenshak, for pushing me each day.

To all my readers for keeping me motivated with their encouragement.

And to my husband Russ, for the unwavering support you've given me throughout the years.

AN IMPORTANT NOTE FROM THE AUTHOR

I feel it my responsibility to issue a trigger warning for this story.

I never wanted to know so much about the very alarming practice known as cutting. When you discover somebody near and dear to you, however, suffering from an addiction, you absolutely must learn as much about it as possible.

It is often misunderstood, mimicked, and criticized, but I've learned that for those who are truly compelled into self-harm, they cannot control it any more than an alcoholic or overeater.

Even more alarming, the more a cutter dwells on it, the greater the compulsion.

For that reason, I find it necessary to recommend that anyone with cutting compulsions NOT read THE PERFECT DEBUTANTE.

I've done my best to write an accurate depiction of a young woman who struggles with cutting and the most realistic means she has to overcome it. Although cutting has been referred to by different names throughout history, the compulsion is nothing new.

I am not a psychologist, nor an expert in any way. THE

PERFECT DEBUTANTE has been written based solely upon my own personally conducted interviews, research, and experience.

I hope you all are edified and entertained by this work of fiction, which is inspired by a real issue.

CHAPTER ONE

THE DARKNESS

*M*iss Louella Rose Redfield huddled on the floor on the far side of the large canopied bed taking up most of her chamber. If her mother took it upon herself to peek in, she would believe the room to be empty and leave.

Which was exactly what Louella wanted—what she needed.

It wasn't as though she were a child! She was a lady now. She had every right to be left alone. She glanced toward the closed door.

Mama would not come now anyhow. Mama and Papa knew she was not at all pleased with them. Not after Papa had told her his decision and given her no choice but to consent to the betrothal he'd arranged for her with their neighbor's son.

And they expected her to be grateful! Of all things!

Anger. Frustration. Disappointment. The hopelessness of this situation made her want to be invisible. Black crept into the edges of her vision.

How could her parents so easily dismiss her older sister Olivia? They couldn't realize the cruelty of their actions. For this slight seemed worse than all the others. To betroth the younger daughter first.

Her.

Cowering behind the bed, Louella opened the bottom drawer of the nightstand and reverently withdrew the sewing basket.

The tattered straw and old cloth lining provided a modicum of comfort, in and of itself.

Her father's words replayed in her head. "You are the beauty of this family, Louella. A perfect English Rose. This is your duty. And your mother assures me the marquess is quite handsome. You'll be a duchess someday, gel. Now stop your blathering." He'd meant to placate her.

A beauty! Perfect?

Louella knew what they saw.

A young girl with an unblemished complexion, shining chestnut hair, and eyes the color of the sky, framed with thick lashes.

But that was only her shell.

She was not perfect; she was not beautiful.

Dizziness gripped her.

Closing her eyes, Louella inhaled deeply before opening them again and unraveling the ribbon from around her wrist. She'd tied the silk loosely, but it managed to leave an imprint on the tender flesh, nonetheless.

She opened the basket and withdrew what she sought. Eyeing it critically, she frowned. The needle was becoming dull from too much use.

She could not access her abdomen during the daytime. Her stays prevented that.

Examining her arm, she located an unscarred section. With practiced precision, she compelled the needle downward. As the sharp point drew a short crimson line, she felt nothing.

She pressed harder the second time, and a thicker line of blood oozed onto her pale, almost translucent skin. A sting. And tingling. *Ah, yes. I'm real.*

And the berating voices swirling in her mind began to subside.

Blood is real.

The blood is mine.

I am real.

She drew another line, this one longer and just the tiniest bit deeper than the first two. The needle stung. It hurt even.

Her racing heart slowed.

It would be okay. Olivia would understand.

She could now feel the floor beneath her and the frame of the bed digging into her back.

The last cut was shallow, barely a scratch, really.

Her vision cleared.

As she watched blood flow and begin to congeal, her breathing slowed as her muscles relaxed. Sleep called to her, the sensation of melting into the floor overcoming all her senses. Still caressing the needle between her fingers, she dropped her hand to the carpet and tilted her head back, resting it on the side of the bed.

She could do this. She didn't want to, but she could. Papa would insist.

After what may have been a few seconds, or several moments, Louella roused herself from the blessed lethargy enough to clean the needle and replace it in the sewing basket.

She then washed her wrist in the wash basin, dried it, rewrapped the silk ribbon, and tied it snugly.

Using her teeth, she managed a fairly decent bow.

Louella had done this before.

The devil didn't dwell inside her.

It was just... her.

* * *

"You wish me to marry *little Louella Rose?*"

Captain Cameron Samuel Benjamin Denning, Marquess of Stanton, barely remembered the girl.

She'd been a child when he left, gallivanting about her father's estate and often his father's property as well.

He vaguely remembered the older sister... blonde, she'd been on the verge of womanhood, sweet and pretty. But he'd been an arrogant Devil at the time. All he'd noticed was that the gel had been cockeyed.

And the younger girl? Louella Rose? She had been all skin and bones, brilliant blue eyes too large for her face, dirt on her dresses, and ah, yes, stringy brown hair. She would have been most unmemorable but for her flashing eyes and violent temper. She'd lobbed an apple at his head on one occasion.

He scratched his chin. If memory served him correctly, he'd done something to provoke the attack. He'd been an ass that summer. Hating his father. Hating his father's new family. Hating pretty much everybody, including himself.

"She's not a child anymore," his father said without glancing up from the papers on his desk.

What had the sister's name been? Olive? No, Olivia, Miss Olivia Redfield, oldest daughter of the Viscount Hallewell. She'd been closer to him in age.

"Truth be told," his stepmother, the duchess, piped in, "Miss Louella Rose is one of the comeliest debutantes in all of England."

Cameron wasn't certain he could believe that. The hoyden had been something of a tomboy, trespassing with her sister almost daily. They'd met with better luck fishing on the ducal lands than their own.

And Cameron had not treated them kindly. Ah, yes, he'd teased the older girl mercilessly for her eye. He winced at the memory.

At the time, he'd barely reached his majority; he'd been an irresponsible youth, willing to do anything to escape his father and all of his ducal expectations.

"What of the older daughter?" Cameron stared out the window, contemplating his past wrongs.

Again, his stepmother supplied the answer. "Something of a spinster. Doesn't move in Society, as I understand. Hallewell keeps her well under wraps. I doubt they've brought her with them to London for the Season. If I were to take a guess, I'd say she's probably simple."

His father grunted.

Cameron knew neither of the girls were what attracted his father to such an alliance. The Hallewell estate sat just south of Ashton Acres. Nestled in the low lands, unkempt and overrun with brush, it was aptly named Thistle Park.

But just inside of its borders sat the true prize.

An abandoned mine.

Abandoned, and branded as cursed by the current viscount's father following a disastrous cave-in decades ago. But that wasn't the end of it. No, the damn thing was rumored to be loaded with gold. A few of the men who'd managed to survive the collapse, but not their injuries, had spoken of a thick vein discovered just before the tragedy. Ancient tales warned that the cave-in had occurred because the treasure had been exposed.

Locals scoffed at the notion of the mine having anything of value. Never, in the history of the area, the entire region, really, had any precious metals been mined profitably.

Viscount Hallewell, like his father before him, believed the mine to be cursed. He'd adamantly refused to reopen it. Until now, apparently.

With pockets to let, and a comely daughter at that... Cameron guessed that Crawford, his own father, had finally discovered the bargaining chip to change Hallewell's mind.

His son.

And, fiend seize it, upon departing a decade ago, Cameron had promised to marry upon his return. He'd not hated his birthright; he'd simply needed to sow his oats. Such a stupid promise to have made.

"Isn't there a boy in the family as well?" Surely, the son would have something to say about all of this. It was his inheritance, after all.

"Not anymore. Died shortly after your departure." Cameron's father had no sympathy when it came to others' misfortunes.

Raising his brows, Cam glanced toward the duchess. She would know more about the family.

"William, I believe they called him, couldn't have been older than six or seven at the time," she replied helpfully. "His mother, the viscountess, was inconsolable for months. But the boy was always sickly. Nearly drowned but then took ill. I imagine he'd have died of some other malady if not for the accident."

Cam rubbed his eyes with the heels of his hands. All of this seemed rather sudden, and yet, he'd known before returning that his father would expect him to marry and set up a nursery. And Cam had promised he'd do just that.

Despite the enmity he'd forever carry for the man purported to have sired him, Cam intended to keep his promise. Because, as backward as it seemed, the one thing he'd carried with him all those years serving his country had been the burden of guilt.

He'd known his stepmother and stepsisters worried endlessly about him.

Well, not him, per se. The male son. The heir.

For the Duke of Crawford had failed to produce a spare with his second wife. She'd given birth to three girls with her first husband but failed to conceive with Crawford.

Cameron was destined to forever be the older brother to three silly stepsisters.

His conscience had berated him to do his best to avoid being killed. He'd not wished to make their circumstances precarious.

But even more compelling had been the desire to thwart the duke by living.

Cameron shook his head, dismissing the passing thought.

Hell.

And as he *had* lived, and he *had* returned, he would marry the Redfield girl.

He could only hope the girl and her sister had little memory of him and his behavior.

Upon reaching his majority, Cam had been filled with angst. He'd returned from school to discover his father remarried. The new duchess had brought with her three small daughters.

Cam had countered by drinking, carousing, swiving whatever he was offered, and then ultimately threatening to enlist himself into the British Army.

Which would have been unheard of.

An unmitigated embarrassment to the duke.

Crawford had taken the threat literally, and to avoid the disgrace, he'd negotiated a bargain with him. With the understanding that when Cam reached the age of thirty, he would return home and marry the bride of his father's choosing, the Duke of Crawford had purchased Cam an officer's commission in the British Navy,

Thirty had seemed a lifetime away.

Cam brushed a hand through his hair.

Damn his twenty-one-year-old self.

"I'm to visit the youngest daughter tomorrow?" he asked. "And she is agreeable? How old is she now?"

He certainly wouldn't force the poor girl to marry him if

she was unwilling. He would make his offer, formally, dispassionately, but... pleasantly. He would not insist, however, and by God, he wouldn't beg.

"She's ten and nine. A most suitable age. We'll visit their townhouse together. For tea," his stepmother responded.

"Of course, she's agreeable. Damned fool girl she'd be if she wasn't," Crawford barked.

The girl must be a social climber then.

Hell, perhaps she'd forgotten him completely!

"Tomorrow, then? At tea." Speaking the words, he could almost hear the chains winding around his ankle.

"She's a lovely girl." The duchess patted the duke on the shoulder. "We'll allow the two of you a few moments alone, so that you can be certain you'll get on well together."

Well, then.

Damn.

"Better yet, you may renew your acquaintance this afternoon at the Snodgrass Garden Party. I wouldn't think the Redfields would miss it."

Perhaps that would make tomorrow easier. Perhaps he could charm her into forgetting his actions before he'd gone off to war. His stupid and churlish behavior.

Might make for a less awkward proposal, anyhow.

CHAPTER TWO

FOR HER MOTHER'S SAKE

*L*ouella's one and only London Season would be cut short. Her papa had informed her that as soon as her engagement was set, they'd return to Thistle Park. Why waste funds after she had a betrothal in place?

The duke and his family would return as well, according to her father. An expedited ceremony could have the mine reopened by early summer.

Louella bristled as her mother led her across the vast lawn behind Snodgrass Manor.

"Over there." Her mother spoke in hushed tones, guiding Louella with sudden purpose. "That's the Earl of Carlisle. Mrs. Pendleton told me he just inherited his title. He was a vicar or curate or something before. I don't imagine he's set his cap for anyone yet. You ought to be kind to him. In case this deal your father's bartered with Crawford falls through."

I'm a deal now.

Wonderful.

Inhaling deeply, she smiled for her mother's sake. And for the fact that the gentleman standing before her was considerably handsome. Blond hair and blue eyes, he possessed the countenance of an angel.

The poor man didn't stand a chance with Lady Hallewell in close pursuit. Louella kept her gaze down at first, embarrassed at her mother's unfettered enthusiasm.

"Such an honor to meet you, my lord! This is my daughter, Miss Louella Rose. Louella dear, make your curtsey to the earl."

"My lord." She bent her leg and dipped daintily. She could have done it in her sleep, she'd practiced so much... and now, she'd miss the remainder of the Season.

"My pleasure, ladies." When Lord Carlisle bowed a lock of golden hair fell across his face. He barely noticed, however, his gaze searching the lawn for escape.

"Such a beautiful day." Her mother's bosom bounced as she tilted her head back to look up at the sky. "Perfect day for a boat ride, don't you think, Louella dear?"

Louella would rather avoid the water. Glancing at the ribbons on her wrist, she plucked at them almost without thinking. "Oh, yes, Mother. The conditions are divine."

Given a choice, she'd provide the earl with an easy escape. But her mother...

Louella could never disappoint her mother.

Lord Carlisle stared across the water and then back at her before clearing his throat. "Miss Redfield." He bowed. "I'd be honored if you would allow me to row you around the pond."

Don't think of what lies beneath the water, how the mud sucks at your feet... Don't remember.

Louella tilted her lips up and forced a smile to her eyes. When he offered his arm, she took hold of it seamlessly. "Don't you simply love London, my lord?"

If she didn't dwell on the murky surface of the lake or the unknown depths in the center, she would be just fine. She needed to think about something else, that was all.

"Papa brought us to London an entire week early so that I

could shop. He insists I dress in the finest England has to offer. You wouldn't believe the dresses I've ordered. Do you like this one?" She released him and halted her steps in order to skim her hands over her skirt and twirl around. Her mother had chosen this gown. Louella knew that it looked the same as every other dress worn by her counterparts that afternoon.

She was babbling but couldn't seem to stop herself.

"It's lo—"

"Because Mother declared the pink perfect but I'm not as certain."

Lord Carlisle nodded and smiled just as something across the lawn caught his attention. A flash of golden yellow, daring for a lady to wear in the afternoon. The woman wearing the gown had not only caught his attention, but she'd also seemingly trapped it.

Miss Rhododendron Mossant.

Tall, elegant, and the last woman in the world Louella ought to be consorting with. Her mother had warned her earlier in the day to steer well clear of the lady.

Nervousness only increased her babbling.

"Miss Mossant has such lovely coloring. I don't believe I could wear anything so bright." Nor would her mother allow it. "But it doesn't look quite so horrible on her. Mother says I'm not to converse with her though. She didn't tell me why. She only mentioned that Miss Mossant was tainted. I'm surprised Lady Snodgrass received her today." She attempted to divert his attention. Mama would have apoplexy if Louella did anything to jeopardize tomorrow's expected offer. "Do *you* know what she's done to kick up so much scandal?"

In response, Lord Carlisle stared at her in disapproval. As though she'd made a grave mistake in asking him to gossip. And of course, yes, to attempt to gossip with *this* vicar was not the thing. Not the thing at all.

"I'm certain your mother is mistaken," he admonished her.

He didn't hesitate or falter as he continued to steer them toward the scandalous lady. Shamed into silence but also a trifle panicked, Louella attempted to swerve him toward the lake once again.

At the same time, she couldn't help being fascinated. What had Miss Mossant done?

"My lord, really, Mother will be most *vexed* if she sees me in her company." Despite her pleas, he did not veer off course. No turning back now.

"Miss Mossant." The earl's attention focused intently upon the lovely young woman.

He released Louella long enough to bow.

"My lord." Grasping the skirt of her brilliant gown in one hand, the other lady curtsied hesitantly.

"Are you acquainted with Miss Louella Redfield? She was just now making known to me her appreciation of your dress."

Guilt rippled through Louella. "Um, yes, Miss Mossant. No one else would ever dare appear in something so bold." She'd meant it to be a compliment, but it didn't come out sounding like one. Most of her attention was focused on hoping to go unseen.

"Why thank you, Miss Redfield, Mr. White. I've grown ever so bored with wearing bland pastels."

Louella winced at Miss Mossant's gentle jibe. Except she deserved it.

The new earl seemed oblivious. "Miss Mossant, you must join Miss Redfield and me for a row around the lake." Without giving either of them a chance to object, in one smooth motion, he was leading both her and Miss Mossant toward the jetty.

Louella lowered her face, hoping no one took notice. Lord Carlisle did his best to include both ladies in conversation, and Miss Mossant's manners were quite genteel.

The infamous woman didn't fawn and flirt with the earl; rather the opposite, in fact. And although the dress she wore was a bold color, the style was not overtly suggestive in any way.

Contrary to everything she'd been taught, a part of Louella envied the young woman. The confidence she portrayed with the determined jut of her chin and the defiant look in her eyes were indeed admirable.

Fumbling at one of the ribbons wound around her wrist, Louella wondered if a woman learned such traits or perhaps was simply born with them.

"Careful now, Miss Redfield." Lord Carlisle offered his assistance in boarding the craft.

Louella clasped the earl's hand tightly and gingerly found her seat on the wobbling boat. Although aged, the wood felt smooth. She was safe, of course. This was all perfectly safe. Without shifting her weight, she nervously spread her gown around herself.

Lord Carlisle turned toward Miss Mossant. The other lady had twisted her mouth into a grimace. She obviously wasn't eager to join Louella on the water. "This really isn't necessary, Mr. White."

"Why do you persist in addressing him as Mister?" Louella did not wish to go on the boat. She hated ponds. She hated boats, and even more so, she hated imposing on the earl's gallant nature. And, of course, her mother would expect a full narrative when they returned to the townhouse her father had leased. Irritation goaded her. "Are you not aware he is an earl? Surely, you insult him, Miss Mossant?"

"I take no insult, Miss Mossant." So smooth, so charming.

The boat rocked. What on earth was Miss Mossant doing? Why didn't she release Lord Carlisle's hand?

He was going to fall. Miss Mossant was going to fall. Louella reached out to grab hold of the other woman's legs but that seemed to only make matters worse. Perhaps her dress was in the way. Louella attempted to pull the material away and—

A tilt to the left and then the right and then… "No!"

Two giant splashes sent a wave of water into the boat, soaking Louella's dress, but even more problematic, the silk ribbons wrapped around her wrist.

"I'm drenched!" Brown-tinged water covered the bottom, and Louella gripped the edges of the boat frantically. It had drifted away from the wooden dock. Miss Mossant had survived well enough and was standing knee deep in the water and appeared somewhat satisfied with this turn of events.

Had she done this on purpose?

Panic rising, Louella watched the shore recede into the distance as she floated toward the center of the lake in a boat that had taken on an alarming amount of water.

Would it sink?

She couldn't swim. She shouldn't have agreed to the boat ride. A shiver rolled through her already chilled form as she imagined the boat disappearing into the depths of the lake. Taking her with it…

Louella looked imploringly toward Lord Carlisle, hoping he might swim out and tow her back to the shore.

"We'll bring her in, Carlisle!" This from a gentleman on a boat so distant that she couldn't even make out his identity. "Sit still, Miss Redfield! Nothing to be afraid of!"

Did the boater imagine her to be an utter fool?

"I'm taking on water!" she shouted in earnest, hoping to induce urgency into the gentleman slowly rowing in her direction.

She was embarrassed to admit that she didn't swim.

Not so embarrassed, however, that she'd fail to bring up the fact if the water in her small craft rose any higher.

"Not to worry. It is Miss Redfield, is it not?"

Who was he? He did seem rather familiar. He was not alone,

of course. He'd been squiring another lady around on the lake himself. Gentlemen didn't undertake to row a boat in the middle of a garden party if they didn't need to.

Or if they didn't wish to have time alone with the lady of their choice.

"Your name, sir! I'm afraid I'm at quite the disadvantage."

He laughed.

When he finally managed to bring his mirth under control, he'd floated to within about ten yards of her. "Lord Stanton, at your service."

* * *

It couldn't be. The rude and boorish oaf.

And he was laughing at her. He obviously hadn't changed at all.

Louella straightened her spine, ramrod stiff, as much as she could without upsetting the boat, and crossed her wrists in her lap. "I'm glad you find my predicament so amusing, my lord."

Her displeasure fazed him not at all. He merely continued rowing and smiling until his craft floated a few feet from hers. She studied his face.

Familiar but not at all the man she'd remembered. His skin was no longer pale and youthful looking. Nothing soft about him at all. He'd obviously spent much time in the sun, darkening his complexion. Chiseled jaw, high cheekbones, and his nose must have been broken a time or two.

The mocking green eyes were the same though—except for the creases at their edges. Of course he was older now. Nearly ten years since he'd run off to join the war effort. The heir to a duke! What had he been thinking? The entire village had been shocked that the Duke of Crawford had allowed it.

Louella shifted her eyes away from his face.

Although he'd removed his coat, he still wore a waistcoat over an elegant white linen shirt, of which he'd rolled up the sleeves.

She couldn't keep her eyes from straying to admire strong, tanned forearms.

"You haven't changed a whit, Louella Rose."

Idiot man. She tilted her chin back. "Miss Redfield, my lord. Now would you kindly tow me back to shore?"

Another chuckle from him. "May I present Miss Winters? Miss Winters, this is Miss Redfield. Her father's estate sits adjacent to Ashton Acres."

Miss Winters was a vision in red—a dry, perfectly coiffed vision in red. One would have thought her hair, an auburn color, might have clashed with the bold colors she wore, but it did not. The combination made her appear rather sophisticated.

It made Louella feel like a drab imposter—a drowned rat.

Swallowing hard, she nodded. "Miss Winters."

"Miss Redfield." Even her voice sounded sophisticated.

A jolt jarred the boat when Lord Stanton rudely barreled his craft into hers. He had lifted the rope tied to her stern and was attaching it to a hook behind him. All she wanted was to stand firmly on dry ground again. And then go home to be left alone, in her chamber.

"You're in no danger of sinking," he announced confidently, serious for the first time. "But you are rather soaked, aren't you?" He reached behind him and then offered her his coat. She would have to lean out a bit to take it from him.

"I'm fine." Only her teeth chose that moment to begin chattering. It wasn't that she was overly chilled, although when the breeze hit her, it penetrated her wet gown unpleasantly.

"Do take it." This from Miss Winters. "You'll catch your death."

Louella grasped the far side of the boat tightly and attempted to reach across the water. At that moment, Lord Stanton lurched forward himself and dropped it around her shoulders.

Both boats rocked unsteadily, causing her to gasp, but then immediately righted themselves.

She did appreciate the warmth. *Darn him.*

"Thank you," she muttered into the fabric. Now if only she could get off the lake. She didn't want to feel grateful toward him.

"I rather think you made out better than Miss Mossant and Carlisle."

"I suppose," Louella uttered quietly. She still wondered if Miss Mossant had done it on purpose. She turned to see the two of them striding away from shore. The other lady's lovely gown was likely ruined beyond repair. Surely, she wouldn't have fallen in on purpose. "A rather unlucky accident," she conceded, louder this time.

Lord Stanton watched her with something of a perplexed expression.

"May we go to shore now?" Louella shivered inside the warmth of his jacket. She wouldn't admit that its masculine scent comforted her.

Soap. Nothing more.

He narrowed his gaze, but then without another word, lifted the oars and turned both boats toward the jetty.

One would have thought it would be awkward to steer two boats, but he did so effortlessly. Even made conversation with the other lady while doing so.

Louella felt like a third wheel, dragging behind them. Surely, her father wouldn't make her marry such a man.

A stranger.

He was so old. Must be nearly thirty by now.

Why would he want to marry her? Oh, yes, she reminded

herself. The blasted mine. Fools. Both the Duke of Crawford and his son. Captain, Lord, whatever he was now.

She watched as the other lady climbed gracefully out of her boat onto the dock, and then stiffened when the marquess tied hers off securely.

She had no choice but to take the hand he offered.

"I'd intended to seek you out this afternoon," he said quietly. It was the first sign that he was aware of the agreement their fathers had made. "If you are not too chilled, would you stroll in the sunshine with me?"

Was he trying to be nice? Flatter her? Didn't he realize she was a certainty? That her father's estate was in financial straits, giving her no options?

In truth, she was no longer chilled. And a walk in the sun was what she had in mind anyhow. Her mother would not be willing to excuse them from the party so early.

She pursed her lips. "Perhaps another time."

CHAPTER THREE

THE PROPOSAL

*L*ouella had given it her all.

She'd wept, she'd sulked, she'd even raged at her father, but he had already given his word to the duke and would not break it. If she wished to remain his daughter, if she wished to keep her dresses and all of the things he'd bought for her throughout her entire life, she must marry the marquess! A boorish, horrid man.

The consequences of her defiance, if she chose to deny his wishes, would be felt for a lifetime. By not only herself but Olivia as well. How dare he use his daughters with no regard to their own wishes?

The home leased by the Viscount Hallewell, innocently tucked away behind a tall hedge on the outskirts of Mayfair, had not been a pleasant place to be that morning.

Louella was all too cognizant of the fact that there was more to this betrothal than anyone was willing to discuss. It was all about the cursed mine.

The duke's desire to reopen it had been common knowledge back home for ages. As far back as Louella could remember. She had no doubts that the rights would be tied into her betrothal.

Unmentioned, of course, were her father's financial woes.

Bringing them all to London had been a calculated risk on Papa's part. He must not have made his deal with the Duke of Crawford before deciding they'd participate in the Season.

She had known her duty to marry a man of wealth before they left a few weeks ago. And she'd accepted it. Welcomed it even. She would be glad of whatever she could do to help her family.

Had she been presented with any other man in the entire world, Louella would have been nervous, yes, but she would have willingly acquiesced to her father's wishes. It was not as though the marquess was an old man, or disfigured, or disgusting—quite the opposite, in fact. It was the man himself. His cruelty to Olivia before he'd gone away had planted bitter resentment in Louella's heart.

That summer, he'd nearly broken her sister's spirit.

She wished Olivia were here in London with her now. She'd know what to do.

Because today Louella could no longer pretend her father would change his mind. The duke, the duchess, and Lord Stanton were expected to arrive for tea that afternoon.

Stanton would formally propose, and she was expected to formally accept.

Or else.

"The ribbons aren't going to cover them all, Miss Louella," Jane tsked as she unraveled the silk from around Louella's wrist and forearm. "You need to be more careful, miss! My heavens!"

Her maid would cluck her tongue and make other disparaging noises, but she'd not tell anyone. Jane had informed Mama only once. Her mother's ensuing crying and dramatic vapors had exceeded anything ever witnessed.

"My perfect, beautiful daughter! How could you do this to yourself? You are ruining your beautiful skin! What is the matter with you?" And then she'd prayed and wept and threatened to call the curate to their estate to cast the devil out of her daughter.

Louella did not want the curate to know about any of this. He gossiped worse than Mrs. Fry. The entire village would know before sundown.

Her face streaming with tears, Louella had solemnly promised never to do it again.

Mama didn't want to know the truth, anyhow. Louella was her perfect daughter. Not *flawed* like she viewed her firstborn to be.

Since then, Mama occasionally glanced at the ribbons wrapped around Louella's wrists, but she'd not mentioned the cuts again. As long as she did not see the scars, she could believe that her youngest and most beautiful daughter was, indeed, perfect.

As long as she didn't see the scars.

Without consciously thinking about it, Louella had cut frantically last night. And she'd been so careless! Lost in the moment, some of the cuts were much longer than usual.

It was springtime. The window to her room was thrown wide open, and warmth wafted through her chamber.

"So, not the cerulean with puffed sleeves?"

"I don't think so, love." Her maid sounded mournful as she withdrew Louella's old standby. They kept it pressed and clean so that it was available at a moment's notice. It was a mint green muslin with puffed but then long fitted sleeves that came all the way down to Louella's knuckles.

"We'll want to tie a ribbon over the sleeves, even," Jane reminded her. "In case one of them bleeds through."

Louella had cut *deeper* than usual as well.

Jane had the right of it. Reddish-brown streaks stained the

21

sleeves of Louella's nightdress. She couldn't be certain the cuts would not bleed again today.

Several young girls in the village back home now tied ribbons around their wrists as well. Ironically enough, Louella had made something of a fashion statement with her silk ribbons.

Other girls her age envied her looks.

They also envied her lineage.

Good Lord, now they'd be envying her for her fiancé.

But that they might envy her tiny dowry.

Louella lifted her hands into the air as Jane assisted her into the gown and then tied it over her stays.

If not for her dratted stays, Louella could have dispensed with the satin ribbons all together and made the cuts on her abdomen.

Her hair required little styling, what with it curling naturally, and so after pinning it up with a few barrettes, Jane stepped back and declared her ready for the marquess. Just in time, too, as the sounds of a coach drawing up outside drifted through the window.

Her time had run out.

Louella picked at the corner of one of the ribbons, wishing again that Olivia had been allowed to travel with them to London.

* * *

"Here she is now, Your Grace. Make your curtsey, daughter."

Louella frowned in her father's direction. She was nearly twenty years old, not ten. She knew what was expected of her in social situations. She wasn't a child!

With exaggerated grace, she took hold of her skirt and turned to face the Duke and Duchess of Crawford. She then dropped into a long, slow curtsey.

She'd had a few opportunities to see them at local events back home but hadn't ever been presented to the elegantly clad couple now seated in her father's tired-looking drawing room. "Your Grace, Your Grace," she made her addresses.

Maintaining her attention on his parents, she ignored the gentleman seated across from them.

Blasted entitled tormentor, that he was!

She'd tried to erase his image from her thoughts as she lay in bed, chastising the part of her that found him handsome. Instead, she dwelled on how he'd treated Olivia. He'd been less virile looking back then, slimmer, much like other noble sons. The abundance of time on his hands that summer had been wasted away on foolishness and seeking out her and her sister to victimize.

He'd caught her and Olivia on the duke's property, fishing, and ordered them off.

More than once. But never without taunting them for being unladylike urchins. He'd dismissed Louella as little more than an annoying child but leered at Olivia.

"You'd really be quite pretty, you know, if you could keep your eye in check." Ah, yes, he'd told this to her sister in the kindest voice.

He'd not always been alone. When he was with the other boy, it had been even worse. "Can you see in both directions at the same time?" He'd cackled mercilessly. The friend had found it endlessly amusing to announce that Olivia must have a fly on her nose.

"So rude," the marquess had said. "To not look at a person when he speaks to you." Louella remembered every last slight. He had been evil. Nasty. Despicable.

It had been that very summer that their parents decided

Olivia would not be presented to Society. They'd said they would use her dowry to enhance Louella's.

Louella had hated their decision.

She would not allow Lord Stanton to fool her with his charm, much as he'd attempted to the day before.

She would not forgive him so easily, choosing to ignore him in favor of studying his parents instead. This was as close as she'd ever been to a duke and duchess.

The duchess appeared to be much younger than the duke. Her light hair wasn't completely white, rather mostly blond. And although a few wrinkles crinkled around her lips and the corners of her eyes, her attractiveness could not be denied.

The duke appeared to be hearty and exuded an undefinable sense of power. His chin was firm, and he had a full head of hair, but his skin looked dry and powdery. He was likely nearing his eighth decade, whereas the duchess looked to be in her late forties.

"Such a delightful girl," the duchess murmured. Louella squirmed.

"Louella," her father grasped her by the elbow to turn her, "you must remember Captain Lord Cameron Denning, the Marquess of Stanton."

Louella kept her eyes lowered, staring intently at the tattered carpet. She did not wish to concede any favor upon this man. *Lazy-eyed Livvy* he'd called her sister.

Holding tightly to her skirts, she dipped into another slow curtsey. "My lord," she forced herself to say.

And then she raised her eyes.

She'd wished he had remained standing, arrogantly looking down his nose at her, but he hadn't. No, he had bowed, and as he rose, he bestowed on her the most disarming smile.

Drat it all. Just as pleasant as it had been yesterday. Even more so with him not finding amusement at her expense.

Hands clasped behind his back, he stood tall and masculine but not in an intimidating manner. In fact, a lock of dark wavy hair had slipped out of his queue, giving him an almost boyish quality. Deep green eyes twinkled as he grinned. And the genuine smile drew her gaze to the firm line of his jaw once again.

He had no right being so pleasant! Louella lifted her chin defiantly.

"Miss Louella." His baritone voice wrapped her in its sincerity. "You are recovered from your dousing yesterday?"

"I am quite well, my lord." She would have left her greeting at that, but her father was watching her sternly. "We are so very grateful for your safe return from service to our country." But then she added, "How do *you do*, my lord?"

He chuckled but eyed her curiously. "Well enough, Miss Louella."

"Shall we all sit down, then?" Her mother tittered.

Mama clasped her hands together tightly. Louella realized that her mother must be nervous that she'd somehow offend their esteemed guests. Even more likely she worried that Louella would decline the proposal.

What would Olivia do? Would she consider Louella's acquiescence a betrayal? They'd hated him together for months after he'd left his father's estate.

But they'd been children... well, Louella had been. Olivia had been closer to womanhood, closer to Stanton's age. Even so, his antics had been horribly childish.

And yet, Louella had a responsibility. And her father, in truth, hadn't given her any choice.

Lowering herself reluctantly onto the settee, she turned attentively to their guests.

Her mother's eyes flickered over the long-sleeved dress she wore. And the ribbons tied over the fabric at her wrists.

"It certainly feels as though spring will arrive early this year, doesn't it?" The duchess' melodic voice broke the silence before it could become uncomfortable.

"Oh, yes, indeed it does," her mama supplied. "Did you bring any of your daughters up to London for the Season, Your Grace?"

Louella had nearly forgotten about the Crawford girls. There were *three* of them! Except that they'd not participated in many local events... whether that was because they'd been too young or too high in the instep, she didn't really know.

"Rothberg's heir proposed to Lady Lillian over the holidays, but she declined, so she was to be on the mart this spring. We don't intend to stay on for long, however." The duchess gave a frustrated glance in her husband's direction. "Crawford is anxious to return to Ashton Acres. And next year we won't have a choice, as Cora will be ready for her come out."

The duke most certainly wanted to reopen the mine quickly if he was willing to cut his daughter's Season short.

"They've grown up so quickly," Mama responded appropriately.

"As has Miss Louella." This from the duke. Upon his words, he rose from the sofa.

The others rose as well.

No! No! No!

"Shall we leave these young people alone for a few moments?" Louella's father offered his arm to the duchess. She took it graciously, while Mama slid her hand in the duke's. Crawford's impatience for this proposal confirmed Louella's suspicions. Of course, this was all about the mine. Foolish man. He'd not find even a sliver. Everyone knew the mine to be nothing more than a deathtrap.

Louella flexed her hand inward. She'd slipped a long needle inside of the ribbon. Yes, there it was.

Seeing them depart the room sent panic racing through her. But what could she do to stop them? What would she say?

What *could* she say? Even if she had the courage to make her objections, nobody would listen to her.

The door clicked shut behind the cluster of parents, and she dropped hopelessly onto the sofa.

Stanton cleared his throat. "Well then, Miss Redfield."

She shifted the location of the needle. She did not wish to have this conversation today.

And yet, the distress that had been on her mother's face prevented her from running from the room. Recalling the empty walls where valuable paintings had once been displayed at Thistle Park taunted her. As did the near threadbare carpets.

Forcing her chin up, she concentrated on the man standing before her and lifted the corners of her mouth. "My lord," she responded sweetly.

No one could deny his near perfect features. He'd always been handsome.

A grimace crossed his most appealing face. She must appear more convincing. *"Please."* This time, she forced the smile to reach her eyes. "Sit down, my lord."

He dropped onto the sofa beside her. The cushions were low, and he was a tall man, which required he lower himself a considerable distance.

"I'd have preferred to court you properly, as you deserve." His attempt to charm her was wasted. She knew of his true character, the brute. Had he forgotten?

"Every young buck in England will have conniptions at me for my audacity. They'll complain that I've snatched up London's comeliest debutante."

Comeliest.

She hated the word.

More likely, the ladies of England would complain of Louella's accomplishment. Lord? Captain? Whatever... Cameron Denning was a *marquess.* He was *heir to the Duke of Crawford.*

As the eldest daughter, Olivia ought to have been given the opportunity to marry first.

The settee groaned under his weight as he shifted.

She didn't have a choice in any of this. Olivia would understand, really, wouldn't she? Olivia would forgive her. She tended to excuse people's rudeness all the time.

Whereas Mama and Papa would never speak to Louella again if she refused the marquess.

Affecting a shy glance in his direction, she fluttered her lashes. "I am just a country girl, not even a lady, my lord."

"Ah, but you are the daughter of a viscount. You are a gentlewoman... and you are one of the loveliest ladies of my acquaintance."

The compliment sent that bleak feeling of shame coursing through her again.

Louella plucked at the ribbon wrapped around her wrist. His voice sounded gruff, as though he truly were attracted to her.

He reached out and stopped her fidgeting. "Miss Redfield." His tone forced her to meet his gaze. "Will you consent to be my wife?"

That was it?

That was his proposal?

Somehow, she'd expected more.

She might not have much choice in the matter, but she could not make it so very easy for him. She widened her eyes but did not speak.

At her silence, he seemed to sense her displeasure.

With an uncomfortable glance around the room, he slid off the settee onto one knee and took hold of one of her hands again. So, he would do this properly, after all, removing the very last of her resistance.

She twisted her wrists and examined his left hand. How odd! He lacked two fingers.

"What happened to them?" As far as she could remember, when he'd left Misty Brooke ten years ago, he'd taken ten fingers with him.

He seemed irritated by her change of subject but answered anyway. "Nothing glamorous. I imagine they made a satisfying lunch for some fish in the Indian Ocean somewhere. Happened a few years ago, nothing serious really."

Not wanting to revisit his proposal yet, she ran her fingertips along the edges where his pinky ought to be. "Does it hurt?"

He didn't look irritated so much by this question, as reluctant to delay the business at hand. "It only hurts where they used to be." He shook his head, as though to shake himself free of his thoughts. "Miss Redfield, despite my gruesome injury, I can assure you that all other... appendages... are present and functioning properly."

Drawing away one of his hands, he tipped her chin up so that she had no choice but to return his stare. "And so, I will ask you again, would you make me the happiest of men and consent to be my wife?"

Louella wondered at the apparent sincerity behind those green eyes of his. Not just green. Blue and gold flecks danced around his darkened pupil. But he'd asked her to marry him. He expected an answer.

"My lord, I am honored."

"And...?" He furrowed his brow at her hesitation.

Whether he desired her consent or merely any answer whatsoever so that he could rise from the floor, Louella wasn't certain.

Her gaze flicked to the closed door and then back at his handsome face. Unable to stop herself, she scowled. "I suppose so, my lord."

His eyes narrowed.

Oh, fiddlesticks. She'd sounded rather as though she'd

consented to clean the chamber pots. On a rush of air, she attempted to correct her manner of acceptance. "Of course, I am delighted at the prospect of marrying such an esteemed gentleman as yourself."

Smile, Louella! Gaze adoringly at him! She fluttered her lashes and tilted her head. And then, feeling rather foolish but knowing what must be done, she leaned forward and closed her eyes. She'd considered the necessity of this. She'd never allowed the boys at home who'd tried to court her any such liberty. But she knew they'd all wanted to.

The marquess would want to.

After hearing five whole ticking sounds coming from the clock that sat upon the mantle, she felt his lips upon hers briefly.

Thank heavens, she hadn't ruined it!

But before her thoughts could go any further, the kiss took precedence over all else.

Warm and firm, his lips teased hers. He did not simply press them there, as she'd expected. They nipped at the corner of her mouth sending a shiver down her spine. When his tongue slid along the seam of her lips, warmth spread to her limbs. He wanted her to… He wanted her to open her mouth!

Almost of their own accord, her lips parted.

And then… nothing.

She opened her eyes to see him watching her, satisfaction in his gaze.

But also, a level of puzzlement.

"You are as curious now as when you were a child."

He had not forgotten! In less time than it would take to blink, Louella forgot all about the kiss and the sensations it had evoked in her. Curious? *Curious?*

"And was Olivia curious? Or was she more of an oddity to you?" Louella could contain her disdain no longer.

***

Miss Louella Rose was not at all as Cameron had remembered.

Not. At. All.

The gangly limbs were now attached to sweet feminine curves, and the too-large eyes now set in the most beautiful of countenances. Yesterday he could not help but notice.

In fact, the observation had eliminated a few of his misgivings. Even if she had seemed a trifle prickly.

She had nearly been dumped into the lake, after all.

His stepmother had not exaggerated in the least. *The girl is stunning.*

To his regret, she also possessed an excellent memory.

Cameron cleared his throat. "I hesitate to say this in the presence of a lady, Miss Louella, but my only defense is that... I was an ass." As though she'd not expected him to respond with any candor or honesty, her perfectly shaped eyebrows rose upon hearing his words. "I'd be honored to be given a chance to apologize to the elder Miss Redfield."

His words seemed to extinguish some of the bristling animosity emanating from her.

"So, you do remember." Her indigo-colored eyes burned with accusation.

"Admittedly, I acted horribly. But to be fair, it was a long time ago, and the two of you were trespassing." He utilized his most cajoling manner, but her scowl indicated a lack of appreciation for his teasing. Bollocks.

He pushed himself off the floor and paced across the room. Not often he came across a lady whose graces he couldn't charm himself into.

"Your bullying devastated her. What with you and your friend and my parents... How was she to feel?" Rosebud lips pouted as she spoke. Lips he'd rather enjoyed.

31

"I'd take it back if I could." Again, he'd like to thrash his younger self.

Miss Louella Rose narrowed her eyes, not ready to forgive him by any means. "You were cruel. As was your friend." She turned her gaze away from him and her admonishment stung.

"Why did you go to war? You are a duke's son."

Her change in subject jarred him.

Why did he go to war? It had taken him years to discover the answer.

He'd blamed his father for his mother's death. She'd been too old to attempt childbirth again. When Cameron returned from school, he had discovered his father remarried to a much younger woman. A woman who filled his home with obnoxious little girls. Cameron had been a selfish and spoiled fool who had considered only himself.

But without going into a litany of excuses, the best he could do was, "I could not remain at Ashton Acres."

He studied his betrothed closely as she plucked distractedly at a ribbon wrapped several times around her wrist—oddly enough—over her sleeve. He'd noticed his stepsisters wearing such a ribbon on their arms but never over a sleeve.

Cameron thrummed his fingers thoughtfully upon his thigh. Miss Louella Rose presented something of a dilemma.

Her initial acceptance of his proposal had lacked any enthusiasm whatsoever. But then she'd fluttered her lashes and offered her lips for a kiss.

Of course, she would accept his proposal! She likely had no choice.

"And you lost your fingers for it." Her voice held no sympathy, rather a pragmatic tone. As though he'd perhaps deserved exactly what he'd been given. "I suppose everybody consoles you by reminding you that at least it wasn't your right hand."

"It is nothing." He turned his left hand over and then made a fist. But she reached forward and slowly pried it back open.

"How *did* it happen?" She held his hand in both of hers.

He didn't have to look to know what she saw. A stub where his pinky had been and a clean cut where he'd once had a ring finger.

The injury was, truly, no real loss at all. Other men had suffered far greater than him.

And then she touched the nub.

His instinct was to jerk his hand away.

Not because it hurt. Oddly enough, the part of his fingers that remained were numb. Any pain he ever felt existed only in his head.

"Were they shot off?"

"Nothing so glamorous." He'd certainly not expected to have this conversation today.

"Hmm." She examined his hand more closely. A whisper of a smile crossed her lips. Was she *flirting* with him? *Regarding his lost fingers?* "The cut is too clean for them to have been bitten off, by either a wild animal or…"

"They were not bitten off by an embittered woman either."

"I didn't—"

"Ah, but you were thinking it."

"I was not!" she avowed, but a definite smile danced on her lips now.

Good lord, but she took his breath away.

He had to ask.

"Are you being coerced into this betrothal, Miss Redfield?" Because although he felt less reluctance as each moment passed, he would *not* marry an unwilling girl.

Her smile fell at his words.

Then, seeming to realize she still held his hand, she dropped it suddenly and went back to fidgeting with the silk bow on her wrist. Just when he thought she wasn't going to answer him, she looked up. "My father will flay me if I refuse."

Even though he felt some disappointment, Cameron would

not do it then.

"But…" she continued.

But?

"But you aren't quite the monster I remembered you to be."

And she blushed.

Damned if he didn't have the strangest urge, at that moment, to thank his damned father for choosing such a precious gem.

Because he liked her.

Breathtakingly beautiful, her nature was sweet, if not a little irritable. She seemed intelligent enough and even had a sense of humor. Good heavens, his father had found him the perfect debutante after all.

* * *

"Ah, yes, Redfield, I'll send my masonry man over later this week to take a look at that." Louella's ears pricked up as the duke's voice floated in from the corridor.

Their privacy would be interrupted in moments.

Louella chastised herself. Where had her righteous anger on Olivia's behalf gone? Was she so easily susceptible to the charm of a handsome gentleman?

Not only had she accepted his proposal, but she'd also, it seemed, accepted his excuse for hurting her sister. What had he said was the reason?

Oh, yes.

He'd been an ass.

Which was—well—difficult to argue with. How did one rebuke a person when said person rebuked himself first?

But he was… sweet.

And his kiss had been… intriguing.

No, he was not a monster after all. And she'd admitted as much to him.

The door swung open and nervous energy returned to the room along with their parents. Louella's father studied her with raised brows. "Did you accept him?" they seemed to say. She tipped her chin slightly.

Captain Lord Stanton took Louella's hand in his yet again.

It was done. And it wasn't as bad as she'd expected. Except that she was going to have to tell Olivia when they returned to Thistle Park.

Olivia would not expect Louella to defy their father.

And, of course, Louella had not. And now it would become real. Despite not hating the marquess, Louella wished to be anywhere else in that moment.

He was going to announce their betrothal.

She'd accepted him. The man who'd hurt her sister with his thoughtless words. What did that make Louella?

She bent her wrist forward and focused for just a moment on the pain of the needle pressing into her flesh.

And then he spoke.

"Your Graces, My Lord, My Lady, I'm happy to inform you that Miss Louella Rose has consented to... a courtship."

A courtship?

Louella's jaw dropped. She relaxed her wrist and the pain disappeared.

At the same time, her father's eyes turned stormy.

"Some tea, then?" Louella's mother always suggested tea when her father's temper threatened to erupt. And they *had* invited the duke and duchess over to *take tea* with them. Louella straightened her spine, vaguely aware of her mother tugging at the bell pull over and over as though that would bring one of their few servants more quickly.

But it was the duke's voice that drew everyone's attention. *"A courtship?"*

Stanton patted her hand, as though sensing the storm he'd steered them into. "Doesn't every lady deserve a proper courtship?"

"Oh, heaven's yes! Yes, so very thoughtful! How wonderful of you, Stanton!" The duchess covered her husband's hand with her own.

"And, of course," Louella's mother joined in, "Louella has consented." This last part directed toward her father.

"I'm to collect Miss Louella Rose the day after we've returned to Ashton Acres, in fact." Stanton slid a glance in her direction, mischief in his eyes. "We'll have a drive through the country, and then a picnic."

At a slight toggle from his eyebrows, Louella nodded in agreement. "Er... yes! A drive." But her father still looked awfully unhappy.

As did the duke.

"In the country," she added. "And a picnic. Terribly romantic..." She couldn't help but add the last part. What would she tell Olivia?

He most definitely was not a monster.

People changed. They grew up.

The duke grunted. "We'll forgo tea, then." His lips were pinched. Not a man who appreciated his plans going awry. "We can discuss the final details next week, Hallewell."

Her father nodded.

"Ah, yes... So much to do this afternoon... Packing for the journey home tomorrow." The duchess rose and allowed the duke to steer her toward the door. "Stanton, are you coming?"

Her not-quite fiancé turned to face her and bowed. "I'll collect you from your home in four days' time then?" He really meant to court her.

"I'll be ready, my lord."

But was she? And if she was, what kind of person did that make her? A girl who would be disloyal to her own sister?

CHAPTER FOUR

HOME AGAIN

$\mathcal{L}$ ouella had promised she'd visit Olivia as soon as they arrived home. Olivia had known what was expected of Louella, but not that their father's plan involved Stanton.

Louella was conflicted.

She wished she could pretend for just a little while that a handsome gentleman had requested to court her. That she was just a normal girl. She did not want to worry that he was the same person who'd caused her sister such grief, even though it had been long ago.

But she had promised. She'd told Livvy she would come right away.

And so, that very afternoon, Jane assisted Louella into her most comfortable walking boots and a warm shawl so that she could walk over to the small residence on the edge of her father's property.

Spring had barely arrived, and a crisp chill laced the air. She would need to hurry so that she could return home before dark. Especially as the path traveled directly past the family burial ground.

Which she didn't mind so much during the daytime, but...

She shuddered as she picked her way through the overgrown path. She owed William a visit, too. Several weeks had passed since she'd brought him any new shiny pebbles.

Or a toy.

Or read to him.

To the eight-year-old boy who'd never reached the age of nine.

Louella ignored the clusters of wildflowers she found in favor of stones. William had been an avid collector of unique rocks. And, of course, she carried the book with her.

Plodding along, her gaze focused on the ground, she occasionally stopped to scoop some sparkling pebbles up and drop them into her apron until she reached the edge of the woods. There, an old iron fence safely enclosed the ancient and not so ancient headstones of her deceased ancestors.

And of her little brother.

As always, she tried not to remember the last time she'd seen him. She tried instead to summon memories from before he'd taken so ill—before he'd fallen into the murky lake.

Cold seeped through her at the memory of that day. He'd been unconscious. His lips had turned blue.

She had no difficulty locating the polished headstone her father had purchased for his only son.

Herein William Elwood Harlan Redfield, Beloved Brother and Son, B: 1813 D: 1821.

He'd been in the ground longer than his short life. As always when she came here, she remembered his casket lowering into the ground. At the age of eleven, she'd been terrified for her brother, frightened to think of him buried beneath the earth... in the dark, in the cold.

"Hello, Little Will." She spoke out loud, her words disturbing the hush of the cemetery. Brushing some leaves away from the ground beside the stone, Louella then dropped her knees onto the tufted grass and pulled the book out of her bag. She'd read it to him a hundred times since. She practically knew it by heart.

"Here we go, Willy. Sorry I haven't visited lately. You wouldn't believe all that's going on." Since she didn't have a great deal of time, she opened the well-worn tome and commenced reading the familiar words. She knew he couldn't hear her. She knew he wasn't really here. But it helped to read a few of the childish limericks.

"Walking around in the woods with his dog,
Alistair would not get lost in the fog,
For canines can smell,
what humans can't tell,
although he might trip on the log."

She turned through a few pages and found another poem about a dog. William had always wanted a dog, but he'd never been allowed one. She read a few more but knew she was merely delaying her visit with Olivia now.

"Oh, Will," she said one last time, pushing herself up from the ground. "I've left you alone too long." She sniffed away the burning behind her eyes. He shouldn't have died. He should be heading off to Eton, with other annoying boys his age.

She stuffed the book into her bag and then brushed the dirt and grass from her dress.

She needed to speak to Olivia. She needed to inform her older sibling that she would fail her as well.

Louella touched her fingertips to her lips and then to the tombstone. "I won't take so long to visit next time, Will."

* * *

Olivia must have seen her coming for she burst out the front door before Louella could even open the gate.

"I'm so glad you are back already! It has been horribly quiet without you!" Olivia's gorgeous blond hair was tied back in a ribbon and flowed down her back, almost to her waist. Although older than Louella, she was nearly half a foot shorter.

Olivia's face lit up as she raced toward her. Louella loved Olivia's smile. And her eyes, not merely a vibrant blue, but violet.

Louella didn't even notice that one traveled on its own sometimes. Except when their mother insisted it be covered with a patch.

Louella opened her arms, eager to embrace the person she loved most in this world. Olivia gave the best hugs.

Louella bit her lip and pulled back. "I am betrothed—well, sort of."

Olivia's eyes locked on hers. "So soon? No wonder Papa brought you home early. Who is he? Does he live nearby? I'll hate it if you move far away. No. Ignore that. I won't hate it. I'll simply move with you. Mama and Papa wouldn't mind that in the least." And then she scrunched her nose. "What do you mean, 'sort of?'"

"Papa insists I give my consent. But the, er, gentleman in question has asked to... court me."

Olivia squealed. "How terribly romantic! Is he handsome? What is his name? He is coming to Thistle Park then?"

Standing in the sunlight, noticing the golden glints shining in Olivia's hair, Louella could not help but believe that her older sister ought to have been the one to become betrothed. She ought to have been given a chance at least.

"Lord Stanton. Crawford's heir."

At the widening of Olivia's eyes, Louella knew no further explanation was necessary.

"Cameron? The marquess? Oh, but, Louella! You shall be a duchess then."

"But he was atrocious before. How can I forgive him for the names he called you? He was awful!" At her own reminder, Louella felt naïve and gullible for allowing him to kiss her.

And even worse for liking it.

Olivia waved one hand in the air. "That was ages ago. Does he seem different now? Surely, he's not such an arrogant blighter as he was before. Youth does that to people, you know. Especially heirs of grand estates."

Olivia was too good-hearted for her own good.

"He said he was, well, he said he was an… a… brute." He had offered to apologize to Olivia, hadn't he?

"So, an apology of sorts."

"I suppose."

"It was a long time ago, Louella." Livvy grasped her arm and peppered her with questions as they entered the little cottage. "Tell me about him. Is he more handsome than before? And he wishes to court you! Do you like him? Has he fallen madly in love with you? Oh, this is so exciting, Louella!"

He'd not fallen in love with her. How could he when he didn't even know her?

"All of this is most certainly to do with the mine." Except for the kiss. Had it affected him the same as it had her? Surely, he'd kissed hundreds of women! Well, perhaps not hundreds. Louella dismissed the imagery. "He's obviously being compelled by his father. You've heard the rumors about the duke's desire to locate the gold. Papa has run out of funds. I'm simply a part of a business transaction."

Livvy slid her a sideways glance. "But he's going to court you! Don't be coy with me. It's not as though you're repulsive."

He'd not treated her as though he'd been repulsed. But what if he knew the truth about her?

"But he did propose? Of course, he would propose. You're

the loveliest lady in all of London—I'd wager in all of England."
She ignored Louella's rolling eyes. "But you are not yet
betrothed? You told him no then?"

"I, er…" She'd never been able to keep anything from Olivia
so she wouldn't even try. "Well, he did—propose, that is—and I
agreed. I wasn't all that gracious initially." She bit her lip at the
reminder of her first attempt at accepting him. "But then I told
him Papa would be angry if I didn't consent. So, I suppose…"
The gesture really had been a gallant one on his part. "When
the duke and duchess, and Mama and Papa returned, he told
them he had proposed to *court* me." Louella touched the ribbon
on her wrist. "And that I consented."

Both girls fell silent as they entered the small parlor and
then dropped onto a cozy settee together. The ticking of the
clock on the mantle suddenly sounded louder than it
really was.

He'd been gracious and charming, and she'd been utterly
undeserving.

And her parents wanted her to marry him. *I have no choice!*

Why was she reluctant, then?

The memory of his mouth coaxing her lips apart ought not
to cause her heart to race. Louella had wanted to dislike the
marquess. She'd hoped she'd have good reason to beg and plead
her way out of this engagement. So far, he'd given her none.

He'd understood her reluctance and delayed announcing
their betrothal. Which was more than she deserved.

I like him.

"He sounds very considerate. Tell me all the details. What
do you feel when you are with him? Could you ever fall in
love?" Olivia drew her knees up to her chest. How could Olivia
remain optimistic, open to goodness after being treated so
poorly by her own parents?

Louella contemplated what facts might be interesting to tell
her sister. "He lost two of his fingers."

Her sister made a face. "Which hand?"

"His left." Louella recalled the smooth thick skin that had grown over the injured area. He'd flinched when she touched it. But he'd said it didn't hurt.

"So, he is no longer so perfect himself." Olivia softened her words with a wry smile. "I don't imagine it takes away from his looks at all. He was quite handsome, even back then."

Olivia was six years older than Louella. She'd practically been a woman before Lord Stanton went away. And despite his horrible behavior, Olivia had sighed over him on more than one occasion. Or was it his friend that her sister had been besotted with?

"I don't imagine much could take away from his looks," Louella replied without thinking, drawing a huge grin from her sister. Why wasn't Olivia more upset about this?

"You will be a duchess someday." This time, it was Olivia who seemed to speak without thinking. But not a trace of jealousy sounded in her voice.

If anyone ought to be bitter, it was Olivia. Their parents hadn't seen fit to allow her a come out. They'd slated her to be a spinster. What man would want a woman with such an imperfect condition? Especially when he could have her younger sister.

Her perfect younger sister.

Gathering her shawl, Louella rose from the settee. "But it should be you! You are the eldest! I hate this! I hate all of this! How could I enjoy being in London knowing you were left behind?" Louella berated herself for looking forward to being courted while her sister was overlooked.

Frustration defeated her. Even if the marquess had turned out to be a monster, Louella could not have declined.

"You have no choice." Olivia would not gloss over the truth.

"You are not upset," Louella stated.

Olivia shook her head side to side. "You have no control

over what Mama and Papa demand of you. I wish you'd stop blaming yourself. If Papa is determined you marry the marquess, you couldn't very well refuse him. If he is kind and handsome, and a man who will treat you well, you might as well be happy for it. Because I know you. Even if he were still a monster, you would insist on doing what would be best for Mama. And for Papa. You always do the right thing. Sometimes too much."

"I want *you* to meet a handsome and charming gentleman. I want you to be cherished, to become a wife. You would make the most wonderful mother." Louella sat back down, tilted her head, and rested it on her sister's shoulder. "I love you, Livvy."

"It isn't meant to be, Lulu, but I love you, too. I always will." Olivia sniffed. "Are you stopping by the graveyard when you go home?"

"I did on my way over."

"William was such a sweet boy. If he hadn't died, Mama and Papa wouldn't be so desperate to marry you off."

Louella swallowed hard. "If only…"

* * *

Lying awake that night, Louella couldn't help but contemplate the truth in Olivia's parting words. William had been her father's only son, his heir.

Not quite three years old when her brother was born, Louella vaguely remembered the joy in the household when the midwife had announced the birth of a boy. Her father had laughed out of sheer joy. And her mama had been so proud!

With their mother abed and so intent upon the new baby, Olivia and Louella had been left to their own devices. As the eldest, Olivia had done her best to keep Louella out of harm's way. She'd told Louella what to wear, insisted she bathe, and attended to duties a governess or a mother ought to have performed. Not much more than a child herself, she'd taken on much of the responsibility for her little sister.

Which had been perfectly acceptable to both their father and mother. They could save on funds and focus what little resources they had on the care of their only son.

Matters continued thusly as William grew from an infant, to a toddler, to a small boy—to a very small boy.

For William had not ever really thrived. He'd often been sickly and confined to his chamber, if not his bed. As a result of his special position in the family, and a somewhat precarious position in this world, he'd been terribly spoiled by their parents.

But the girls had loved him, nonetheless.

Often selfish, demanding, and a pestilence, he was, nonetheless, their little *brother*!

Olivia helped their mother and the nursemaid care for him, and Louella had spent many hours reading and entertaining the small boy who was hardly ever allowed to play outside for fear he'd sicken more.

When he reached the age of seven, he seemed healthier than he'd ever been. He'd even been given permission to walk in the garden occasionally. He gained weight, and his skin wasn't so sallow.

And then Olivia and Louella had taken him out to the lake.

If only... She pushed the memory away.

Louella fluffed her pillow and turned onto her side.

Tomorrow, Captain Lord Cameron Samuel Benjamin Denning, Marquess of Stanton, had promised to take her on a drive and a picnic.

She'd asked her father his exact title, and her father had pulled out the betrothal contract for her to see. *Captain Lord*

Cameron Samuel Benjamin Denning, the Marquess of Stanton, a rather magnificent name, really.

Cameron.

"Are you being coerced into this betrothal, Louella?" he'd asked her. She'd thought it hadn't mattered to him. She'd thought he cared as little for her feelings on the matter as the duke and her father did.

But she'd been wrong.

Because he'd not announced their engagement.

Why would he announce a courtship if he didn't wish to consider her feelings?

But then Olivia's words echoed in her head. *Of course, he would propose. You're the loveliest lady in all of London.*

Louella threw off her covers and sat up. Unable to bear her own thoughts anymore, she pulled out the sewing basket.

CHAPTER FIVE

A DRIVE

"*R*ise and shine, Miss Louella!" Jane drew back the curtain to reveal a cloudy, gloomy day. Mist hung in the air, hiding any sunshine completely. Louella pulled the covers closer around her face and snuggled into the soft mattress.

Not the best of days for a picnic.

"Do you think he'll cancel, Jane?" Louella asked.

Jane paused and stared out the window. "A hint of blue sky over there in the west. I think you'll be having your picnic."

It had been late before Louella fell asleep. She groaned.

"Oh, Miss Louella! Not again!" Jane had turned from the window and was staring in exasperation at the blood stains on Louella's sleeping gown. "Always I'm soaking this or that gown of yours! Sit up, miss. The sooner I get this in water, the easier it will be to clean."

Louella had thought she'd cleaned the new cuts well enough before coming back to bed. But it had been dark. She'd not wanted to light a candle, lest somebody see light from beneath her door.

"Oh, miss," Jane moaned as she pulled the gown over Louella's head.

Looking at her arms, and the dried blood, some on the sheets even, Louella flushed in embarrassed remorse.

"I didn't mean to." She knew her cutting bothered Jane. Now she would make additional work for her maid as well.

Jane, sworn to secrecy, seemed to understand somehow that it was not something Louella could stop doing.

She just couldn't.

And when she tried, she only did it more.

Louella wet the handkerchief by her bed and began brushing at the streaks on her arm.

"Don't worry, I'll have a bath made up for you anyhow. At least it's cold outside, and you can wear one of your warmer gowns without it seeming... odd."

Louella shivered in her thin nightgown.

Jane dropped a shawl around her shoulders before pulling the partition screen across the room. "I'll get you some breakfast and order hot water and the tub. You might as well climb back under the covers."

Louella did as her maid suggested, tears threatening to overflow. She didn't deserve to marry a handsome man like Stanton. She was the last person in the world who ought to someday become a duchess. She pulled her knees up to her chest, feeling ashamed and most unworthy.

Even now, she craved a needle.

* * *

Louella had thought her father would be present when the marquess arrived to collect her, but he'd gone out today, leaving her alone with her mother in the drawing room awaiting Captain Lord Stanton's—or was it Lord Captain Stanton's—visit? Why could she not remember something so simple?

Her mother pretended to read, and Louella was adding the final embroidered details to a gown she had sewn for Olivia made of soft cotton muslin. She'd threaded tiny stars and moons in a myriad of colors around the hem.

She tried ignoring her mother's critical gaze. But then her mama sighed heavily. "Long sleeves again Louella?"

Louella shifted uneasily. *Not today! Please, not today!* Her mama didn't normally comment on her choice of gown. But today, of course, she worried over the pending betrothal.

Louella glanced down at the gown Jane had selected for her. Made of a dark green sturdy cotton material, it had thin gray pinstripes running vertically from the waist to the hem. The pinstripes ran diagonally on the bodice and puffed sleeves. The sleeve lengths were solid green. The dress was in good condition and would be warm and comfortable for a picnic. It was very practical and certainly deserved no criticism from her mother.

"It's cold outside, Mama. We'll be riding in the open air."

A lining ensured she would not need the silk ribbon today.

"Besides," she added. "I love this dress."

"I suppose." Mama then closed her book and gave up altogether on pretending to read.

"Louella."

"Yes?"

"I want to know the truth. Did you refuse his proposal?" That pinched look was back.

"I did not. Perhaps he wishes to know me some before declaring himself."

Suspicious eyes narrowed.

"Mama! I swear to you, I did not refuse him!" Louella was glad she could be honest in this.

But this conversation would end at that, for a commotion of horses and vehicle rose up from the front of the house.

Her heart skipped a beat at the thought of seeing him again. It shouldn't. It should sink into her shoes. How could she manage to feel so guilty and yet excited at the same time?

And what would they talk about? He'd traveled the world. She must seem terribly young and countrified to him.

* * *

Cameron wondered if his memory had embellished Louella's good looks. Had her beauty been enhanced by a trick of the light? Had his mind remembered her as more attractive because he'd been relieved to see that she was no longer a child, but, in fact, a grown woman?

No, he'd not been mistaken.

And damned if she didn't curtsey prettily.

A few chestnut curls fell forward, decorating her exposed neck and décolletage. The rest of her shining hair piled atop her head, held in place with various pieces of jewelry, but that was not where his eyes were drawn.

Brilliant blue eyes confirmed that he'd not imagined her beauty at all, nor the physical effect she had on him. And today, her rosy lips temptingly teased him with a hint of a smile.

He bowed. "Miss Louella. Your beauty increases with each meeting."

"Thank you, my lord." Her voice was pitched lower than many girls. Which bode well. He'd prefer not to listen to high-pitched screeching from his wife.

"My lord." This from the viscountess.

"My lady." He bowed again before turning back to the younger girl. "The clouds are clearing so we ought to see the sun soon. I think we'll have fine weather for our drive after all." Good Lord, he must be smitten. He never discussed the weather. His opinion had no effect whatsoever upon it and nothing could be done to change it. The extent to which English conversation revolved around meteorological events boggled his mind sometimes.

"I'll fetch my spencer and bonnet." She dropped her lashes shyly.

Which left him alone with her mother.

Who was eyeing him suspiciously.

"Louella assures me she did not refuse you in London." She clasped her hands below a generous bosom but worry lined her face. The lady's hair, which must have once been the same color as her younger daughter's, had faded with age. The eyes peering up at him weren't as blue as they must have once been, but they showed intelligence.

He would not dissemble.

"She accepted me, my lady." Had his declaration to court Miss Louella Rose caused trouble for her? He'd intended it to do just the opposite. "It was I who decided we must familiarize ourselves with one another before making an official announcement. I'd prefer not to enter my marriage with any qualms. I'd prefer my bride not do so either."

At his words, Lady Hallewell exhaled a long breath.

"No, my lady. Your daughter did not refuse me. She was willing to do as her parents requested."

"She's a good girl." The older woman stared down at her hands.

A good girl.

He was bothered to think that was the only reason she would accept his proposal.

But then again, he supposed, this was the way of the world. Not everybody was given the luxury of long romantic courtships, but he'd do his best.

He felt her presence the moment she returned. The air grew a little lighter, the colors in the room brighter.

"That bonnet is quite attractive on you, Louella," the viscountess addressed her daughter with some approval. "How long, my lord, before you plan on returning Louella home?"

His companion for the afternoon blushed at her mother's question.

Cameron stared at Miss Louella Rose. "If you are up for it, I thought we'd drive to the edge of my father's property. There is a lake there. It's quite picturesque and makes a delightful spot for a picnic." At her nod, he turned again toward her mother. "Perhaps a few hours then, my lady."

The viscountess scowled but did not argue. She would not.

And upon his words, Miss Louella Rose took hold of the arm he'd not even been aware he'd offered. He covered her hand with his.

A most unremarkable butler opened the door and held it for them to exit onto the street.

"Shall we?"

Her smile took his breath away, as she nodded and then allowed him to lead her down the steps. Cameron hadn't felt so much anticipation in… he could not remember when.

And the gasp she made upon seeing the vehicle he drove gave him no small amount of male satisfaction. He'd purchased the curricle on a whim just a few weeks before. It was a High Flyer, painted a deep scarlet color, and barely sat two people.

Which ensured no maid could accompany them. After a few moments of tense discussion, the maid, who'd discreetly followed the young miss outside, muttered under her breath and returned inside.

Miss Louella Rose did not seem overly disappointed as he showed her where to place her feet to climb on. High Flyers had the added benefit of allowing him to place his hands on her waist for assistance as well as get a glimpse at slim, stockinged ankles. He was honest enough with himself to admit to enjoying the view.

And once he sat beside her, the entire lengths of their bodies touched.

"It's not all that practical, is it?" She took hold of his arm as he settled himself beside her.

Cameron laughed. No, it was not practical at all. And it represented his last gasp at bachelorhood.

"No, Miss Louella, it is not." He urged the horses forward, and with a jerk, they rolled away from her parents' home. "But it is fun."

She gripped his arm tightly. "It's also quite high off the ground!"

He slowed the horses slightly. "Are you frightened?" He didn't want to scare her. He'd become accustomed to giving his team a loose rein.

It was she who chuckled this time. "Not if you know what you're doing." But her grip on his arm held like a vise. "I imagine if you've captained a British Navy ship, you can manage this contraption well enough."

"I imagine." He'd only been captain those last two years. His first commission had been as a lieutenant on a small man-of-war ship, which he'd eventually commanded but relinquished when the opportunity to work on a larger ship had opened up. At the time, he'd thought he'd make the navy a lifelong career, which had been foolish.

His father was a duke.

It would have been ungrateful and irresponsible to stay away.

"My lord—"

"Cameron."

"My Lord Cameron?" she teased.

"Louella Rose," he countered.

But then she sobered. "How *did* you lose your fingers?"

He'd not told her that afternoon. "Bloodthirsty, aren't you?" He chuckled at her tenaciousness.

"You don't have to tell me if you don't want to."

"No, it's a little embarrassing, that's all. It was my own fault. Captain of his ship ought to know when to let go of a damn rope." He peeked over at her.

She was grimacing. "Ouch! And afterward, did you fall ill?"

"I suppose you could say that." Not wanting to appear weak before his men, he'd wrapped the wound and gone about his business for the remainder of the day. Early the next morning, he'd awoken with a raging fever. And the day after that, he'd nearly died. "The surgeon on board was either very skilled or I was very lucky. After less than a week, I was back on deck."

"Well I, for one, am glad you recovered."

Cameron cleared his throat. She had him talking about himself, something he normally avoided. He supposed that he had, after all, suggested this outing so they could come to know one another better. He flicked the ribbons as they turned off her father's property onto the main road. "You were a child when I left, Louella. Tell me, do you still climb trees?"

She slapped at his hand playfully. "Of course not. I haven't climbed a tree since... last summer!" He felt her laughter in his chest somehow.

She quickly regained her composure. "Papa wouldn't be so happy to learn of it, though."

Ah, her papa. And her mother had told him that Louella was a "good girl." Cameron couldn't help but study her again. A smattering of freckles dusted the bridge of her nose, but her profile couldn't have been any more perfect; a pert nose and a sweet, delicate chin, not too pointed nor too rounded. Nothing too prominent to mar her features.

God, but she was young.

"It's not always a simple manner to please one's papa." He

referred to hers, but she apparently made the connection with his own.

"When you left... Why were you, as you said, an...?"

"Ass?" He finished the sentence so she would not have to.

He could have groaned at her question. He'd prefer even to be discussing the weather, or the next assembly to be held in the village.

But she persisted.

"I remember that your father had remarried, and his new wife was a mother to all those little girls. Did that have anything to do with it?"

Cameron wondered at her accurate assessment. "How old were you when I left, Louella? Eight? Nine?"

"Nine and a half," she supplied, then added, "I'm surprised you even remember me."

Ironically, he remembered her more so than most. Perhaps because she hadn't been a young lady throwing herself at him. Perhaps because of her very innocence.

"I remembered you, Louella."

"Before that last summer, you'd never singled us out in any way. You weren't overly friendly but not cruel either," she surprised him by saying. "Until you were." Ah, but she would land the dagger.

He shifted in his seat, uncomfortable under her scrutiny.

"Why did you leave? It had something to do with your father, did it not?"

He'd not understood his reason at the time. But he supposed she deserved an explanation of sorts. What could he tell her without revealing all the skeletons hiding in his family's closets?

"When I returned from school, I learned that my father had established for himself a new family. I hated him for it. He'd done it while I was away and still grieved for my mother. I suppose I was overly sensitive to it all. Add to that my own selfish rebellion… wanderlust… That's my only excuse, Louella, really. I wish I had something better than that."

He couldn't blame her for holding his atrocious behavior against him, could he?

She sat silently as they drove. He wished he could take his words from all those years ago back. He couldn't even remember all that he'd said. He knew he'd been a terror though. Hell, he'd known it at the time but simply hadn't cared. And now, he'd stumbled on consequences he never would have foreseen.

"Did you really see us that way? So below you? Olivia is a beautiful lady, I'll have you know. You'll see for yourself. Perhaps be sorry you have offered for me."

He slid her a sideways glance, unable to hide his roguish inclinations. "I doubt it, Louella Rose."

"Hmm…" Her lips pinched together.

He steered around a rut, not wanting to snap one of his wheels off. But then he focused his attention on her again.

"What do you mean by that very cryptic sound?" This time, he would know what *she* was thinking.

"We all do things sometimes that we are sorry for later." She spoke reluctantly, as though she would rather not reveal this information to him. And then she surprised him with more candor. "Tell me the truth. You have been very… kind to me. Not unpleasant at all. But you are only offering for me because of the mine, aren't you? I'd rather know beforehand."

CHAPTER SIX

THE MINE

"*T*hat bloody mine." Cameron's language had certainly suffered for his years spent in the navy. But she rather liked it. Hearing such coarse words come out of his mouth made him seem less an heir to a duke. Earthier... dangerous....

But, of course, he wasn't.

Regardless, she needed to know the truth. She didn't want to have unreasonable expectations.

"It does complicate matters between the two of us, and I'd rather go into this with my eyes wide open," she persisted.

He shook his head, almost imperceptibly—not an answer really, and then let out a loud sigh. "Do you think there's any truth to the rumors?" he asked in a sincere tone. He had been away for the past decade. Was it possible he really didn't know?

A farmer's cart approached them, so he steered his vehicle closer to the edge of the road.

"Which ones? The curse or the gold?" She'd heard variations of both for as long as she could remember. She also noted that he'd evaded her question.

He grimaced, still focused upon his driving. "The gold. I

imagine the curse amounts to no more than the result of poor engineering and bad luck."

Louella stopped herself from snorting at the notion of gold trapped somewhere on her father's ill-fated property. If such was the case, he'd have opened the mine years ago... decades...

But ought she to tell this to the marquess? After all, it was likely the root of the duke's desire for an alliance between their two families.

And if Lord Stanton's father discovered there was no gold, he'd seek an altogether different bride for his only son.

Which would certainly solve most of her problems.

And add to those of her parents.

She'd already caused them plenty of grief. Could she live with herself if she caused them more?

As she contemplated the notion, she realized that the man seated beside her was shaking with laughter. "Oh, Louella, such beautiful irony. You don't believe there is any gold in there either, do you?"

Oh, no!

"Well, nobody knows for certain." Best to try to leave some doubt in his mind.

He peered at her sideways, mischief lurking in his gaze. "Have you ever visited it?"

Surprisingly enough, she had not. Going to the mine had been forbidden, but even that had not been necessary. Years of stories of ghosts and curses had been enough to keep her and Olivia away. She'd been curious enough, certainly, but never had the courage to go on her own.

Shaking her head, she returned the question. "You?"

"A few times, with some other lads from the village."

They'd just come upon a clearing and he began turning his fancy vehicle around in a tight circle. "We'll see the lake another time," he explained. "Since this mine is 'complicating' matters, as you say, I think you ought to, at the very least, get a good look at it."

She wasn't quite sure what she thought of this impulsive decision he'd made. Was such a characteristic in a gentleman, a prospective husband, a good thing, or a bad thing?

She wasn't sure.

But she did know one thing. Her heart felt lighter now. In fact, it had jumped at the novelty of doing something so new and different.

"Isn't it just a hole in the ground?" she asked. She ought to put up some sort of protest.

What would her father say if he found out she'd gone?

"Oh, no, Miss Louella Rose." His voice was serious, but there was a glimmer in his glance as he looked over at her. "It's an adventure!"

And his statement proved true as soon as they turned onto the road leading up to the mine. Having gone mostly unused for decades, the road—if one could even call it such—had been overrun with grass and weeds, and in a few spots, eroded by trenches made by storms.

But the marquess maneuvered his expensive vehicle commendably, avoiding most of the bumps and ruts. Only a few times did she have to push leafy branches aside so they did not snag her bonnet off her head. She found herself laughing.

This *was* exciting! *An adventure!*

As the road climbed, the views from a few precarious places took her breath away.

But she was not afraid.

He was in complete control of the horse and seemed to understand the capabilities of the vehicle.

Perhaps she ought to have been afraid but having him by her side eased her mind. Deep in her bones, she knew that Captain Lord Cameron Denning, Marquess of Stanton, would sacrifice his own self in an instant, if need be, to protect her.

He'd do the same for any lady.

If he was not certain of his ability to keep her safe climbing this neglected road upon her father's property, he would not have taken her on it.

Even so, she breathed a sigh of relief when they arrived at a clearing.

They'd not spoken much as they'd gotten closer. She'd been glad of that, allowing him to concentrate fully upon his driving.

At one end of the lot, a boarded-off building leaned against the side of the hill, tracks and aged wooden cars parked haphazardly around the closed-up mine. A few hammers and axes rested upon a long wooden bench, rusted and splintered.

"There is no way to look in, is there?" she asked.

"There is a trail we can take to the right. It leads to another opening. It's not far, a few hundred yards." He glanced at her feet in approval. "I'm glad to see you've worn practical shoes. Not that I'd mind carrying you, but you'd miss out on the satisfaction of achievement one gains from such a hike." The corner of his mouth ticked upward.

Was he joking with her, or was he *flirting*?

"Right you are, sir." She played along with him. "And who'd carry our picnic? You did bring a picnic, did you not?" This she said as he ambled around to her side of the high-perched seat. Rather than allow her to climb down, much the way he'd shown her how to board, he held his arms up to her.

"Put an arm around my neck, Miss Louella. Easier that way."

As she did, he caught her weight and then let out an exaggerated groan. *He's teasing me!*

He toggled his eyebrows. "Now that I've got you, what should I do with you?"

"You should sit me down, my lord, lest I demand you carry me all the way up the hill, after all."

She joked, but her heart raced.

The pure maleness of him assaulted her senses. His scent unlike anything she'd experienced before. For it wasn't simply the leather spicy essence of cologne, but the warmth of him, the strength, and... safety.

She'd wrapped one arm around him when he'd taken hold of her. The sinewy chords of muscles in his shoulders and neck flexed beneath her arm. She placed her other hand upon his chest, just below his cravat.

Rather than set her down, he shifted her in his arms and placed one booted foot upon a nearby boulder. And then the light in his eyes changed from laughter to something else, something... intense.

His lips hovered inches from hers, and his eyes gave her nowhere to hide. She studied the different colors around his pupil; olive, with dancing gold lights and a few flecks of brown and blue. His pupils dilated, and something flared that she didn't quite understand. Or maybe she did. Could it be desire? Lust?

The urge to bury her head against his shoulder nearly overwhelmed her.

It was either do that or close her eyes and offer her lips again.

Which was not something she'd set out to do today. She'd wanted to gain a better understanding of him. Of his character, not this.

Whatever it was.

"I could always return later for the basket." Warm breath mingled with her own as her lips parted. The heady taste of his breath was like a drug. Heat swept through her.

He'd kissed her boldly before, with their parents possibly waiting on the opposite side of the door. How might he kiss her knowing they had certain privacy?

Was he going to kiss her again?

Because, dear God in heaven, that was exactly what she wanted.

"But then I'd miss out on all of that satisfaction... from the walk... and such..." Her voice rasped, practically a whisper. How had this happened? So quickly? He'd mesmerized her.

"I thought I could deny myself until we finished our picnic..." His voice emerged low and gravelly.

"Deny yourself of what?"

"Kissing you."

Her heart skipped another beat. Several, in fact.

"Far too much value is placed upon self-control these days." Had those words really come out of her own mouth?

Surely, this broke every rule of courtship, but held tightly against this man, feeling the heat of his breath already on her lips, she didn't care.

Louella leaned forward, shortening the gap between their lips by half.

He'd yet to move, but his gaze settled intently upon her mouth.

And then there was no more talking. No more thinking.

How could a person talk or think once she turned to pudding? Which was what happened when he claimed her lips at last.

So different from London. This time, he was holding her fully, her arms twined around his head and neck.

This time, her lips parted to taste him before the kiss had even begun.

And taste him, she did.

The sensation of not thinking, of simply feeling and touching and kissing, magically cast her under some sort of spell. It awakened inside of her a new want, a new need.

She would fret about everything else later. About William, her father's failing estate, her mother's nerves and megrims, Olivia, the darkness inside her...

"Umm…" His mouth sent vibrations into her own as he moaned. Was that the same pleasure she felt? Did he enjoy this as much as she did?

"Damn, Louella. Perhaps a quick betrothal isn't such a bad idea after all," he muttered as his lips abandoned hers to create new havoc along her throat and the lobes of her ears.

He would marry her, knowing nothing of her but this.

Knowing nothing of all her imperfections. Knowing nothing of her weakness and shame. He'd tie himself to her forever. He'd proposed while in London knowing nothing of who she was. Believing her to be as beautiful on the inside as she was on the outside.

And yet nothing had changed. She suppressed a shudder at the thought of him knowing…

"If it is something you wish," she barely managed to whisper between the hitches in her breath.

He pulled back and looked at her curiously. His hair was mussed where her hands had been, and his lips glistened, appearing fuller than they had before. He shook his head as though to clear his thoughts and then lowered her to the ground.

She thought he might say something, but then he turned back to the curricle and reached up to grab the picnic basket.

Bowing slightly, he gestured toward what must be the path he'd referred to earlier. "This way, madam."

Had she done something wrong?

They'd been having such a spectacular moment, and then he'd stopped.

What had she said? Only that she would do what he wished. Perhaps he'd grown tired holding her. Perhaps he was hungry. Perhaps he regretted mentioning the betrothal again.

Louella lifted her skirts a few inches and marched forward, her head swimming from being in his arms.

She searched her mind for something to say; anything to

disperse this new tension pulsating from him, but she could not come up with a single thing.

"It is cooler up here," she said finally. Thank God for the weather! Good conversation was an accomplishment all young ladies understood, and when at a loss, one could always safely turn to some meteorological comment.

He grunted behind her.

Louella quickened her pace.

What had she done?

"And yet we must be closer to the sun." That might explain why her face felt hot and flushed.

"An acute observation." He'd kept pace easily and spoke from directly behind her. If only she could turn around and look at him, perhaps she could read the expression on his face.

She halted and, feeling a slight breeze, reached up and removed her bonnet. He would stop as well. Gentlemen did that. Closing her eyes, she reveled in the cool air as it caressed her face. "Ah, but the breeze is nice."

He remained silent.

She opened her eyes to see that he ignored the spectacular view below in favor of scowling in her direction.

"Is it not something you wish, Louella? Do you not wish to marry in general or is it me, in particular, you have an aversion to?" He bristled with an altogether different intensity—more along the lines of exasperation. "I know this entire... alliance has been arranged in a most calculated manner, but I'd thought that perhaps..." He turned his head away from her at this point. "God damn it, I'll not marry a chit who's being coerced."

An aversion to him?

"I'm not a martyr!" she answered. How else could she respond to that? She'd accepted his initial proposal because she'd been told that she must.

Did *he* consider *himself* a martyr for having to ask for her?

But he seemed to care about her feelings. *"Is it not something* you wish, Louella?" he'd asked. Did she wish it? What did she wish?

God, she wished she knew!

"I have no aversion to you, Cameron. I'd have thought you'd perhaps concluded this by now."

He scrubbed one hand across his face. "I have. I had. I thought anyhow." He finally looked back over at her. "Is this still because of how I treated your sister? Because there is nothing I can do about that now. It's over. It's done. I've already told you I would apologize. But I cannot take it back." He seemed so very sincere! "Would it help if I met with your sister? If I apologized to her?"

Surely, he'd be irritated for having to take such a measure.

Louella could no longer pretend that she had not forgiven him. Olivia herself had admitted it was a long time ago. And yet, Louella wanted him to meet her sister again. She wanted to see his reaction to her sister's goodness and light—if he recognized it even.

And he'd possibly begin to see the truth in her.

An ache twisted her gut.

"I think an apology couldn't hurt."

He turned to look at the scenery and then let out a long, hard sigh. He then brushed a hand over his face again. "An apology," he stated.

"Yes," she answered.

* * *

There was always a catch. This couldn't be so simple as he'd wish it to be.

When Cameron first realized he was expected to marry in the very near future, he'd been concerned that the lady would not be to his liking. And when he'd heard the identity of the bride selected for him, he'd been concerned that she was still something of a child.

And then he'd gotten an eyeful of Miss Louella Rose.

Not a child.

Definitely to his liking.

Perhaps too much so.

Of course, he would apologize to Miss Olivia Redfield. He only hoped it was enough to dispel the resentment Louella still held toward him.

"And you will be satisfied by this?"

Louella smoothed her skirt and then stared back up at him solemnly with those crystal blue eyes and a sweet pout on her lips. Lips that parted far too easily beneath his own and tasted of sweet, sweet woman.

What were they talking about?

Louella had removed her bonnet, and wisps of shining brown hair fluttered in the breeze. Her cheeks were flushed and those lips of hers appeared pinker than they had earlier, and a little swollen...

He stepped forward and took her hand in his. "When would you have me make this apology then? Tomorrow?"

She nodded.

Damned if he wasn't already wrapped around her little finger. "Are we going to have this picnic then?"

She smiled and nodded again. "I'm famished!"

CHAPTER SEVEN

THE APOLOGY

The next morning, Louella dressed early, and without waiting to share breakfast with her mama, she slipped outside and strolled leisurely across her father's property. Sleeping had been practically impossible. Every time she'd closed her eyes, all she could do was think about *him*.

Such a silly afternoon!

Such a wonderful afternoon!

After their tense discussion, she'd allowed herself to give into the enchantment of his company. How long could it last? Rolling her shoulders, she rejected the doubts that assailed her. Likely, he'd quickly see her for who she was. He'd see through to her weak character.

And when that time came, she'd likely be his wife.

Spending the afternoon with him had felt almost magical.

Louella opened the iron gate and wove her way around the various headstones. Flickering sunlight dappled the grass and ornamental monuments as a breeze stirred the trees above. Walking through a graveyard ought to make a person uneasy.

It soothed Louella. No doubts here. Only truth.

She propped herself against William's headstone and

opened her satchel to remove the book. As the rhyming verse rolled off her tongue, it almost felt like a song or a prayer.

And as though she'd performed a penance, her heart settled into a calm rhythm.

"He will be kind to Olivia this time. He is a good man, I think." She plucked at a blade of grass growing at the corner of the stone. "I wish…" Sometimes she wished she looked different. Plainer. Not as pretty.

But she didn't really. What if people looked the same on the outside as they did on the inside? She flinched at her thoughts.

And that was the crux of the matter.

William would not answer her. He wouldn't argue or expect her to be something she was not. "One's outward appearance can be deceiving, as you well know, and I fear that is all he sees when he looks at me." And then she groaned. "But I do like him, Will."

She sighed and watched the soft stirrings of the branches around her until the ground felt damp beneath her bottom and her back ached from sitting against something cold and hard for so long.

"Wish me luck, Will. I love you." She ran her hand along the top of the rough stone before turning to go.

It did not take long for Louella to walk the rest of the way. This time, she found Olivia outside, working in her garden. Catching sight of Louella's approach, her sister stood and pushed her large floppy hat back. How could her parents not see how beautiful their eldest daughter was? Standing amidst her flowers and other plants that would produce blossoms in a month or two, Olivia shone with goodness.

"You went for a very long drive with him yesterday." Mama must have made a rare visit to the cottage for Olivia to know this. "Did he kiss you?" Olivia's eyes danced teasingly as she removed her soiled gloves.

Louella could do nothing to prevent the heat from traveling

up her neck into her face. Olivia would notice despite Louella's bonnet.

He'd kissed her. Several times. While sitting, enjoying their picnic, he'd leaned forward on more than one occasion and pressed his lips against hers. He'd fed her slices of an apple and the simple act had felt far more intimate than she would have guessed. Had Louella behaved imprudently? She'd certainly allowed Cameron liberties she'd never given any other man who tried to court her.

And before driving back down, he'd pressed her against the side of his vehicle for one last ardent embrace.

She'd opened her mouth for his kiss. Disgraceful! Shameful!

Exquisite.

He had been oh, so charming.

And he'd seemed utterly sincere. He'd not pushed her to do anything she didn't already want.

He'd promised to come here today and apologize to her sister for a ten-year-old offense. No man would do such a thing if he lacked character.

He'd thought she still resented him for the hurt he'd inflicted with his words nearly a decade ago. It was what she'd allowed him to believe, but in truth, she'd mostly forgiven him already. And her sister didn't act as though she held any ill will from so long ago.

"Livvy...?" she ventured tentatively, uncertain as to how her sister would react to the news that a marquess would be coming here to apologize.

Olivia's eyes narrowed. "What have you done? Tell me you haven't done more than kiss him?"

"Haven't what? Oh! No. Not that! Never that!" Louella shook her head at Olivia's question. Her sister never had been one to wax eloquent.

But would Olivia appreciate what Louella had come to say?

"Er, well." She might as well spit it out. "I asked Captain Lord Stanton to come here and apologize to you."

Violet eyes widened in surprise. Since moving out of the main house, Olivia did not receive formal visits, least of all from titled gentlemen. "When? I mean, I wish you'd asked first. And to apologize!" She placed both hands upon her cheeks. "How mortifying! And look at me! I'm covered in dirt!"

"He won't arrive until later this afternoon. Plenty of time for you to prepare."

Olivia's mouth opened and closed once, twice, again.

"He has told *me* how sorry he was for his ill behavior, but I am not the person he must apologize to, am I? It is you who deserves the apology."

Olivia moaned but then seemed to reconsider. "I certainly don't expect an apology, but I would like to meet him, ensure he's good enough for my little sister."

"Mary can help, too." Mary was Olivia's housekeeper and maid. Her parents couldn't exactly send their eldest daughter to live down here all alone, after all. "We shall have a bath prepared. And you can wear one of your finer gowns."

Olivia removed her hat altogether and tossed it onto a bench near the porched entrance. She was so real—always genuine! Louella plucked at the ribbon around her wrist and followed her sister inside.

* * *

Two minutes before the appointed time, the clop-clop of a horse's gait came through the open window. Mary had done something to add shine to Livvy's hair, curled it, and piled most of it atop her head. A dab of rouge and just a touch of lip stain made her look prettier than ever. Olivia had claimed it was all too much trouble for a casual visit, but Louella had insisted.

At the sounds of his arrival, both women remained in the parlor, but they each sat up a little straighter when the knock sounded at the door.

"Miss Redfield is expecting me, I believe." His voice carried through the foyer. "Captain Lord Cameron Denning, Marquess of Stanton."

Louella suppressed a smile when she heard him state his full name and title. Later, she would play it over and over in her mind.

She shivered. He spoke to Mary with a great deal of authority, sounding quite out of place in Olivia's little abode.

And he had come because of her! Because she'd asked him to!

"Right this way, my lord," the maid addressed him with due respect. His steps grew louder until Mary pushed the door open to the small parlor. "Captain Lord, I'm sorry, Stanton, was it?" At his nod, Mary gestured for him to enter and then clicked the door shut behind him.

With a barely perceptible wink in Louella's direction, Lord Stanton approached Olivia as she stood and bowed over her hand. "Miss Redfield."

"How do you do, my lord?" Olivia dipped into a curtsy, keeping her eyes lowered.

Louella, feeling suddenly awkward, joined them in the center of the room and dropped into a curtsy as well. Studying the two of them from beneath her lashes, she could not help but remember that her sister and Captain Lord Stanton were closer in age than she was to either.

"I am well." He stood at his full height, appearing uncomfortable but still quite charming. "It has been a long time."

With her face turned away from him, Olivia laughed

nervously. "Almost ten years. I imagine your family is pleased to have you home safe once again."

Louella released the breath she'd been holding. Her parents ought not curtail Olivia from participating in society. Her sister didn't always say or do the expected, but she delighted those who knew her.

"My father has admitted his relief on more than one occasion." Cameron twisted his lips into a sneer for just a moment, but he quickly replaced it with a smile. His sarcastic lapse gave her reason to wonder about his relationship with the duke. They'd spoken on numerous topics the day before, but he'd avoided saying much, if anything at all, about his father.

"Do sit down." Olivia gestured to the open seat beside Louella.

Which also brought his attention around to her again. "Miss Louella Rose." He ignored the seat for the moment to lift her hand to his lips.

Lips which had tasted more than the back of her hand barely twenty-four hours earlier.

"My lord." Yesterday, she'd called him Cameron. She couldn't bring herself to do so today. Profuse emotions beset her at his touch. Pleasure. Excitement. Uncertainty.

He held her hand a moment longer than he'd held Olivia's, his gaze traveling over her person and then returning to her eyes, expressing satisfaction.

But he does not know me, a tiny voice taunted. *He only knows what he sees.*

Breaking the connection he seemed to be seeking, Louella took back her hand and sat primly on the seat as far from him as possible. He distracted her far too easily.

"I take it then that Miss Louella has informed you as to the nature of my visit?"

* * *

Although the elder Miss Redfield avoided his gaze, Cameron couldn't help but notice the knowing glances the two sisters exchanged.

Had he never met Louella, not found himself caught up in his attraction to the younger woman, he imagined he might have been drawn to her older sister. Blonde and petite with voluptuous curves, she possessed an allure all her own. But his thoughts had not strayed far from Louella since he'd conveyed her back to Thistle Park yesterday afternoon.

Odd, really. He hadn't been besotted with one particular woman for ages. Looking at her now, he wasn't so sure she returned the feelings.

Miss Redfield sat relaxed, a smile of mirth dancing behind her lips while Louella could not have sat any straighter if a board was placed along her spine.

Two girls could not have been any more different in demeanor or in looks.

When the blonde girl finally met his gaze, her left eye meandered ever so slightly. How had he forgotten the color of this young lady's eyes? Violet blue, vivid and laughing.

God, he'd been an ass. He'd probably been attracted to the chit all those years ago but had known his father would not approve.

Louella didn't meet his gaze. She seemed nervous as she fidgeted with the ribbons wrapped around her wrists.

She confounded him. Taller, thinner than her older sister, she seemed afraid of joy. A beauty, by God, but he longed to unlock the sunshine inside of her. He'd experienced glimpses of it yesterday and before, when he'd met with her in London.

Cam swallowed the large lump that had suddenly formed in his throat.

"Miss Redfield, I have been reminded that in the past, before my commission, in fact, I treated you—" He'd rehearsed this in his mind the entire ride over. Now that he'd begun, he could not remember a word.

"It is forgotten." The blonde girl interrupted his apology before he'd even begun to make it, and she dropped her lashes and smiled sympathetically. "To be perfectly frank, I hardly even remember it. It bothered my sister far more than myself." She glanced sideways at Louella, pure sisterly affection in her teasing smile. "However, I thank you for going to the trouble of coming here, at her request, today."

Cam searched his memory for those days just before he'd left England. From what he could recall, he'd come across Miss Olivia Redfield and her much younger sister dangling from trees that reached over the fishing hole he preferred. He'd found the best way to escape his stepmother and her daughters had been to fish in the lake that adjoined Viscount Hallewell's estate with his father's.

At the thought of Louella as a child, rolling her eyes at something the older girl said, Cameron nearly smiled. He'd winked at her on a few occasions. As though both of them were in on a joke that Miss Olivia Redfield did not understand.

But he'd become angrier and angrier with his father. With his lot in life. He'd missed his mother and felt his father had betrayed her in the worst possible way.

"My memory of that time is not without a few holes. It was a long time ago, Miss Red—"

"Olivia." Her tone broached no argument.

Oh, yes, he remembered this about her now. She'd addressed him in a familiar manner, but had been sweet and kind. He'd repaid her with insults.

"Olivia." He was to make an apology, after all. He cleared his throat.

Feeling Louella's eyes upon him, he would not be deterred.

"The manner in which I spoke to you on a few occasions was not well done at all. I likely believed it to be sport on my part, but I now realize it was cruel, and…" He shook his head in disbelief at his younger self's conduct. "I beg your forgiveness."

Silence, but for the ticking of the clock on the mantle, settled on the room.

His intended's sister pursed her lips in deep thought. "You were not alone," she reminded him. "You were with another boy."

Something he'd completely forgotten. "Fellowes. Earl of Kingsley, now." Whereas Cameron's unruly behavior had been motivated by angst and spite, Fellowes had seemed driven by an unnatural recklessness.

Cameron hadn't met up with Kingsley since he'd returned. As memories flooded in, he cringed. They'd been terrors that last summer.

Miss Redfield nodded slowly. "Yes. He was a delight, too."

Cameron cleared his throat and shook his head. He didn't quite know how to respond regarding Kingsley. "But do I? Have your forgiveness, that is?"

This time, she nodded firmly. "But, of course, you have it, right, Louella?" Olivia addressed her younger sister solemnly.

Eyes that reminded him of the sea at dawn blinked slowly as she nodded. "Thank you, my lord."

She'd spoken his given name freely yesterday. He supposed she felt uncomfortable doing so when they were not alone.

"As long as you treat my sister with due respect, we shall get along splendidly." An odd warmth stirred in Cameron at hearing Louella's sister make such a proclamation. His relationships with his own stepsisters barely merited polite comments in passing and during social functions.

The lady he planned on marrying smiled sheepishly. Louella carried far too much responsibility on her young shoulders. Perhaps more than he'd initially realized.

"She is a good girl," her mother had said.

She'd been pressured into accepting him. For the family? For her father's estate? That was a great deal of weight to bear for one so young.

And she'd been willing, loyal, almost to a fault. A rare quality he could hardly comprehend.

His father certainly hadn't exhibited any loyalty to his mother. On board ship, allegiance to one's comrades existed to a point, but they'd all known self-preservation to be the great motivator.

His stepsisters seemed close enough to one another. He'd barely acknowledged them before taking on his commission. And since returning, he'd been preoccupied with matters other than getting to know his younger siblings.

Perhaps he ought to take some time to do so. He'd returned home. He would have a wife, and then a family. And someday, all of his father's burdens and privileges would become his own. That would include caring for his sisters.

He wanted more than his father had had.

He wanted affection. He hoped Louella would be the woman to provide it. She'd already shown him she could be warm and sweet and charming. She was not weak-willed. She would make a wonderful mother, he had no doubt. She'd champion her children, turn all of that loyalty toward them.

And him?

He had no idea.

* * *

After asking dozens of questions that Louella wished she had thought to ask herself and consuming tea and several small sandwiches, Olivia placed her hands on her belly and groaned.

"I'm positively stuffed!" Her innocent pronouncement was made without much thought for propriety. "How about you, Louella?"

Louella smiled at Olivia's lack of inhibitions. "It was lovely, indeed."

She'd not done much more than nibble at the corner of one cucumber sandwich. She'd been enthralled listening to Cameron's answers. She'd known he lived on ships for most of the past decade but hadn't realized the extent of hardship one faced while at sea. Of course, storms would be harrowing, and boredom would eventually set in, but upon listening to some of Cameron's descriptive answers, she realized he'd faced dangers she'd never considered. And she couldn't help but wonder if she would become ill if ever she had an opportunity to travel by sea herself.

But she also learned that, as challenging as the existence had been, he'd loved it.

The corner of his lips turned up and excitement lit his eyes as he spoke of the winds and currents, and what a sunset looked like with nothing but ocean to reflect its light.

Her own life experiences, in comparison, were rather limited. When he mentioned docking in France and Portugal and India even, she wondered that she held his attention at all

Other than her looks, what about her could possibly be of interest to him?

So caught up in her imaginings, she startled when he rose from his seat and bowed toward Olivia. "I cannot remember when I've enjoyed a more delightful afternoon." He lifted Olivia's hand to his lips.

Olivia laughed in that carefree manner of hers and thanked him for coming. Louella was happy to see her sister meet his gaze directly by the end of the meeting.

Lord Stanton had treated Olivia with the utmost kindness, charm, and respect. This was not always the case with strangers, and Louella hated nothing more than watching a person deem Olivia unworthy of their attention because of one minor flaw. Not even a flaw in Louella's mind.

It made Olivia even more of a special gift.

"Louella."

The depth of his voice so near startled her.

His eyes caught hers. That warmth she'd seen in them remained.

"Will you show Lord Stanton out?" Olivia prompted. Her smile was a sign of her blessing. Olivia never withheld anything Louella wanted, and yet she never asked for anything for herself, never demanded her due.

"Of course." When Louella took his arm, the same excitement she'd experienced at his touch yesterday coursed through her.

He patted the top of her hand gently before wishing Olivia farewell. "Thank you again, for your kind hospitality, and for not being nearly hard enough on me for the past."

"You are always welcome, my lord." Olivia made no move to accompany them from the room. "We all make mistakes." And with a mischievous smile, she picked up some crocheting that she'd set aside earlier. "Take your time."

Louella could not suppress a grin at her sister's audacity.

Whatever would she do without her?

Louella could find no more excuses to resist this increasingly provocative gentleman. She smoothed her skirts as they stepped outside.

"Your sister has cultivated quite the gardens here." He squinted his eyes and stared up at the sky. "Walk with me?"

How could she decline? It had only been one day since their picnic at the mine and already she craved his company. No, she craved being alone with him. She rebelled against her conscience, which urged her to end this brazen behavior.

She wished she understood herself. It was all rather confusing.

Louella nodded.

"I believe your sister has forgiven me." He did not *sound* overly pleased as they strolled beside the house. "Can you?"

But she had!

"It was a lovely apology."

He'd looked like he might be angry with her but shook his head as though to clear his thoughts instead. "You have not answered my question."

Of course, she'd forgiven him. "I have. Yes," she tentatively began. "What do you think of Olivia?"

They strolled slowly through the walk leading around the house, so she was able to make out the furrowing of his brows.

"She is lovely. And kind. I hate the notion that I caused her grief through my own self-importance and thoughtlessness." He rubbed at his jaw. "And I'd nearly forgotten about Kingsley."

Louella no longer worried about the past, but the future. Cameron was a handsome heir; charming and kind. She deserved none of this. "But what do you think of Olivia now? She is my father's eldest daughter. I cannot imagine our fathers would care which daughter you married in order to secure their contracts."

He turned her so quickly that her breath caught.

With both hands pressed flat against the bricks above her shoulders, he caged her against the wall. If she wished to escape, she'd have to duck under his arms. Louella tried not to squirm as he looked off to the side and then back down at her.

Intensity blazed from his eyes; they appeared almost black. "Tell me if you do not wish to marry. I do not find you to be interchangeable with your sister."

Was it possible he wanted her? Wanted Louella for herself? Or was he enamored with her looks as every other person seemed to be?

"Why not?" She feared the glimmer of hope she felt.

He scowled.

"Why am I not interchangeable with my sister?"

He dropped his hands and turned away from her. "You're beautiful, of course." He inhaled sharply. "But..."

"But?" Louella held her breath, waiting for him to complete his statement. She touched his arm tentatively. "For what it matters, I, too, have forgiven you. It was long ago and you are no longer that same person." She needed to be perfectly honest with him.

"It was inexcusable," he maintained. Another breath, this time a little shaky.

"But?" Louella wanted to know what he'd been going to say before.

He swallowed hard. "I don't know. I expected to resent the woman chosen by my father. I expected to dislike you."

And then a bemused smile from him. And an earnestness in his gaze, so intense that she could not hold it. He grasped her hands between the two of them, cradling them protectively.

"But?" she urged him.

"No, no buts this time." He leaned forward and kissed the corner of her mouth. Sweet, warm tenderness she never could have imagined. "Can we move beyond this?"

When he held her, she could not deny him..

He crouched down so that he peered directly into her eyes. "What do you say, Louella, shall I speak to your father tomorrow?"

Oh, yes. She held his gaze this time, searching for reluctance on his part and seeing none.

The decision had been made days ago but, to suddenly be given a choice... She couldn't admit to feeling joy or an abundance of pleasure, because then she'd feel the imposter again.

"You may."

"And you no longer feel coerced into marriage with me? It is something you can look forward to?"

Could she hide her darkness from him? Could she push away her guilt? Could she do it less? Because she didn't want him to have a disgust of her. Ever. For some reason, this mattered a great deal.

She was already more than halfway in love with him, which was ridiculous. She'd gone from hating him to practically loving him after four brief meetings. Could he ever love her?

And did it matter anyway?

Her father most certainly did not think so.

He tilted his head and grimaced. "Ah... She hesitates."

Louella did not wish to disappoint him. She didn't want to be contrary or difficult. He was being so very *kind* about everything, and he most certainly did not have to be!

"When I believed I had no choice but to marry you, and I believed that you were a despicable person, I had decided I was not going to be happy in my marriage. But I was going to do it anyway. For my parents. But then I met you." He was not only handsome, with his sparkling green eyes and reassuring smile. Oh, no, he was so much more. "And you are *not* a despicable person. Quite the opposite, in fact. You did not have to take me for a drive in your shiny new vehicle yesterday, nor did you have to make an apology to Livvy today."

How could she explain that, in his kind gestures, he'd planted a new hope inside of her? He'd planted something quite wonderful but had also opened something of a Pandora's Box?

Because, now, she not only hoped she would not be *unhappy* with her father's choice of husband, she wanted far more. She wanted to believe that she might be *happy* with that choice.

She couldn't bear marriage to this man if he felt indifference, or worse, toward her.

The thought was a chilling one, indeed.

"Louella. If you are no longer *un*happy at the prospect of marrying me, what causes you to waver now?" His voice, not quite a whisper, didn't taunt her with frustration or impatience. He asked as though he truly cared what her answer would be.

This tall, strong nobleman who'd captained an entire ship of men, traveled throughout the world, now stood before her, wanting her to tell him what would make her happy.

She wished she knew!

"What of you, Cameron? Are you unhappy at the prospect of marrying a lady your father chose? Surely, you bristle at the thought of marrying a bride who is not your own choice?"

As she spoke, understanding dawned in his gaze.

"You want the same reassurances I seek. I've no wish to marry an unwilling bride any more than you want a reluctant husband."

She nodded. But there was more to it than that. "Well, almost," she corrected herself.

She wanted the two of them, if they were to marry, that was, to care for one another—to come to eventually love one another even.

But one could not just come right out and ask a gentleman if he might ever love her—especially when she felt so uncertain herself.

"Do you suppose... well, is it possible... that you might someday be the sort of husband who might come to love his wife? Sometime in the future, of course, the very distant future..."

The idea was so close to perfection that it frightened her. Because if everything were perfect than perhaps one day, she'd not feel the need to...

That was as far as her thoughts were allowed to go. Because Captain Lord Cameron Denning, the Marquess of Stanton, swooped in and began kissing her with an eagerness even greater than before. And when Captain Lord Cameron Samuel Benjamin Denning, Marquess of Stanton did that, all her doubts were swept away.

She barely registered that her back and arms pressed into the sharp brick of the house behind her, or the prick of the pin stored beneath the ribbon tied about her wrist.

All she felt was warmth seeping through the wool of his jacket. The crisp soft strands of his hair between her fingers. All the hardness of his male body as she melted into him.

Oh, yes, and the texture and warmth of his tongue as it trailed a path around her jaw to her neck, the heat of his breath teasing her skin.

Until he stilled, his face tucked between her shoulder and throat. "Well, Louella." He spoke against her skin. "Of course, there is this."

Oh, God, yes. She didn't need to ask him what he meant by "this."

This delightful burst of adrenaline and bonelessness that affected her whenever he was near.

And he didn't need to be near for her to feel it. Sometimes it happened simply at the thought of him.

"Is it possible for me to become a caring husband? In the very distant future, who perhaps could come to love his wife?" He would answer his own question as his mouth found hers again. Speaking against her lips, he whispered harshly, "It all depends upon the woman I marry."

Oh.

Oh!

"So, perhaps?" she whispered, almost afraid to hear the answer.

"Most definitively."

And then he released her lips and rested his forehead against hers.

"So, yes?" His voice carried a hint of pleading.

The intensity in his questioning gaze was overwhelming. She lowered her lashes for a restorative moment before meeting it again. "Yes." She tilted her wrist slightly and felt the sting of the needle. She didn't deserve such a magnificent opportunity for happiness. But she answered him again. "Yes, I can be happy at the prospect of this marriage."

CHAPTER EIGHT

THE MEANING OF HONOR

"*I* need you to lock up this marriage business, Stanton."

Crawford was in high dudgeon. They'd just finished the evening meal and Her Grace and his three sisters had withdrawn so that the duke and Cameron could take their port alone.

But there'd been a tension in his father throughout the meal. Cameron had wondered when Crawford would broach the subject of this engagement again.

Fortunately for Cameron, he was beginning to feel keenly about "this marriage business" as well.

"Working on it," he stated noncommittally. Even after having been away for nearly a decade, Cameron struggled to keep resentment out of his voice.

The duke took a sip of the burgundy liquid and then stared intently into his snifter. "Of course, you realize I wouldn't insist upon an alliance with Hallewell if there wasn't a great deal at stake."

At these words, Cameron understood two things.

One, that, of course, his father had somehow verified the existence of gold in the mine.

And two, that the viscount knew nothing of it.

"You've sent experts down, haven't you?" And then he pressed, "Exactly how much gold is there?"

Crawford was shaking his head, marveling it seemed. "My engineers assure me it's one of the largest veins they've encountered. They say they can reinforce the integrity of the structure itself and mining will pose no more danger than usual."

"Hallewell knows nothing of this, I presume." Cameron considered that Louella's father had seemed something of a desperate man, willing to sell his daughter off. But he needn't be so desperate after all.

"He's a fool," his father scoffed. "To believe tales of gypsy curses and such. It's his own damn fault for not looking into this himself."

Cameron had thought the boards on the back entrance to the mine seemed out of place. They hadn't had the aged and worn look of the boards on the front.

His father had sent men down that shaft without the viscount's consent or knowledge. He intended to benefit from his neighbor's weaknesses.

With Cameron's help.

And Cameron had, only a few days before, practically assured Louella there could be no gold. They'd laughed at his father's absurd obsession with reopening it.

"This betrothal contract you've drawn up, the one I've yet to sign. It includes a transfer of the mining rights then?"

"In exchange for a hefty annuity for his wife and daughter. He needn't worry about their security upon his death."

But Louella's father would surrender his land's greatest resource.

Taking a sip of his own port, Cameron mentally confronted

the idea of crossing the duke. "I'm to meet with the viscount tomorrow… and his daughter."

"Good, good. This could keep the ducal coffers full for decades to come, generations even."

Cameron placed his snifter upon the table. He needed something stronger than port tonight. Pushing his chair back, he rose. "If you'll excuse me, Your Grace." He was none too proud of his father at that moment.

"Stanton." Crawford's voice stopped him before he could exit. "Don't do anything that could spoil this for me."

Cameron clenched his jaw tight. He'd been home less than a week and already he was feeling the suffocating effects he'd always known as Crawford's heir. Pressure to put the title first. More important than friendship. More important than health. It was more important, it went without saying, than love.

And in one particular instance, it had been more important than life itself. Anger rang in his ears.

As long as Cameron could remember, he'd been aware of Crawford's incessant disappointment in himself and then his mother, who had failed to present him with a ducal spare. Even as a boy, he remembered the darkness that fell upon the house whenever she'd miscarried yet another babe.

And yet the brute had not given up.

His mother, well into her forties, had died in her attempt to please the duke—in her attempt to secure his succession with a spare.

Bolstering the lineage was imperative in the event Crawford's eldest did something stupid and got himself killed.

Cameron swallowed, shaking the ringing away and then nodded.

"We'll have the banns read on Sunday then." Crawford rubbed his hands together. "And mining can begin next month."

In a manner far more controlled than his thoughts, Cameron nodded and then closed the door silently behind him.

He'd been summoned away from his classes and told of the death of his mother by two of the school's highest administrators. He'd wanted to return for her funeral, but the event had already passed. She'd been in the ground for two weeks already when the duke had finally seen fit to send word to his heir.

By the time Cameron was allowed to come home, his father had remarried.

Ironically, the duke's second, much younger wife, hadn't experienced any success at securing the line either.

Would his father have purchased his commission if he'd known this would be the case?

Good God, Cameron had been a mess that summer.

He'd like to make excuses for himself. Miss Redfield had been too forgiving. He hadn't deserved her kindness.

He definitely shouldn't deserve her sister's hand. But he had it. And he'd never considered himself a martyr.

He'd carry out the promises he'd made to Louella. Every damn one of them.

Was he merely following the urgings of his lower anatomy? Or was there more to it than that?

He'd not felt such attraction in a very long time—if ever. And he had promised his father he'd make her an offer. It was all so convenient. It was all too perfect.

She seemed all too perfect.

But such doubts vanished when he was with her. In those moments, he only thought to make her his, in every way.

And to make her happy.

Rather as though she'd cast some sort of a spell on him. Which was ridiculous.

She expected him to ask for her hand again tomorrow, to follow through with his promise to meet with her father.

Had he actually said that he might eventually love her? By God, he had.

He located a footman and requested a mount be brought around. He needed away from his father's home tonight. Away from the clawing vines wrapping around him.

As he waited, his mind conjured the image she'd presented sitting in her sister's parlor. She'd been dressed in a thin cotton dress, which had revealed more of her curves than he'd seen before. The sleeves were short, but she'd had the silk ribbon wrapped around both of her wrists.

She'd quite stolen his breath. Although he'd found her sister to be surprisingly pleasant, he'd anxiously awaited an opportunity for them to be alone.

She'd had more questions for him.

Could he love one woman for the rest of his life? She'd asked. And with her sweet scent in his nostrils and her soft skin beneath his lips, he'd believed himself capable of doing just that.

Maybe he'd simply waited too long between women. Throughout his journeys, his missions, he'd been witness to too many of his men succumbing to *lues venerea,* or syphilis, to allow his baser urges to get the best of him at every port. He'd limited himself, instead, to a few specific courtesans. The ladies he lay with, he'd made certain, were selective in who they took on as customers.

Would have served his father right for him to succumb to a disease he'd caught with his prick.

"Your mount is out front, my lord," Cogsworth interrupted his musing.

There weren't any courtesans near Ashton Acres, but he'd find a willing female at The Dog and Pudding Pot five miles down the road. The last time he'd stopped, one of the serving wenches had seemed more than willing to… meet his needs.

He'd have a few drinks, take a room there. If he were soon

to retire his bachelorhood, then perhaps he'd find some satisfaction tonight.

Clear his head, so to speak.

* * *

"Stanton! I didn't think I'd see your ugly mug around here anytime soon. Thought you were sailing around the world!"

As though summoned by Olivia Redfield's mentioning his name earlier that day, Gabriel Fellowes, Earl of Kingsley, rose from the bench where he'd been sitting and approached Cameron with an outstretched hand.

Kingsley and he had known one another most of their lives, and they'd become chums while attending Oxford. And, of course, there had been that last summer.

Cameron imagined they'd both done their fair share of growing up in the past decade. He hoped so anyhow.

And yet, here they were again, in a taproom tucked away in a less than proper inn. Much as they'd done that last summer.

"Kings? What brings you to the Dog and Pudding? I thought you were out of the country."

Kingsley grinned at the question and wrapped one arm around a rather buxom barmaid. She had been reclining on Kingsley's lap before he'd pushed her aside to greet him.

"On my way from Brussels. Thought I'd make the best of my time before duty calls. What a happy coincidence indeed?"

Misgivings niggled in the back of Cameron's mind, what with the part Kingsley had played in his past treatment of the Redfield ladies, but it was satisfying to see a familiar face, nonetheless.

Kingsley ordered a round and dismissed the maid. After several pints, his old friend ordered a bottle of whisky. And once that had been consumed, they began discussing events in their lives that really mattered.

Women.

Fathers.

Kingsley had been betrothed for nearly a decade to a female chosen by his father. She was a lovely gel, but every time they set a date, a close relative managed to conveniently die, preventing them from going ahead with their nuptials. "Planned the first wedding the year after her come out. Luck would have it, one of her sisters passed a few months prior. The next year, it was her grandmother. After that, her father and then her mother. We've set a new date for the end of the Season, but…" Kingsley shrugged. "I've little confidence in the health of her family. More than likely, another one will give up the ghost before we make it to the altar."

After postponing the last time, Kingsley'd decided to take a tour of the continent. It was this holiday from which he now returned.

"Do you want to marry her?" Cameron couldn't help asking. Kingsley had never discussed the lady before. He certainly hadn't acted like a betrothed gentleman.

Hadn't and didn't still, Cam noted.

"She'll make a fine countess," the other man admitted. "Lovely girl, and she's been through so much. I've every intention of going through with it." But then he winked. "But until then, nothing to keep me from enjoying a little feminine company."

Cameron had a hard time imagining Kingsley limited to one woman.

His own tongue loosened by spirits, Cameron confided the news of his own betrothal. "Only good thing Crawford's ever done." He shook his head. "She's damn near perfect. Beautiful, of course, but more than that. Intelligent, entertaining." He'd not disrespect her by mentioning her lack of propriety. One aspect which had reassured him immensely.

He did not speak of the gold, nor the mine. He'd have liked to obtain another opinion on the complication, without sharing his father's treachery with anyone.

For that was precisely what he considered it to be.

Treachery.

For the good of the dukedom.

"Marriage," Kingsley commiserated before finishing the contents of the bottle he'd been working on. "At least she's not an antidote or a harpy—that you've seen. She could turn on you yet. Women have these ways... That being said, if you're determined to fulfill your famil—fam—il—yal..." he eventually got the word out, "obligations, might as well, er, 'enjoy' the chit while you can." He toggled his eyebrows at this.

Which was no doubt something Cameron longed to do... enjoy Miss Louella Rose, that was.

"What if," he asked, staring into the amber liquid remaining in another bottle that had somehow appeared on the table, "her father betrothed her based upon misinformation? Information that benefited your own estates, but... diminished his own? Would you be compelled to expose it?"

Kingsley's grin fell away at Cameron's hypothetical question. "Now, we're talking about honor."

Cameron nodded. "Honor and duty."

But Kingsley was shaking his head. "What good is duty without honor? Do you not fulfill your duty in order to preserve your honor?" And upon these words, Cameron surmised Kingsley had indeed done some changing. Despite the carousing, the raucousness, honor came first.

And that was the crux of it.

That was what he needed to hear.

"Absolutely, my friend." Cameron raised his glass in a toast. "To honor first."

Kingsley clinked his glass. "And then duty."

* * *

At home late that night, lying in her bed, Louella tried convincing herself that she ought to feel relieved. Cameron had met with Olivia in a civilized manner, and she'd dismissed his slights of a decade ago.

He still wished to marry her. He'd even admitted he might someday love her.

And he was to speak with her father tomorrow.

But she did not. Feel relieved—that was.

She didn't deserve him, or any of this. Anxiety squeezed her heart. Her skin felt jumpy, as though she needed to be moving, walking, running. Thoughts raced frantically around her mind.

None of this could be trusted.

She would not sleep easily. Not with this black cloud of doom hanging over her. Louella burst out of bed, the cool air chilling her through the cotton fabric of her night rail.

Pulling the heavy drapes away from the window, Louella examined the moonlight as it fell across the room. There was barely enough light. A candle would not be necessary.

In a determined calm, she crept around the bed and knelt, almost reverently, on the rug.

Promised relief beckoned as she withdrew the sewing basket. Ah, yes.

The oozing liquid seeped black and shiny creeping along her pale skin. But it was not black, she knew. It was red. Blood.

Her blood. More pressure. Another line.

William's blood had been brighter. She would never forget the minuscule dots. Sometimes larger clumps appeared when he had coughed into one of the white handkerchiefs he'd held in his small fists for days on end.

She tilted her arm to prevent drips from staining the carpet or her gown. She didn't want to wipe it away just yet.

After a few moments, watching, focusing on the stinging, her breaths came more evenly. She wished there were something else she could do, something that didn't leave marks, or the thin white scars afterward.

But she knew of nothing. And she wasn't hurting anyone, really. Why should it matter?

She cleaned her arm and wrapped it carefully. This time, when she lay down, her eyes drooped and her body relaxed. She could sleep.

He would come tomorrow, and she would accept him.

Mama and Papa would be happy with her. They would be relieved.

Feeling better than she had for days, Louella slept.

CHAPTER NINE

MOTHERS

"*L*ouella Rose." Her name sounded ominously at her bedside.

Not Jane.

Louella opened her eyes to stare up at her mother's contorted face peering angrily down at her.

"Louella Rose, if I must watch over you every waking second myself, you will never, ever take a needle or razor to yourself again. It is evil! Pure evil! And I'll not have a daughter of mine sent off to Bedlam!" her mother choked on a sob.

Oh no!

Oh, no!

Louella's arms flew up as her mother pulled back the covers and gasped. "Why would you do this to yourself?" One of the bandages had come undone and the fresh cuts could be seen through the thin material of her nightdress. Blood had seeped onto the sheets through her gown.

It looked so much worse than it really was.

"He's coming today. He has made an appointment with your father. He's going to be your husband, Louella. *He will have access to your body.* It will be impossible to keep something like this from him if we don't take drastic measures immediately." And then in a loud shriek, "Jane! Come here at once! At once!" She turned back to Louella. "If he discovers you doing this, he'll send you away, Louella! Do you understand?" Her mother's voice shook in anger and fear.

Jane rushed into the room, curtsied, and then winced when she caught sight of what her ladyship was hollering about. Louella's mother had grasped her arm and pulled the sleeve upward, as high as she could. Hundreds of white lines zigzagged beneath the newer scabs from earlier this week, and the fresher cuts from last night. From her palm to halfway up her forearm.

Another sob from her mother. "Why, Louella? Why?" And then, "Let me see the other one."

Feeling ashamed, Louella obediently held it out. She knew what her mama would see. She'd cut on the left arm for longer and those white lines traveled from her palm nearly all the way up to the crease of her elbow.

"You promised you'd stop, Louella. I don't understand any of it. What is the matter with you?" Her mother shook her head mournfully. "What in God's name drives you to do this?" It was as though Louella had betrayed her in the worse way.

Barely awake, and stunned by the early morning assault, Louella had no answers to give. She lifted her shoulders in a noncommittal shrug.

She had no idea how or why this compulsion overcame her.

She understood it, and yet she didn't. It didn't make sense, and yet, it did.

Her mother dropped Louella's hand and began pacing the room. "The banns will have to be read, which gives us a month." She then turned to the maid. "You will make certain Miss Louella has no access to any razors or needles or anything sharp from this day forward. You will sleep in this room. I will personally check my daughter every morning to ensure she is not doing this horrible thing! If I discover she has done it again, you will be sent packing immediately. Is that understood?"

Jane was nodding emphatically and then curtsying again. "Yes, my lady. Of course, my lady."

"But Mama!" Louella found her voice. "You cannot blame Jane! It is not her fault! She has told me to stop, over and over again! You cannot sack Jane for something I do!"

Her mother asked the impossible. If Louella could have stopped, she would have done so on her own. Mama asked too much!

And Jane knew it as well. Tears hovered in her maid's eyes. She looked as terrified as if her employment had already been terminated.

"I can and I will, Louella Rose. If you so much as make one more cut on your body, I will send Jane packing. Is that understood?"

Surely, her mother wouldn't really inspect Louella's skin, her body? Was nothing of her person to be respected? She wrapped her arms around herself and shivered, feeling exposed, vulnerable, and utterly hopeless.

And angry.

"I'll check you every morning, Louella. Don't think that I won't. There is far too much at stake. Do you understand what I'm saying?"

"But... why?" Why now?

Her mama dismissed Jane to prepare a bath and then sat down on the seat beneath the window. She waited a few moments before addressing Louella again.

"The duke and the duchess are very powerful people. If it is discovered that you are... doing this... they will send you away. This practice... It will not be tolerated. It isn't right. You will be locked up. Do you understand me?" She stared down at her wringing hands. "After you marry, your husband will be intimate with you. He will see the scars, the cuts. I don't even pretend to understand why you do this. I had prayed you'd stopped when I discovered it before. But, my dear, sweet, beautiful daughter," she implored. "I would die to think of you in an asylum. That is what your husband and his family would do."

Would he?

Louella looked down at her arms and studied them, seeing what her mother did. Not perfect. Broken. Scarred. Messy scribbling. Raised ridges. And yet along with the shame, she felt a certain amount of... pride. She was a real person.

Stopping was... impossible. The harder she tried to stop, the greater the battle.

And she always lost. Every single time.

But... she could not be the cause of Jane's dismissal.

Could she stop? Her heart raced at the thought. Sweat broke out on her brow, and the air seemed to disappear from the room. Was she still breathing? She must be.

"I cannot, Mama," she whispered.

Her mama pulled the chair forward and took both of her hands in hers. "You must."

* * *

Louella couldn't eat.

Her stomach was tied up in knots. When attempting to read, she could not concentrate. She could not find any comfort pacing the manor, nor strolling through her mother's unkempt garden. The minutes dragged by as though they were hours, and her brain flitted between how she could protect Jane and sharp objects that might go undetected.

When she returned to her chamber, Jane awaited her with an anxious look in her eyes. Louella shook her head, attempting to reassure the maid. The woman who'd provided her with steady support and assistance for so long had done nothing to deserve any of this.

Louella's mother could not have chosen a more effective punishment.

Both she and Jane were unusually silent as they prepared Louella for Cameron's arrival.

The excitement and exhilaration she'd felt yesterday at the prospect of becoming betrothed had been squashed. While Jane curled and pinned her hair, Louella's mind wandered to the needles tucked into her sewing basket.

And when Jane slipped out the door to order a bath, and before her mother could order everything sharp removed from Louella's room, she hastily retrieved the basket, tugged aside the coverlet, and transferred three of the needles to a safer location.

They beckoned her.

More so, it seemed, than ever before. She needed to protect them.

"You can do it, Miss Louella. I have faith in you." Recalling Jane's attempts at encouragement, Louella groaned. While her maid would do everything possible to keep Louella from falling into her dark abyss, Louella was contemplating when she might be left alone long enough...

"I'm so sorry, Jane." Louella nearly began crying again.

Her own tears annoyed her. She'd let many fall this morning already.

Lord Stanton was expected around tea time.

Jane twirled and pinned curls and braids with more deliberation than she ever had before. It was as though she hoped to protect her position through sheer force of will. Louella knew that Jane had three younger sisters and an ailing mama at home. She sent most of her pay for their care.

The dress they'd chosen for today was more of an evening

gown than something one would wear during the day. But it was a special occasion.

A very special occasion.

The bodice, cut low, had fringes of lace all along the edges. The puffed sleeves were short.

Jane had made a bow of lace to cover her arms. They looked to be natural adornments, with the delicate strands matching the lace on the dress itself.

Watery blue eyes stared back at Louella from the mirror. Eyes which were only slightly less puffy than they'd been before soaking them with lavender water.

A delicate hint of paint on her lips, and she was ready for his arrival.

Just in time, too, it seemed, as her mother appeared in the doorway to her chamber.

"He's late." Her mother's eyes were somewhat puffy as well. "Why don't you come down for tea, and we'll await him in the drawing room?"

Louella nodded solemnly. Wouldn't it be ironic if he failed to show?

Sitting in the drawing room, awaiting his visit with her mother, Louella experienced the sensation that she'd done this before.

Only this time, he was very late.

Just when she was certain she might explode from nervousness, an approaching horse sounded in the distance. The rider would be none other than Lord Stanton. The day was chilly and cloudy, but he would not arrive alone in a carriage.

Knowing he was coming and would be cheerful and pleasant, Louella fought a tremor that threatened to run through her body. She'd not realized how wound up she'd become.

Your husband will be intimate with you. Her mother's warning echoed in her mind.

Masculine voices drifted upstairs as Lord Stanton requested

he meet with the viscount. Louella and her mother unapologetically eavesdropped.

A bit of shuffling closer to the drawing room and then her papa's voice beckoned the younger man into his study. With the sound of the nearby door closing, silence ensued once again.

Mama sat her book aside and rose. "I expect they won't be overly long, Louella. I'll make myself scarce."

Nodding, Louella lifted her tea to her lips with shaking hands. Thankfully, the normally hot liquid had grown tepid because some of it splashed onto the saucer.

Anxious not to spill on her dress, she set both cup and saucer aside and reached instead for the gown she'd been decorating.

She'd stuck her embroidery needle through the material earlier.

Another needle her mama had missed.

Overcome by the thought of this morning's events, she blinked away a few tears and forced herself to stitch another half-moon. She'd sewn the moon and two more stars before her father's and then Lord Stanton's voices echoed from the other side of the door.

Uncertain, she stood. When she went to smooth her skirt, she realized she still clutched the gown in front of her.

But then the door opened, and Cameron stood in the threshold. He towered over her father, and his presence filled the room.

And for the first time all day, she was not thinking about sharp objects, or her mother, or Jane.

She licked her lips and drank in the sight of him. He'd dressed for the occasion but upon closer inspection appeared unusually pale with dark circles beneath bloodshot eyes.

This was the man who'd touched her, just yesterday, so

tenderly, so adoringly. Was it possible that the same man could send her to Bedlam?

He'd kissed her, whispered promises to her. But did she know him? He did not appear the carefree gentleman who'd met with her yesterday. He seemed less approachable.

The needle pressed into the back of her wrist for a fleeting moment before she realized that those bloodshot eyes had crinkled at the edges.

He was smiling and once again seemed less a stranger and more the man who'd kept her awake as of late.

She curtsied. "My lord."

She could say no more than that. Her father lurked directly behind him.

Cameron bowed and then stepped into the room at the same time her father shuffled backward and closed the door, leaving the two of them alone.

Oh, how very different she felt since the last time they'd been alone together in a similar room—less than one week ago!

Was she foolish to have fallen for him so easily?

"Louella." His voice broke into her thoughts.

* * *

At first glance, Louella presented herself as the perfect debutante, a vision in yellow and lace. Most girls might appear bland in such a color, but not Miss Louella Rose. For her dark hair and shining blue eyes contrasted sharply with the bright material, except…

Was her nose just slightly red at the tip? And were her eyes rimmed with pink and a little swollen?

She smiled tremulously. "You came." Her voice sounded little more than a whisper. She cleared her throat.

Cameron's head was killing him, and the perfume from a bouquet of flowers in the room threatened to unsettle his lurching innards.

And yet he still experienced desire.

"I have."

She clutched some fabric in both hands, almost defensively.

A wave of nausea washed over him, and he rethought his fleeting amorous urges. Instead, he wished to lay upon the sofa, preferably with his head in her lap and take a long nap. She could run her fingers through his hair soothingly and it would not go unappreciated.

When he'd opened his eyes that morning, Cameron had found himself alone and fully clothed in a sparse room he must have rented for the night. His head ached, his mouth was dry, and his stomach heaved when he moved too quickly. He remembered little of the early morning hours except that he'd invited Kingsley to stay at his father's estate, take a look at the mine. Kingsley had generously declared that he would stand up with Cameron at the ceremony.

It went without saying that she'd accept him.

Seeing her now, however, his confidence wavered. He'd arrived late, he realized this, and she looked none too happy.

"Forgive my late arrival." His body no longer tolerated copious amounts of alcohol as easily as it had when he was younger.

She stared at him more suspiciously than she had before his first proposal.

When Cameron finally shifted a glance toward the sofa, she jumped.

"Er, oh, yes. Shall we sit then?" She motioned for him to come into the room and then lowered herself into the far corner of the settee.

He followed tentatively. The meeting with her father had

been as tedious as he'd expected, but he was satisfied with the outcome.

No doubt, there would be fireworks when Crawford read through the amended contract. Hell, he'd have apoplexy.

This was of no matter.

Kinglsey had had the right of it.

Honor first.

Cameron's muscles protested as he sat. He had vague memories of brawling in the taproom. Oh, yes, he'd wrestled about on the floor with a few scoundrels who'd insulted one of the maids.

As had Kingsley.

Perhaps he ought to limit time spent in the blighter's company.

Cameron turned so that he mostly faced this lady who'd taken over his thoughts. "You look beautiful today."

She didn't respond but glanced down at her hands and let out a long-suffering sigh. "I... Thank you," she said, oh, so half-heartedly.

Cameron studied her. She did not look to be well. In fact, she looked as though she might have suffered a worse night than he had. "Louella? Are you ill?"

She peeked up at him. "I... did not sleep much. I have been... nervous... I suppose."

Was this the same lady who'd only yesterday told him she was happy at the prospect of marriage to him? And then she reached out and touched his hand. His gloves were stuffed in his back pocket, where he'd placed them earlier when signing the contracts.

Her own gloves were made of lace. "What of you?"

Her delicate touch nearly sent him into a trance.

Damn, but the cushions and her soft lap beckoned. "I had a late night myself." Which was putting it mildly.

He lifted his other hand and covered hers. He felt no small

amount of relief when she chuckled. "A late night with spirits, I presume?" But she was smiling. Her eyes sparkled with... was that relief?

He nearly shook his head but stopped himself before he sent it throbbing again. "I'm afraid so. I ran into an old friend and..." He would not go into great detail.

She laughed some more but then sobered. "A *lady* friend?"

Was that jealousy in her question? Although pleased that she cared, he unexpectedly experienced the sensation of a noose tightening around his neck. What matter was it of hers if he'd spent the night with a lady friend or not?

Pearl white teeth bit down upon her lower lip.

Before he could stop himself, he shook his head and then moaned.

But he answered her question. "An old school chum."

Some of the tension left her body.

But as he looked at her more closely, he was certain she'd been crying earlier. What reason did she have to cry?

"Are you still... not unhappy at the prospect of marriage to me? You appear... bleak this afternoon."

She entwined her fingers with the two of his that remained. She didn't flinch. She hardly seemed aware that two of her fingers clasped a stump. "I am not unhappy at the prospect... quite the opposite, actually." She smiled brightly. Was it just a little forced?

And then she reached up and traced a line down his jaw. "You have a bruise here." Such delicate fingertips...

Very well. It was time. He needed to do this.

He was exhausted.

He'd like to have made love to her, right here in her father's drawing room. But even if he had the stamina to do so today, her parents could very well be listening at the keyhole.

And if his stomach didn't settle, he could quite possibly

embarrass himself in the most objectionable manner possible. He needed to get this over with.

Gathering his strength, he dropped to the floor, onto one knee, still holding her hand.

How did one do this? He'd heard more than one account of what was considered to be the perfect proposal.

Appreciate her lovely countenance, gaze into her eyes. Yes, and infuse affection into his voice.

"Miss Louella Rose," he began.

She gazed back at him, a hint of bewilderment in her eyes.

"You have captivated me. I cannot wait any longer. Make me the *happiest of men*, won't you please, and consent to marry me?" He hoped his speech didn't sound overly cliché.

She puckered her lips, giving the answer great consideration. Hell, she was taking longer now than she had the first time. And then she rubbed her nose. "You are not feeling quite the thing today, are you?"

"Louella..." He would strangle her if she played games with him now!

"It's just that you have turned a tinge green. I hadn't thought my prospective groom would look so very... sickly."

He dropped his head and buried it in her lap. Whereas the smell of flowers in the room had caused his stomach to lurch, the scent of her, the scent of Louella, soothed him. He took hold of her lace-covered hand and pressed it to his lips.

And then he felt her other hand in his hair. Massaging him. Comforting him.

"Please?" he begged. Yes, he begged her to put him out of his misery.

Was that her mouth on his forehead? Oh, yes, and her sweet, hot breath.

"Of course," she finally answered.

CHAPTER TEN

BETROTHED

*P*erhaps her situation wasn't as dire as she'd imagined it to be this morning.

Louella found it nigh impossible to believe that this man, his face buried in her lap, would ever do anything to cause her pain or unhappiness. He'd begged her to marry him.

She slipped off one of her gloves so that she could touch his hair with her bare hand. Crisp, soft, and clean, it bounced back into place as soon as her fingers threaded through it.

He most certainly had consumed too many spirits the night before.

She didn't blame him. In fact she wished she could have done the same.

"My lord, Cameron?" Had he fallen asleep?

He burrowed deeper into her lap and mumbled something she didn't understand.

"Cameron?" she tried again.

"Um-hm." He hummed his answer.

"You know that people aren't always as they seem? Sometimes…" Maybe she could find some reassurance from him. If she could tell him… explain…

"Um-hm." His face remained buried, his shoulders relaxed, and much of his weight leaning into her.

"And sometimes, people have faults. Faults that aren't so apparent."

Cameron stirred, but finally turned his head to meet her eyes. "Are you trying to tell me you have a few bad habits, Louella? That you are not the perfect debutante, after all?" The lazy smile dancing on his lips jumbled her thoughts.

He was so very handsome, even after a night spent deep in his cups.

Louella tried to focus. "I am not perfect. I am so very far from perfect. And I just wanted you to know..."

Loud footsteps sounded at the door. By the time it opened, her now official fiancé sat three feet away from her, at the other end of the sofa. Despite winking at her before standing to greet her parents, his complexion was still tinged a tad green. "My lady, Hallewell." Although he held the higher rank, he bowed respectfully and then stepped closer to Louella with an outstretched hand.

He did not release hers even after she'd risen. "Your daughter has made me the happiest of men by consenting to become my wife."

He'd barely spoken the words before her mother began fluttering about, smiling and making plans. Her father shook Cameron's hand enthusiastically. "Well done, my boy, well done."

Cameron's thumb massaged the back of her hand, unseen by either of her parents. She concentrated on his secret seduction, suddenly overcome with the need to escape.

"I am a lucky man, indeed." He looked away from her father in order to meet her gaze. "Very lucky." He squeezed her hand.

She smiled tremulously. This was what she wanted. Yes, of course, it was. She could almost convince herself that he'd never need to know her secret.

Almost.

* * *

The Duke and Duchess of Crawford would be delighted to host Lord and Lady Hallewell as well as Miss Louella Redfield for the evening meal on the morrow, at six o'clock, at Ashton Acres. The invitation arrived less than an hour after Lord Stanton's departure.

Now that the betrothal was official, it seemed all of the planning decisions were out of her hands. The banns would begin being read that Sunday and a modiste was being summoned to take measurements for the gown Louella would wear on her wedding day.

And looking quite pleased with himself, upon informing them of the invitation, Louella's father declared he would spare no expense for his daughter's wedding. His declaration weighed like a stone in the pit of her stomach. It reminded her of the financial arrangements surrounding her nuptials. It reminded her of the mine. She knew she hadn't much of a dowry, and half of it ought to have been Olivia's.

Her mother had beamed at her father's announcement. They'd both looked at her, expecting an equal amount of enthusiasm but she'd only been able to summon a tight smile.

Any mention of money tainted the romantic gestures by her betrothed. Although normally a practical girl, she preferred to believe that feelings of affection and romance drove her nuptials. She liked to imagine her prospective groom was first and foremost motivated by the prospect of spending his life with her.

Not by the prospects of an abandoned mine.

And not because he'd found himself fleetingly attracted to her for her looks.

Olivia failed to be of any assistance in these matters. Lord Stanton had impressed her quite thoroughly. She surprised Louella, even, with an impromptu visit the very next day, tracking her down in the overgrown gardens surrounding the manor.

If the various trees and shrubs could be considered as such, that was. A good deal of brush, plants, and dried blooms had yet to have been removed from seasons past. The only surviving flowers grew so hardily that one could easily call them weeds. They'd crept out of their beds, onto the trees and in many cases, onto the paths. Some hid thorns on their vines, camouflaged by tall grass and dead leaves.

But it was precisely for these reasons that Louella found the location to be perfect.

Having just removed her slippers, she quickly slipped her feet back into them and rose when she saw Olivia approaching.

"Come into the sunshine," Olivia laughed, "What are you doing on the ground, anyhow?"

Louella brushed her skirts, keeping her gaze lowered. "Um...I thought I saw a button."

"Oh, was it? Wouldn't that be a boon if it were gold?"

Olivia moved forward, peering into the shade. At her sister's enthusiastic perusal, Louella shook her head. "If what was gold?"

"The button, you goose!"

"Er, no. Just a... beetle." Louella took Olivia by the arm and dragged her to the bench in the sunshine. Caught between her feelings of affection and unworthiness, Louella found her nerves were frayed as she contemplated the evening ahead.

"Father is pleased." Olivia slid her a sideways glance. "You are betrothed," she added slyly.

Louella couldn't contain a smile at the memory of Cameron kneeling before her, his face pressed into her lap. "I am."

"And you are happy?"

Again, Louella nodded. "I am." Which, oddly enough, was true.

Both girls sat silently, listening to the sounds of nature, contemplating the full magnitude of change that lay ahead, until Olivia released a sigh.

"I must tell you something." Her words came out sounding foreboding.

"What?" Anything to take her mind off her own troubles.

"Miss Cline stopped by for a visit. She was full of all manner of gossip. Work began up at the mine this morning." Olivia didn't need to explain what this meant. Their father never would have opened it up of his own accord.

Of course, Louella had known about the mine. *But already?*

"She said Lord Stanton is overseeing the operation. That Kingsley, the other one, remember?" At Louella's nod she continued. "Well he is assisting your fiancé and they are contracting workers left and right. Apparently the vicar has heard rumblings that Papa's been wrong all along. The men in the village are talking about nothing else. They say a vein, nearly a foot thick, is down there. Not coal and not iron, Louella, but gold." She reached out and flicked a leaf out of Louella's hair. "I hope Papa knows what he's doing."

Louella shifted uncomfortably, but then a thought occurred, and she nearly laughed. There wasn't any gold in papa's mine. Even Cameron had scoffed at such a notion just a few days ago.

But if he had, a suspicious voice whispered inside her, why such a hurry to open it up?

Louella squirmed uneasily on the bench. She didn't want to think about Cameron misleading her.

She would change the subject. She hated to be troubled by something she had no control over. She'd already accepted!

Must her dreams be thrashed against some stupid mine so quickly?

Olivia spent the next twenty minutes regaling her with other gossip. "Luke Smith's wife died in childbirth two nights ago."

Louella winced. "But he's three other boys to care for as well, doesn't he?"

Olivia nodded. "That's why I came over this morning. Cook's preparing a basket."

"And the babe?" She'd met Mrs. Smith on several occasions. Although she'd always seemed tired, worn out from caring for her family, she'd never failed to be friendly and pleasant.

And now, the children were without a mother -- and one of them a newborn.

"Miss Cline says she thinks there's an aunt up north. Ought to come help once she gets word."

Louella rubbed her hands over her face. Her problems seemed utterly insignificant when she heard the trials of others. She had been so very blessed to be born into her family. She ought to be forever grateful to be engaged to Lord Stanton. She ought to be able to do whatever was necessary to ensure a peaceful and fruitful marriage.

She ought to be able to...

"I imagine it's ready now. I asked Mama if you could come with me, but she said you had a dinner to prepare for." Of course, Olivia would not have been invited. Louella would change all of that after her marriage.

Or sooner, even!

She smiled at the thought.

* * *

The two families had been neighbors for generations, but Louella had never actually set foot inside of the Duke of Crawford's mansion, set picturesquely upon the highest point of the entire estate. Although several sections had been rebuilt, one could still identify the older structures by the moss on the stones and the faded brickwork.

Most of the estate at one point had been surrounded by a massive wall. The title was one of the oldest in England.

Awestruck, she followed her parents into the foyer where the butler greeted them. "Their Graces await your arrival. Please come this way."

Up a grand rounded staircase and then along an endless cold corridor, past more displays of suits of armor than Louella could count, they required several minutes to make their way to the chamber where they would be presented to their hosts.

The room was more crowded than she'd expected and she only recognized a few of the other guests. Louella ought to have insisted Olivia come along. She ought to have realized that Cameron's sisters would wish to be present. Presumably, the occasion merited a complete inspection on all their parts. While the duchess performed all the necessary introductions, Louella only hoped she could remember names and faces.

For Cameron's sisters were all quite similar in appearance. Blonde, delicate girls, they wore the finest and most fashionable of gowns, and all seemed to possess the grace and presence of their mother.

The youngest, Lady Martha, looked to be in her early teens. The next youngest was Lady Cora and then Lady Lillian.

Lady Cora and Lady Martha both wore silk ribbons about their wrists.

Louella glanced at her own. Since she'd chosen a short puff-sleeved dress for the evening, Jane had wrapped Louella's wrists in transparent lace. No fresh cuts threatened to bleed through, making the delicate material an adequate option. The lace sufficiently covered the pink and white lines left behind from the week before.

Both Jane and her mother had beamed approvingly.

Cameron watched her from a dark corner. Relief swept through her when he pushed himself away from the wall to come and greet them.

CHAPTER ELEVEN

A WEDDING TO PLAN

*S*itting in the duchess' favorite drawing room, Cameron studied his father from his vantage point against the wall. The duke's demeanor proved he had yet to discover the changes Cameron had enacted to the betrothal contract. Cameron presumed the flames of hell would rain down upon him when the terms became known.

Until then, it was all he could do to keep his father from going into the mine himself. He'd been so anxious to begin operations, Cameron had worried the fiend would ignore important safety measures in his haste.

To ensure safety, Cameron opted to oversee the mine's excavation himself. His conscience could not handle any more blood on his watch. He'd seen too much of that over the past decade.

Before the sun had fully risen, he and Kingsley had met with his father's engineer and then made it known in the village that workers would be needed soon. Mr. Compton, the man who'd overseen the project up until then, pointed out the weaknesses that had caused it to collapse in the past. Several issues needed to be addressed and secured before any further exploration could begin.

They would require constant monitoring.

And somehow, the determination of a haul had become public knowledge as far as three villages over. This meant they'd needed to arrange for security, armed guards even. He'd barely made it back this evening in time to bathe and change for dinner.

Awaiting the arrival of his fiancée's family, his sisters peppered him with questions. Would they like her? Was she as nice as she was pretty?

Martha held her arm up, displaying the silk around her wrist. "It was Miss Louella Rose who first began wearing the wrist bow."

Even Miss Crawly, their governess, knew about it.

Lillian was concerned with far more practical matters. "We only hope she is intelligent and good-hearted. For you will one day be Crawford, Cam. And she will be the duchess."

"Not anytime soon, God willing." Her Grace shushed them all. "You'll meet her and see for yourself. There is nothing to worry about."

Almost on cue, the door opened and Frederick announced their arrival, "The Viscount and Viscountess Hallewell and Miss Louella Redfield."

Cameron's heart jumped when he saw her, this rush of feelings still too new for him to harness. He wondered if he'd become accustomed to her beauty. Slim and graceful tonight, she seemed quite ethereal, dressed in a white gown with silver lace and puffed, gossamer sleeves. Pearls draped around her slender neck, emphasizing the alabaster-like skin revealed above her bodice. Skin he'd pressed his lips against.

Refusing to look in his direction, Louella dropped into perfect curtsies with each introduction. His eldest sister seemed stunned. Martha had an "I told you so" sort of look upon her face.

He could not help but claim her.

"Miss Louella." He stepped forward and bowed over her hand. Again, she wore gloves made of lace. He imagined his wedding night, when he'd begin unwrapping her layers of clothing, beginning with the bows around her wrists.

How had she managed to transform such mundane features into sensual and hidden delights?

"My lord." Her voice tore straight to his groin. He'd been alone with her for all of thirty minutes yesterday and been unable to steal a single kiss.

Tonight would be different. He'd walk with her in the garden after the meal.

Her fingers squeezed his. Was she seeking reassurance or giving it? He led her across the room and sat beside her across from his sisters.

"Miss Louella." Martha was lucky to have been allowed out of the nursery this evening. Except she wasn't a little girl anymore. "I like your ribbons." And then she dropped her gaze, suddenly embarrassed. Such enthusiasm wasn't at all the thing.

"Why thank you, Lady Martha. I think your ribbons are pretty as well. Who would have thought to use more than one color at a time?"

Louella *was* intelligent, Cameron couldn't help but think. She *was* kind-hearted. She would be a perfect duchess. With a few thoughtful words, she'd put Martha at ease immediately. Martha even rose from her seat to come sit on the other side of Louella. She would show her the ribbons more closely. And could she please see Miss Louella's lace as well?

Louella hesitated and then presented her arm to Martha. Martha fingered the lace, almost in awe but then peered more closely.

Louella laughed brightly. "This lace comes from one of my

mother's dresses. From when she was a girl. It was made in Italy." She pulled her arm away and clasped her hands together in her lap. "I love taking something old and forgotten and turning it into something new."

She seemed a little jumpy.

Cameron would have liked to slide closer and wrap his arm around her shoulder.

He'd not considered how very young she was. A full decade. And everything had happened so quickly between the two of them. He'd found himself so acutely attracted to her that he'd forgotten her inexperience and age.

As though reading his mind, she sent him a tentative smile.

And yet she did not seem immature. She seemed level headed and compassionate. She had a sense of responsibility to her family but also cared about her sister's feelings.

His father was pouring a drink for the viscount. There were several different conversations in the room. Cameron managed to slide closer to her.

"I've missed you, Louella," he said softly near her ear.

She did not meet his eyes, but he was satisfied to see a smile dance at the corner of her lush, pink lips.

"Do you like to sew, Miss Louella?" Cora asked.

Barely sixteen, Cora pressed the duchess at every turn for an early come out. The prettiest of all the girls, and also the most daring, she was certain to bring his father a great deal of grief.

"I prefer embroidering. As a matter of fact, I am just embellishing a gown for Olivia, my sister." In an animated state, Louella took his breath away. She glowed as she spoke of half-moons and what-nots she was adding to some sort of gown she'd sewn.

"I dreamed of touching you again," Cameron whispered behind Louella's ear as Cora described a project of her own.

A subtle flush crept up his betrothed's neck. And then she shivered.

"Dinner is served," Frederick announced at the door.

His father offered the viscountess his arm, and the viscount presented his to Her Grace.

Protocol demanded Cameron escort the next highest-ranking guest. He smiled ruefully at Louella and abandoned her to escort the eldest of his sisters, Lillian, into the dining room. Damned if several hours would pass before he'd be allowed any time with Louella again.

* * *

Having absented themselves to leave the men to their port, the ladies settled into the drawing room, and talk immediately turned toward the upcoming wedding festivities. The duchess, Louella's mother, and Cameron's sisters excitedly discussed details of the pre-wedding ball. It must be held at Ashton Acres, of course! But ought the wedding breakfast be held at Thistle Park? The duchess looked pained at the thought. So many details that Louella ought to care about. Just as she had throughout all of dinner, however, she found it difficult to concentrate on the conversations around her.

Cameron's whispered comments had been comforting, disconcerting, and yet worrying all at the same time.

In a room full of family, he'd secretly told her that he missed her.

She'd wanted to tell him she'd missed him as well! She wanted to go on another picnic, just the two of them, so that she could understand him and know him better. She would even be happy to sit alone in her sister's garden with him.

And then he'd told her he dreamed of touching her again.

All sorts of sensations spiraled inside her at those words. She'd pressed her knees together, heat spreading through her limbs, and fought a consuming desire to lean into him, in spite of his sisters and their parents' presence. Dare she call this what it was? Lust?

Was it so different from romantic love? Why had she never felt such intensity for any other gentleman of her acquaintance? She wished she had more experience to base her emotions upon because embarrassment and shame accompanied it all.

"What is your opinion, Louella, dear?" the duchess interrupted her musings.

"Er, I think that would be fine." She had no idea what she'd agreed to.

"Oh, wonderful! We'll hold all the festivities here at Ashton Acres, then." Her mother gave her a look as though she were a traitor. "And just in time. It sounds as though the gentlemen are finished with their port."

Cameron entered behind the other elegantly clad males, as though he were in no hurry, as though he had no reason to be. His attraction was not only due to his excellent looks. He walked as though he owned the world, as though anything he wanted was his for the taking. And when he looked at Louella, his gaze lingered with sensual confidence. She did not remember any of this from before. His years away had changed him. She could not help but believe him when he'd told her he was not the same as when he left as a young man.

The sight of his approach caused her heart to pound. Could others nearby hear it?

Whatever this was, it was powerful—and possibly a little dangerous. For it caused her to stop thinking about her virtue and reputation—her darkness. She'd already allowed him far more liberty with her person than she should have.

And yet, given the opportunity, she would do it all again.

He wasn't dangerous. Everything he had said or done demonstrated he was good-hearted. All their conversations certainly showed he cared about her feelings.

And he'd be hers. Perhaps forever. Could she tell him? Trust him?

"A stroll?" He reached for her. He knew she'd not refuse him.

Taking his hand, she stood. "I'll need my wrap."

"Of course."

It must be expected of them, as an engaged couple, to abandon the party for a few moments alone. Nobody questioned them. She half expected Lady Martha to jump up and follow, though.

She did not.

Cameron took her wrap from the footman, dropped it over her shoulders, and then led her out the grand front entrance, her hand tucked on his arm.

"I'd seen the estate from a distance, of course. But until tonight, I'd never actually set foot on it."

He sent her an admonishing sideways glance.

"Except of course—I mean—" She stumbled over her words, and then they both laughed. Pleasure spread through her that they could joke about this now.

"As I was saying, it's even more magnificent than I'd thought it would be." She relaxed. "Did you miss it while you were away?"

"I didn't at first. At the risk of revealing how spoiled and selfish I was, it represented all the shackles I'd resented for as long as I can remember." This wasn't something he was proud of. He didn't laugh about it or charm his way around it.

"So many responsibilities fall upon the eldest." She was thinking of Olivia. Her mother and father ought not to have neglected their daughters so much. Olivia's childhood had ended quickly.

Cameron glanced sideways at her. "Rather astute of you to recognize, as the youngest."

Not the youngest! "But I am not—was not. William was the youngest."

"I'm sorry. Of course." He patted her hand comfortingly. "Were you close to your brother?"

He was her baby brother, and yet she'd often resented him. "I loved him," she insisted. "My parents were devastated when he passed." But he'd been oh, so spoiled by them. And by the girls as well.

"He was your father's only son." Cameron surely guessed what such an unfortunate death had meant for her papa.

"Even before he fell in the water, he was sickly." She swallowed hard, remembering the horror of that day. Remembering how helpless she'd been. The pain of feeling utterly useless. "His physician gave him permission to join us outside for a picnic. But some old boats had been left on the shore. He'd been closeted inside for so very long that when he began playing on one, I didn't stop him. And then it drifted... He nearly drowned. Livvy pulled him to safety." His lips had been blue, and he'd lain so still on the shore. Louella had thought he was already dead. "Afterward, he took a chill though. Never recovered. He could be demanding at times, but he was only a child. I wish I'd been more understanding."

"But you were a child yourself. Weren't you?"

"Nine years ago. I should have known better." She hated thinking about this. "He would have been Lady Martha's age now."

He dropped her hand and placed one arm around her shoulders. "You've always been a serious little thing, from what I remember. Great big eyes that missed nothing."

His warmth spread all along her side and his fingers squeezed her arm slightly. His nearness, denied all evening, suddenly made her a little dizzy.

"Did it make you happy? Leaving England?"

"It ought to have." A dry chuckle. "I was angry at Crawford, but ironically enough, I was also angry with my mother. For dying. She'd died trying to please the bas—As long as I can remember, she was either carrying or recovering from losing a baby. She wanted to provide Crawford with a spare. *Duty was everything.*"

She heard something else in his voice. *Wasn't I enough?*

Covering his hand, she clasped onto it without thinking. His injured hand. "So, if leaving wasn't the answer, what was? What finally made you happy, then?"

They'd arrived at a garden bench, and he pulled her down to sit beside him. The stone was cold, but she felt warm with his arm wrapped around her, a beautiful night beneath the moonlight.

"I'm not sure happy is the correct word. Content, perhaps, or accepting. The challenges I met forced me to grow up. To accept the nature of my situation and realize how fortunate I was. To realize what matters most to me. I've even come to be involved in some reform laws coming up. Labor laws involving children." He turned her to face him. "But enough of all this. I am sitting in the moonlight with a beautiful girl who happens to be my betrothed, and I've yet to have stolen a single kiss." A devilish glint danced in his eyes and he, oh so tenderly, caressed the side of her face.

His thumb traced the sensitive skin around her mouth. "Such a perfect mouth." And then his lips substituted where his thumb had been.

She'd rather enjoyed talking to him. She'd wanted to protest the end of their conversation and yet this carnal side to her lit up when he'd mentioned kissing. When he'd looked at her with those hooded eyes.

And so, she succumbed more enthusiastically than a proper miss ought. She allowed his tongue to explore wherever he wished. She tilted her head back when he trailed fiery kisses down her neck, across her collar bone, and along her décolletage.

They always came back to this; this all-encompassing passion she'd never known before.

Could she trust it? One of his hands was gathering the material of her skirt upward, exposing her legs to the cool night air of early spring. And then his hand settled upon her knee.

"Cameron." She tried to tug the material down, but his hand had trapped it against the bench. His head was buried against her chest so that she felt the heat and moisture of his breath upon her skin.

They could be interrupted at any moment. Did he not care about her reputation?

"Is there gold in the mine?" she could not help but demand. It had been all she could think about since Olivia's visit. Had he lied to her?

He stilled but did not answer immediately. Her traitorous body felt bereft when he set himself away from her. His hooded gaze focused as desire faded.

"You told me you did not think there was any gold. And yet I am told you are the person reopening it. And you've wasted no time in doing so." She'd not meant to ask him like this, her voice sounding accusing.

A cloud passed in front of the moon, leaving his face in shadow. She wished she could see his eyes. Had she angered him with her question? Was she trying to ruin everything with her suspicions?

Was she *testing* him?

"Who told you all of this?" *So, it is true?*

"Olivia. The vicar's sister told her this morning."

He made a scoffing sound and sprang to his feet. He paced away from her and then just as quickly returned but paused and stared across the shadowed garden. "Louella." It was the harshest tone he'd ever used with her. "You are going to have to trust me. I'm merely fulfilling the obligation I have to my father." He growled a little beneath his breath. "I've not misled you. About anything."

But this was no answer!

She'd only really known him for a couple of days. Good heavens! And he now would ask her to trust him blindly? Her heart pounded violently. She wanted to believe him.

And she did, oh, but she did!

But the gold? He'd not answered her question. He had turned his back to her. *Had* he misled her?

What had she been telling herself just the other day? That Lord Stanton was a good man. Hadn't she convinced herself that he was a *goodhearted* man?

She would trust him for now. She would not allow her doubts to poison their betrothal.

"I'm sorry." She rose and stood behind him.

At her words, his shoulders relaxed. And then he ran one hand through his hair. "I don't want you to worry about the mine. It has nothing to do with us."

But it did, didn't it? They never would have become betrothed if not for its existence.

His fingers curled around hers, and he let out a deep sigh. "I am the one who is sorry." But he made no move to hold her again.

Louella stood looking at him, awkwardly. "Shall we walk some more?"

He didn't move. "I'm not perfect, Louella. I'm going to make mistakes. I'm going to do things that make you angry. But I do not lie."

"I'm not perfect either! Just because I'm..." She hated to even say it. "Just because I'm... pretty, it doesn't mean I'm not flawed. It doesn't mean I'm not ugly sometimes." She wanted to tell him everything.

But at her words, he finally took hold of her. Tilting her head back, he pressed his forehead against hers. "Neither of us is perfect. Perhaps it would be wise for both of us to remember this." And then he grinned. "But I'll not believe you have any ugliness. And I'll challenge anyone who says differently." A soft kiss on one of her eyelids. And then the other.

It was so much easier when she gave in to this.

Because when her body trembled with need, her mind was silent.

CHAPTER TWELVE

THE DAY OF THE BALL

"*I*'m so proud of you, Louella!" Mama gushed.

Tomorrow was Louella's wedding day, and the pre-wedding ball was being thrown that night. And then she would no longer be forced to tolerate these morning visits.

Invasive. Intrusive. They left her feeling exposed and vulnerable.

Her mama had entered bearing chocolate and biscuits, as though to share a cozy breakfast with Louella, but the truth of it was that she came for one reason only: to check her daughter's sheets for blood—and her body for scratches.

Louella fiercely resented it. Standing by her bed, she shook off her mother's hands.

"And the salves have done wonders! If you douse the candles before bed, he'll be none the wiser. We've done it! I didn't want to be hard on you, darling, but aren't you glad, now, that I was? Such a disgusting habit. And now that we can put it behind us, you'll be able to dispense with those silly wrist ribbons and whatnot."

One more day, and her mama would not be coming into her room every morning. As relieved as she was, the thought summoned a shimmer of tears to her eyes. "Yes, Mama. I am glad." She didn't know what else to say.

"And a ball tonight! So exciting! But so much to do." Mama turned away from the mirror and kissed Louella on the cheek. "Rest up this morning. We don't want you overtiring yourself. You'll be the belle of the ball, of course! My very own daughter, a future duchess!"

And then, with a flourish, she disappeared.

There was so much to do and yet, as the prospective bride, Louella was expected to do absolutely nothing. Wonderful, more time to herself. More time for second-guessing.

Many distant relatives had arrived this week. Her mama and the duchess had invited enough people to fill the local church twice over. Not all would be attending the ceremony. But the breakfast and ball, scheduled to be held at Ashton Acres, were both to be lavish affairs.

Papa had even purchased a new gown for Olivia. A crystalline blue silk, unlike anything Louella had ever seen her sister wear before. Livvy hadn't been allowed to attend any of the local country dances and had admitted earlier that week to being nervous. Of course, their mother had been adamant that Olivia not look anyone directly in the eyes.

Their mother had first given Olivia this order shortly after William's funeral. Louella hadn't understood at first.

Olivia had.

Of course, Olivia would be uneasy about attending the ball. She feared forgetting their mother's directive, she'd confessed. She'd glance up at the wrong person. They'd stare at her strangely. She didn't want anything to ruin Louella's special evening and this made her nervous.

Nothing Oliva did could embarrass Louella. She'd done her best to reassure her sister on this point.

Louella was nervous for an entirely different reason.

She had hardly spent a moment alone with Cameron since

the engagement dinner. Any chance they'd had to see one another, they'd been surrounded by others. If not her mama or his sisters, then the steadily growing number of family that had traveled to attend. She'd met more people over the past few weeks than she had in her entire life.

In those rare moments when she wasn't required at Ashton Acres, she'd visit Olivia, who was not involved in the wedding plans. Louella had suggested she come and sit in at the meetings with the duchess and her daughters, begged her even, but her sister had held firm.

Mama didn't want Olivia presented to the duke and duchess quite yet. She wanted nothing to jeopardize the betrothal, and a "flawed" sister such as Olivia might give them pause to reconsider.

Her mother had explained this to Louella on more than one occasion, and no doubt, Olivia had had to suffer through such ridiculous reasoning as well.

The weeks had been something of a trial. But they were almost over!

And then she would see so much more of Cameron. As her husband. They could come to know one another and develop the trust and confidence she yearned for.

Couldn't they? Wouldn't they?

From what she heard, he spent every day at the mine. He'd contracted workers from all over. He'd apologized for his lack of availability and promised her they would go somewhere together after the wedding. Wherever she wanted, he told her.

She'd told him London. Far from the mine and her mother. She only wished she could bring Olivia along.

Foolishness! One did not bring one's sister along on one's wedding holiday.

Cameron had promised to make arrangements, their separation leaving no chance for her to know.

But she would see him tonight. They would dance. And

perhaps they could slip outside to the vast ornamental gardens at Ashton Acres again. And this time, she would not stop him from kissing her. She would relish in his touch, knowing there was only one more day until they could be together always.

Because there were times when they were apart that she worried he was a stranger.

But he was not!

Louella shook her head to clear away such thoughts and removed one of her older dresses from the wardrobe. She needed to breathe. She needed to be outside of this room.

At least Olivia had been given permission to attend the ball and the ceremony. It was one of the only wedding details that Louella had insisted upon.

When they returned from London, Louella would insist Olivia become a part of Society. Louella would be a marchioness. That would provide her with some influence, wouldn't it?

She donned a pair of well-worn half boots and slipped the dress over her head. She would not call Jane.

Jane would have a bath brought up later today. And then she would prepare Louella for the ball. She was busy helping her mama and other guests this morning.

Now was Louella's chance.

Outside of her room, maids and footmen were busily rushing about. But no guests had emerged yet. Using the servants' stairway, she avoided any early risers who might be wandering the foyers, and then slipped out the backdoor to the garden.

Sunshine filtered through the vines and trees. Spring was in the air.

Louella followed the path she'd worn down in the previous weeks until she located her secret place. A long-forgotten bench sat in an alcove of dangling vines and branches.

Ah, privacy.

* * *

Opening the mine was far more complicated of an undertaking then any of them had foreseen. For the same reasons the mine had collapsed all those years ago, it posed a constant danger reopening it now. And in the last week, they'd had to mitigate three significant leakage issues.

In addition to the problems involving the actual operations, the rumors as to the wealth to be extracted had spread like wildfire. Round the clock guards were required as a result. Not only did Cameron fear the loss of gold, if a thief were to enter the mine, he feared the loss of life and damage that might result.

He was going to do all that he could to prevent injury and death in this endeavor.

His father's impatience made matters all the more difficult. He'd not realized the extent to which his own management and oversight would be required, even with Kingsley's assistance.

As a result, he'd neglected his delightful little fiancée. On the few occasions when he'd managed to steal some time away from the mine, the two of them had been required to attend various social functions. And as the prospective bride and groom, all attention had fallen upon them. Being alone with her became impossible.

But that was all about to change.

Kingsley had indeed, delayed returning to his own fiancée until after the wedding and had remained at Ashton Acres. Always a whiz with physics and engineering in school, his assistance was proving invaluable. And even though he refused to be housed in the manor, electing instead to lodge in an old gamekeeper's cottage, he provided yet another barrier between the mine and his father's unreasonable expectations.

Even so, Cameron wasn't totally satisfied with the safety measures they'd established. He'd have to be soon, though.

He'd asked Louella where she'd like to go after their wedding.

London, she'd said!

He'd made plans for the two of them to visit London, and then travel down to Dover and take a packet across the Channel. They would spend time in Brussels and later in Paris.

He intended the two of them to be away from family and mines for two months and they'd not return to Misty Brooke until just before Kingsley had to travel to London for his own wedding.

The journey was to be a surprise for Louella.

Her mother knew, as did her maid, and when they rolled away from Ashton Acres, her trunk would be packed accordingly.

He'd worked frantically over the past three weeks so that the trip would be possible.

And when his father finally read over the amended marriage contracts, Cameron intended that he and his marchioness be long gone. Guilt nagged at him over this decision, but he'd shoved it away. Crawford would have a few months to come to terms with it before Cameron saw him again.

Tonight, he would behold his betrothed. He would dance with her and then twirl her outside of the ballroom and onto the terrace. He would guide her away from their guests and onto a quiet and secluded path in the garden, where he would show her something of what was to come the following night.

He would taste her lips, touch her flesh, excite her just enough so that he could hear those tiny little gasps he'd gotten a taste of before they'd become engaged.

Just thinking about this scenario aroused him uncomfortably. He knew his plans to be somewhat dishonorable, unconscionable really. But he'd been kept so busy the past few weeks he felt she'd welcome the affection as she had with him initially.

Again, that niggling of guilt took over his thoughts.

With so many family members, friends, and acquaintances in residence, Cameron was confident Crawford would not have time to read the contracts until well after the festivities. He'd never consider that his dutiful heir would think to amend them. However, he knew Crawford would reread them eventually to savor his victory. He'd want time alone to read over the details carefully.

Cameron's blood ran cold at the thought of the duke's response to the changes, but he did not regret his actions. He'd done the right thing, and long term, Cameron believed his decision would ultimately be the best for the ducal estate.

Eventually, the devil would see matters his way. How could he not? Cameron was doing everything expected of him. He was marrying the woman chosen by his father. He'd taken on the very huge burden of exploration of the Hallewell mine, as well as numerous other estate responsibilities. Hell, he'd even hired himself a valet, Mr. Longley. A gentleman's gentleman sent all the way from London.

Longley wasn't so bad, after all. In fact, Cameron thought as he viewed himself in the mirror, there were definite advantages to allowing certain matters to be attended to by a professional.

His hair was more neatly trimmed than he'd had it for as long as he could remember. His shave was close and his cravat a work of art. Even his nails had been clipped and buffed to a high shine.

He was on the verge of becoming a dandy.

"Don't forget your handkerchiefs, my lord." Longley carefully arranged one in his breast pocket and stuffed another into his waistcoat. "One for your lady and another for yourself."

Cameron laughed. God help him, but he hoped Louella would not be needing his handkerchief tonight. The only cries he wished to hear coming from her were cries of passion.

CHAPTER THIRTEEN

RUINED SLIPPERS

The receiving line went on for hours—or so it seemed, anyhow, to Louella. With her parents on one side of her and Cameron on the other, they greeted well over two hundred guests. Although Lady Lillian participated in the line, Olivia had been excluded.

Louella had tried to object, but her mother insisted Olivia could not greet the guests without meeting their eyes. Rather than argue, Olivia had told Louella she was happiest to sit with the other wallflowers.

At least her sister was here tonight.

Dismissing her worries, for now, Louella curtsied and smiled and made inane conversation with people whose names she'd never remember.

Her feet were killing her, and there was dancing yet to come. Not just a few dances, but for the bride to be, the belle of the ball, not a single dance had been left unclaimed. She'd been allowed two sets with Lord Stanton, who looked more elegant tonight than ever before.

Tonight, he looked like a marquess. Tonight, one would

have no trouble whatsoever in believing that he was one day to become a duke.

But first, something more important.

Tomorrow he would be her husband.

And although they were surrounded by onlookers, she could tell by the fire in his eyes that he was just as eager for their marriage as she. When he took her arm, he held it longer than necessary. When he placed a hand at her back, he allowed it to linger and caress her as no man had ever done.

He would be allowed to place his hand in hers and another at her waist, when the two of them initiated the dancing with a waltz. She did not care that all eyes would be upon them. She cared only that it would bring them that much closer to the end of the numerous activities she'd had to endure leading up to their nuptials.

She would have fulfilled her obligation to her parents. She would be able to enhance her sister's opportunities.

Her loyalties would be exclusively reserved for her husband. By law and by God. Louella longed for this.

She also longed to sit down but was to find no reprieve for now.

He leaned down and whispered in her ear, "You are well?" The heat of his breath drew a shiver. How could she think of anything but him when he was so near?

She met his gaze and nodded. Tonight, his eyes reminded her of a dense forest. Dark but with dancing lights where the sunlight broke through.

"Of course." And then she shifted her weight from one foot to the other. "New slippers. My feet aren't used to them yet." She grimaced at the fact that she would say something so mundane when she'd yearned to be near him for so long.

His low rumbling chuckle was one of her favorite things about him. It melted something around her heart. "Poor

Louella. Are you trying to convince me that beauty comes with a price?"

If he only knew. Jane had tied her corset tighter than normal tonight. The lace on her dress was making her itch, and one of the pins in her hair felt as though it was stabbing into her brain.

The only comfortable items she wore were the satin bows around her wrists. She would not give them up yet.

But he'd called her beautiful, hadn't he? This might have bothered her in the past, but when spoken by him, the word didn't cut quite so deeply. She could almost believe he saw inside of her.

Everything had been worth it. Everything was going to be perfect.

And then he winged his arm. "I believe this is my dance."

The orchestra had been making a few tuning noises but went silent. Apparently, the leader had given Cameron some sort of signal.

"It is." Her voice caught on the words.

Louella curtsied deeply to the man she was to marry tomorrow and then clasped onto his proffered arm. Standing before the crowd, she knew that every unmarried woman must envy her something fierce.

Not only was he the heir to a duke but breathtakingly handsome, and something else. Something indefinable that caused a woman to lose all care for her virtue.

He led her to the floor, lifted her hand with his, and placed his other on her waist.

The hand she clasped was his imperfect one, and for some reason, this put her at ease. He knew she was not perfect, just as he'd told her that neither was he.

They both had scars.

As the music began, he exerted a slight pressure at her side and guided her into the dance.

She'd only danced the waltz with the local dancing master. It had seemed dull and slow.

A dance with Captain Lord Stanton was far different. Decidedly wonderful.

As the music rose and fell, her soon-to-be husband showed her everything that made the waltz so very special.

Twirling her, steering her, he guided them both across the gleaming parquet floor. But the magic of the dance did not end there. While taking long, elegant steps, his eyes caressed her. In between a turn and step, his confidence comforted her.

Was this what marriage would be like?

This silent communication, his eyes asking if she was ready to be spun, his hand catching her so that her momentum didn't carry her away, and his legs propelling them to the counts in the music.

Eventually, others joined them on the ballroom floor. As the crowd grew, Cameron had to be more watchful of others around them.

But his thumb massaged her palm and occasionally, he pulled her closer than he ought.

If only that had been the last dance of the night.

When it came to an end, she could have cried. Partly because she would not be dancing with him again for a few hours and partly the pain.

Her feet were killing her.

* * *

As the evening progressed, Louella deeply regretted the weaknesses she'd allowed herself over the past few weeks. She danced with the duke. She danced with some cousins she'd not seen in years, and with some relatives of Cameron's who declared him to be the luckiest of men. She even danced with Lord Kingsley, the fellow who admitted he'd been with her fiancé the evening before his unusually romantic proposal. If she'd not been dying silently inside, she would have enjoyed teasing him for nearly causing said proposal to not have been accepted.

But she had been.

Dying, that was. Only she wasn't really dying. She was simply suffering an excruciating agony. If only she could be allowed to sit with Olivia. Tonight, of all nights, she wished she could be invisible.

By the time Cameron presented himself to her again, she could barely see straight.

He took one look at her and frowned. And then, clasping her by the hand, pulled her most unceremoniously out onto the terrace. By the time he'd dragged her what felt like several miles down one of the dirt paths, she was nearly in tears.

He finally stopped, took her by the shoulders, and through clenched teeth said, "What has happened? Why do you look like you're facing the gallows tomorrow?" When she didn't answer, he shook his head. "What on earth is the matter with you?"

She hated that he looked so angry. She hated that he thought this had something to do with her feelings about their wedding. But she couldn't seem to put any of this into words.

"My feet..."

And then she collapsed into his arms.

* * *

If he'd not been holding her, she would have buckled onto the ground.

But he was there. And he would not for the world allow her to fall. With a strange terror clawing at his heart, he scooped her into his arms and carried her to the nearest bench he could find. She was not unconscious, but she was trembling. And she felt warm, a little feverish.

"I'm so sorry, Cameron," she apologized over and over again. "I'm so sorry. We will be missed."

"Why did you not say you were ill?" He knew why, of course. There was a wedding scheduled for tomorrow, and Louella was the bride.

"I'm not ill," she insisted, but then she added, "My feet. It's my feet." A sob caught in her throat.

He set her carefully upon the bench and dropped to the ground. Damned women and their idiotic fashions. He couldn't imagine what kind of shoes could cause anyone so much pain. If they'd hurt her so much, why hadn't she changed them out for a more comfortable pair?

But when he lifted the hem of her skirt, he froze. Blood oozed through the satin around the soles. Her feet were bleeding!

Lifting her leg carefully, he untied the lace from around her ankle. But when he went to pull off the offending piece of footwear, she drew her feet back, tucking them beneath the bench. "No!"

Her expression revealed horror at his touch.

"Let me take a look, Louella." His own voice came out gruffer than he'd intended. He did not give her the chance to disobey as he grasped her ankle to draw it forward once again. She'd said her feet hurt, as though she'd danced too much, or her shoes were a size too small.

With a muffled cry, she grudgingly allowed him to take hold of her foot and remove the slipper.

"Don't say anything! Please, Cameron? It was stupid of me. I... I... was walking in the garden and got caught up in some thorns. Mama will be so angry if she knows I've done it. Please, please don't say anything to anybody. I'm so embarrassed."

Thorns? Good God! He almost wondered that his own eyes were not tricking him. But as he stared in disbelief, her pleas grew nearly hysterical.

"I won't say anything to your mother, Louella. Now let me have a look at them."

Except to see them properly he was going to have to remove her stocking, which, he believed, extended nearly the entire length of her leg. These were not the circumstances he'd envisioned when he'd imagined getting under her skirts.

Without lifting the hem any farther, Cameron slid both hands along her calf, past her knee, and along the tender skin of her thigh. Locating the garter, he unhooked the silky material and rolled it carefully back down. Damn his baser instincts.

He swallowed hard.

An unplanned swim in a frigid lake. The smell of a fish that has been left sitting too long. An angry papa chasing after him with his blunderbuss. Cameron forced his brain to focus on such thoughts to keep his mind on the task at hand.

For his fingers itched to continue along the silky skin inside her thighs until locating the sweet, wet cavern between them. Disgust unfurled at his lustful thoughts. She was injured. Crying, for Christ sakes!

As he slid the stocking over her ankle, she winced and let out a hiss. That did the trick. All he ought to have done was keep his gaze on her bloodied feet.

"It's dried onto them," she explained unnecessarily.

He needed water. If he attempted to remove the stocking while dry, he might reopen the wounds.

And it would hurt like the devil.

He handed her the shoe and stood up. Before she could protest, he'd lifted her into his arms and headed farther away from the ballroom and their guests.

"Where are we going?" But she wasn't protesting. She'd wrapped her arms around his neck and clung trustingly as he strode along the path.

"There is a gamekeeper's hut out here. Mother's opened it for Kingsley. There will be water and something we can use to dress the cuts inside." Hopefully some sort of salve, too. He didn't wish to upset her by locating her parents, but if he thought a doctor needed to be located, he'd not take any chances.

His promise be damned.

She buried her face on his shoulder. "I'm so sorry, Cam."

"Why are you sorry? Love? You've nothing to apologize for." She had an injury. She'd attempted to endure her own pain so as not to inconvenience anybody.

Although he wanted to strangle her, he couldn't help but admire her courage.

"I didn't want to upset anybody."

Except he would have her speak up in the future. He'd not want her to force herself into such uncomfortable or painful situations as his wife. In the future, he'd have her upset whoever she damn well pleased.

"Poor sweetheart." He dropped a kiss upon her head. "We'll bandage these up, and no one will be the wiser."

Kingsley had left the hut in darkness, which was expected, but when Cameron pushed at the door, it swung open.

The hut consisted of only one room with barely enough space for a fireplace, a bed, a table, and a chair. He lowered Louella onto the bed and struck a flint to the candle. The moonlight had provided more illumination outside, but ah, yes, there was a filled pitcher by the washstand. He wet a piece of linen and knelt at Louella's feet once again.

It struck him that he'd taken up this position more than once since they'd met.

Now that he had water, it didn't take long to soak and

remove her bloodied and crusted stockings. And although she sat silently observing him, he knew the process had not been painless.

"Running through thorns, Louella?" he gently teased as he tenderly pressed a clean cloth to the sole of one foot. "What shall I do to keep you out of such mischief after you've become my wife?"

"I like going barefooted, and before I realized it..." she explained somewhat haltingly, "I thought I'd caught sight of a snake..."

Oh, well, that would explain it.

Cameron lifted her foot and placed a kiss upon her ankle. "Can't say I blame you. I've never been overly fond of the creatures myself." He assisted her then, so that she half lay on the bed with her feet up on the mattress while he rummaged through some cupboards. "I believe there is some salve here. Oh yes, here it is. I wish I had more light so that I could see better. We don't want the cuts to putrify."

He'd brought the candle over to the bed, but her feet were still mostly in shadows. Doing his best, with what little light was available, he dabbed the salve so that the soles of both her feet were covered. He then did his best to fashion bandages around her feet and located a pair of Kingsley's overly large stockings.

While he did this, she watched him curiously.

"Your friend won't mind that you've rifled through his belongings?"

"For a pair of stockings?" Kingsley would never notice. "Most definitely not if he was aware of the cause. Now let me see those slippers."

She handed him the soiled slippers and smiled ruefully. "Do you think all the guests have gone into supper yet? Do you think our absence has been noticed?"

She no longer looked pinched and pale. As long as she was

no longer suffering, he didn't give a rat's ass if their absence was shouted from the rooftops. But matters such as this were different for women. Of course, her mother would have noticed their absence, as well as Her Grace, and damn, most female guests.

He wiped the slippers as best he could and then set them aside to dry. His stomach rolled suddenly at the sight of them. Not that the sight of blood made him ill, but the thought that she'd been dancing for much of the night, smiling all the while. "I would have you share something like this with me in the future, Louella." He dropped himself on the bed and took her in his arms.

A shiver traveled through her. "I didn't want to ruin everything." Her voice came out apologetic sounding. "All the planning—the guests—and your mother's decorations. Even now, we ought to be sitting down at supper." Another tremor. "I've made a mess of everything."

He appreciated her sense of responsibility, knowing she'd someday be his duchess, but he also longed for that carefree side of her personality he'd experienced with her on a few occasions.

Tomorrow at this time, they'd be husband and wife. They would spend the remainder of their lives cleaved unto one another.

He suppressed the jolt of anxiety that shot unexpectedly into his limbs.

"You are disappointed in me." She had been watching him.

Was he? Disappointed in her? His gaze took in her wide eyes, fringed with thick brown lashes. The hue of pink that tinged her cheeks. Ah, yes, she was just as much aware as he that she lay on a bed and they were alone. They were to be married tomorrow and tomorrow night they would consummate this union orchestrated by their parents but agreed upon by one another.

Small, perfect white teeth worried the plump flesh of her bottom lip.

"Are you?" she persisted.

He'd forgotten what she asked. Oh, yes, was he disappointed in her?

"When I saw you looking pale and unhappy, I was. I thought you regretted our engagement," he answered her honestly. "But now. No. I am not disappointed in you, Louella. I feel angry at myself, for not making my will clear to you."

Even now, his words drew a confused expression from her. "Your will?"

"I don't want anything to ever hurt you. Nothing. I hate the idea that you endured pain in order to avoid inconveniencing anybody. Your wellbeing comes first."

"That is your will?" She tilted her head to one side.

"You will be my wife."

She stared back at him for what seemed like a long time before nodding slowly.

This time, when he found her lips, they were already parted, waiting, reaching. He didn't quite understand what this was, these feelings, these yearnings. Over the past decade, and even before that, he'd been attracted to women of all nationalities. He'd lusted for them and admired many as well. But he'd never felt...

This.

This desire to protect, to explore her completely, body, mind, and soul.

God knew he wanted her body. He practically trembled as his hand cradled her breast. He knew they could not find satisfaction tonight. In fact, he didn't want to. On a practical level, that was. His body would disagree if given a vote in the matter.

But in his heart, he wanted to be with her when they could savor one another. He'd enter her tomorrow night, bury himself inside of her, and then soothe her afterward. She was, of course, a virgin. Although he would do his best to bring her pleasure, she would experience pain.

No, he could not take her tonight, on a bed that was little more than a cot. When they could be discovered at any moment.

She moaned and arched her back. Ah, yes, she wanted him. She ached for him.

She was coming to trust him.

"Cameron," she said on a harsh whisper.

As his hand once again skimmed the length of her thigh, he allowed himself to enjoy the sensations she evoked this time. He imagined his lips where his fingertips were. He imagined her thighs tightened around his face.

She turned her head away and brought her knees together, stopping him.

He was an ass to touch her like this before they were wed. To imagine she'd drop her knees open for him. To imagine his hand on her warm, sweet velvety flesh.

Jolts of arousal hardened his cock to an almost unbearable state. He knew she'd be wet for him.

Instead of following his wayward inclinations, he removed his hand from her leg and met her gaze searchingly.

Beautiful. It was as though she'd been made for him, a perfect match. She trembled and buried her face in his chest.

CHAPTER FOURTEEN

AN EARLY NIGHT

*E*motions poured through Louella in a deluge. Never had she imagined she would want to be touched the way she wanted *him* to touch her. Her heart raced at what she'd nearly allowed.

In addition, she'd disappeared from the ball—from her *betrothal* ball for nearly an hour now. Her parents would surely notice. They might even be searching for her this very minute.

And then even more shame.

She'd lied to her fiancé. She'd lied to the man she was marrying tomorrow. And he believed her. He'd more than believed her; he'd sympathized with her and helped her and soothed her.

And she'd nearly allowed him to touch her more intimately than she'd ever touched herself. She'd wanted to open her legs for him.

Elation, fear, remorse, and shame. She turned her head away from his penetrating gaze.

"You're very quiet, Louella." His voice interrupted her thoughts. "What's causing you to hide your face from me?"

His hand rested casually on the bed between them.

And then she felt his lips on her hair. "You are feeling shy?" That chuckle again.

She knew she was going to have to look at him. But how should she answer? That she was a liar and a fraud? That she'd nearly welcomed his touching her and would have him do other things to her—wicked, wicked things her evil mind had conjured up? That she'd made up a story about getting caught in rose bushes so he wouldn't know her weakness?

"A little," she admitted.

"Have I told you how much I've missed you these past few weeks?" His voice sounded gravelly. "Would it be presumptuous of me to think you've missed me as well?"

"Oh, yes! I mean, no!" She had missed him dreadfully. "Not presumptuous at all." She did not want him to mistake her silence for apathy. She forced herself to meet his eyes. "I am so happy all of this wedding uproar is nearly over."

His eyes crinkled. The candle provided just enough light to see his teeth flash in a grin. "So, you are not looking forward to our actual wedding?"

"I had thought that I would," she answered honestly, a little surprised. "But so many people. Everyone always watching..." She'd had people notice her for most of her life, since she'd become a lady, anyhow. It ought not to bother her. But knowing she was hiding something awful, and dangerous even, she was no longer comfortable with the notion.

"I'm looking forward to our trip up to London. Do you think that we can go to the Tower? And Vauxhall?" Perhaps if she could anticipate something frivolous again, she might ease fears of what was to come. Of how she could keep it from him.

He seemed to relax at her words. "Anything you wish. We'll have Crawford House to ourselves, and I'll have you know that I plan to make the most of such advantageous circumstances."

After this, after tonight, she could imagine what he had in mind. She would insist upon darkness. "That sounds absolutely wonderful." Surely, she was making this into more than it deserved. It was the not knowing—the waiting.

But for now, she must worry.

"We'd best return to the ball." When had her life become so complicated?

"Yes, I suppose so." But he didn't move and neither did she. "Only you won't be dancing anymore tonight. You can feign a twisted ankle or fatigue if you wish. You're the bride and for the rest of tonight and tomorrow, the world will dance around you." He swung his legs over the side of the bed.

"Ah, here they are." He'd located her slippers and held them to her feet. Surprisingly, they fit over the bandages and Kingsley's stockings. She'd purposely worn them thinking the extra room would alleviate her pain.

"Still, no dancing," he ordered.

Only he didn't sound arrogant or controlling. His tenderness caused her guilt to return. "I won't, I promise."

At least her feet felt better.

* * *

Surprisingly enough, she'd not been met with any recriminations upon returning. Cameron had escorted her to her parents and explained that she was unwell. "It would be best she not overtax herself for the remainder of the evening," he'd said. They had a big day tomorrow. Her parents had taken one look at her and readily agreed. Perhaps she looked flushed, or pale. Perhaps they could tell she'd been crying earlier.

Nonetheless, her papa had ordered their carriage brought around before going to find Olivia and Louella's mother sent a footman to locate all of their wraps. Cameron had set her down outside the terrace door, and she'd managed to delicately make her way to the front foyer.

The flowers and festive decorations she left behind panged her conscience. She'd not managed even to stay for the duration of her own betrothal ball. Such pain, though. What an ninny she was to have caused it in the first place.

It had been her only option though, and she'd somehow managed to keep it from her mother.

She was *not* going to have to dance with anyone else tonight. Relief flooded her again at the thought.

Awaiting the carriage with her, Cameron promised he'd extend her regrets if any gentlemen came looking to claim their set. "I rather prefer it this way," he teased. "In less than twenty-four hours, you'll be all mine."

How could she not smile when he flirted like this? While her mama fussed with their wraps, Louella skimmed a finger along the back of his hand. "Thank you," she whispered. Her voice caught on her words.

He'd been *absolutely wonderful* tonight. He'd been her knight in shining armor!

His lips brushed along the line of her jaw. "My pleasure." And then as the team drew to a halt out front, he offered his arm and assisted her into the carriage. He encouraged her to lean upon him so that she wasn't putting all her weight upon her feet.

"Until tomorrow." He stepped away from the door. Her mama climbed in after Olivia, followed by her father. Her parents looked at one another with knowing glances.

They were not going to admonish her! They approved of Lord Stanton's stealing her away! Did they know? Oh, they could not.

Perhaps they imagined an embrace, but not in a million years could they have any idea as to how inappropriate they'd been.

Thank heavens the darkness hid the flush spreading across her face.

By this time tomorrow, she would be a married woman!

How was she going to sleep tonight?

* * *

Her mother did not even check her arms and legs. She must be satisfied, at last, that her threats had succeeded.

For this bright sunny morning on the third Sunday in May was her wedding day. Jane had packed up most of her belongings, some for travel but many to be moved into a suite that she would share with her husband at Ashton Acres. The bedchamber she'd slept in for most of her life now felt rather empty.

Mama had brought her chocolate and biscuits and had made use of their time together to advise her as to what would be expected in the marriage bed. Her mama, it seemed, was likely blushing more than Louella had the night before. Her instructions were vague at best.

"It will all feel rather awkward but not to worry. Simply allow the marquess to do what he must, and it will be over quickly. Try to relax, it's always better that way..." And then she'd scurried out of the room, abandoning her daughter to sort out the rest.

Jane entered shortly after.

The maid's lips tightened. Louella had hidden the bloodied slippers behind the wardrobe, but Jane would have had to be blind to not see the cloths Cameron had wrapped around her feet.

Louella burst out of bed. "I'm so sorry Jane. I tried, I really did. Mother hasn't seen a thing. Your position is safe because, of course, you'll be coming with me to Ashton Acres. Please don't be angry with me."

"I'm not angry, miss." But Jane's voice held disappointment and that was even worse. "I'm sad for you, that's what I am."

But it was her wedding day!

"Don't be sad. Please? It's a beautiful day, and I promise you everything is going to turn out perfectly." Even Louella could believe this after the kindness shown by her fiancé last night. "And we are leaving for London tomorrow!" Of course, Jane would be coming with her. "We'll be staying at Crawford House. You have cousins in London, haven't you? Have you sent word to them that you'll be in the city? I'll speak with Lord Stanton so arrangements can be made for you to visit with them!" *This is not bribery. This is gratitude.*

And, of course, she would have insisted her maid find time to see her family in London anyhow.

"It's all right, dear. You mustn't go to any trouble for me. I just hate to see…"

"I'll be fine, Jane. And it is no trouble whatsoever. Now stop fretting. There's far too much to be done! The ceremony is barely three hours away!" Which was all true. At which point, Louella's attention was caught by the opening of her chamber door.

"Happy wedding day!" Olivia peeked around with a mischievous smile. "You are awake! I can't believe my little sister is marrying today! And to such a fine gentleman at that!"

Upon seeing Olivia dressed in a lovely sprig muslin, her hair styled beneath a cheerful straw bonnet, Louella's heart lifted. "You look perfect!" The words swooshed out on a breath of relief.

Olivia crossed the room and wrapped her in a warm hug, rocking her side to side. "You are going to be so happy. I know it. My only regret is that I doubt you'll find time to visit your recluse of a sister quite as much. You'll most certainly be traveling all over England; attending lavish house parties and you'll receive the most coveted invitations while in London." She sniffed on a short laugh, her violet eyes unusually bright, while Louella shook her head in denial.

She'd always find time for Olivia!

She was her sister! The one person who'd loved her more than anyone else. If Louella, as the Marchioness of Stanton, received invitations to house parties, she would deuced well take her sister with her, as she would to the most elaborate of balls.

Olivia drew back and blinked unshed tears away. "I suppose Mama regaled you with all sorts of horror stories as to what you ought to expect tonight." At Louella's wince, a mischievous smile dance on Olivia's lips as she withdrew a well-used book from her satchel. "Don't tell Mama but I've been waiting for the perfect time to bring this to you. You'll definitely want to flip through the first few pages before waltzing down the aisle to meet that prince of yours."

"He's a marquess, you goose." Louella cautiously opened the well-worn book, titled *Aristotle's Masterpiece,* and immediately flipped open to a few pages that had her blushing to the roots of her hair. This most definitely was not a book on philosophy!

The drawing on one page depicted a strangely proportioned male with his pants around his ankles standing over a female whose skirts had been flipped over her head. She'd never imagined or seen anatomical drawings with such intricate detail—scandalous detail!

"This is *not* philosophy. Where on earth did you find something like this?"

Olivia grimaced. "It's not really written by Aristotle." Olivia's eyes danced. "Someone thought it great fun to leave it on the cottage porch, but the joke is on them. It's provided me with no end of entertainment and education. It ought to be informative for you as well. I believe its initial purpose was a guide for midwives."

Olivia took the book back and, shaking her head, thumbed toward the front. "See here." She pointed to an image of a man and a woman lying on a bed beneath what appeared to be a heavy coverlet and then skimmed along the written text. "'The chaste woman may or may not experience pain upon initial penetration...' Read this. '*However,* eventually, the lady ought to find enjoyment as well... with stimulation...' See here! '*La petite mort.*' That means the little death in French. It sounds rather fantastic. Do you think it's something of a myth? You'll have to tell me after."

How was it Olivia could speak of such things without any apparent embarrassment? Louella bit her lip and examined the book more closely. The ladies depicted in these drawings were mostly unclothed while the male counterparts watched intently.

While the males looked on—*seeing* everything.

Louella snapped the book closed firmly. She didn't want to worry about her scars this morning. Marital relations took place in total darkness, beneath the counterpane. He'd see nothing.

She forced herself to swallow around the suddenly huge lump in her throat. "I'll know soon enough. Now hide this before Mama comes in. She'd have apoplexy if she saw it. Have you heard anything about Luke Smith's children? Have their mother's relations arrived?" She'd change the subject and satisfy her curiosity at the same time.

"I've gone over there nearly every day to help and as far as I know, no one has come forth. Miss Cline says it might be necessary to split them up—send the youngest off separately—but nothing's been settled yet. Mr. Smith has a few other options... It seems far too soon after just losing his wife, but if he were to remarry he could keep the children with him."

Jane took that moment to draw Louella away to sit in front of the vanity and begin fussing with her hair. "Nothing a young lady needs to be worrying herself over on her wedding day." She shot Olivia a scowl.

"They would send the baby away?" Louella frowned into the mirror as she ignored Jane's reprimand.

"And the youngest. If nobody comes forward, Mr. Smith won't have a choice. He needs to make a living, and the older boy will have to work as well." Olivia shrugged.

It didn't seem right. Despite her father's financial woes, they'd never had to worry about where their next meal would come from. Where they would sleep.

Olivia had been moved out of the main house, but neither of them had ever worried over keeping a roof above their heads.

They'd worried about where the money would come from to repair the manor's foundation, whether they'd be able to hire landscapers. They worried over who would inherit upon her father's death.

Louella was a selfish, greedy girl, thinking only of herself. She glanced down at her hands while Jane twisted and tugged at her hair. There were hundreds of families in straits nearly as dire as the Smith's—probably thousands. Perhaps opening the mine up would be a good thing. It could provide additional employment for those struggling to make ends meet by working their holdings.

"Oh, I like that, Jane." Olivia complimented the maid's skill. "You're going to be the most beautiful bride. Now, where is the gown?

Already the day's preparations had begun. And so much help. For the next few hours, Olivia, Mama, and Jane fussed over her. Sewing buttons, training curls, and changing out the ribbons on her wrists at least three times.

Even so, by the time Louella climbed into the open

barouche provided by the Duke of Crawford, she felt as though they surely must be running late.

Dressed in a simple but elegant gown, Louella smoothed the material on her lap all the while sitting beside her father. Instead of a bonnet, she wore a wreath of flowers on her head and carried a matching bouquet. She'd even added some flowers to the silk wrapped around her wrist.

As they approached the church, Louella tried not to gape at the onlookers who crowded the street and the building. Why had she not considered this? Lord Stanton would someday be the duke and the woman he married would someday be the duchess. The wedding was a grand event, indeed. She wished Olivia and her mother had ridden with her. They'd left earlier. Olivia promising with a wink that she'd flay the bridegroom if he was anything other than a quarter of an hour early.

He would not be late.

Deep breaths.

"Stanton will reward them with coin after the ceremony," her papa informed her.

Louella nodded.

Her father winked with a smile. Louella didn't often see this side of him. "Folks want a glimpse of the future duchess."

Indeed.

She nodded and swallowed hard.

The crowd parted, and the driver parked them directly outside the church doors. She wished the ceremony could have been held in the chapel at Ashton Acres, as was originally suggested, but with so many guests, the idea had not been a practical one.

The village church, a towering structure hundreds of years old, built of mortar and stone, was a more logical venue.

Nobody seemed concerned that they were a few minutes late. In fact, a few cheers went up when she stepped onto the pavement with her father's assistance.

Olivia and Mama would already be seated inside. Along with Mama's sisters, Louella's aunts, and several other uncles and cousins.

Louella took hold of her father's arm. So many people pressed in around them that she breathed a sigh of relief when the large church doors closed behind them.

CHAPTER FIFTEEN

I DO

*E*very pew was filled. Her heart beat loudly in her ears when a hush fell upon the sanctuary. As the congregation rose, hundreds of eyes turned to where she stood.

Hundreds of eyes looking at her.

She would step away from herself and watch from afar, if only she could. Instead, she seemed to float within herself. It was another Louella who was marrying. Another Louella with a smile frozen on her face.

Organ music shook the building, and her father urged her along the aisle. She moved her feet woodenly. She would float away if her father's grip weren't so strong.

The volume of her own heartbeats rose, drowning out everything else.

But her feet kept moving.

She would not look at all the people. She could not look at the aisle runner on the floor.

She focused on the altar.

And then she saw him.

Lord Captain Cameron Samuel Benjamin Denning. Her fiancé.

Blue eyes twinkling, a smile lurked behind his gaze. He was every woman's dream. He tilted his head and a lock of hair fell along his jaw.

Clad in gray and silver, he had baby blue trim on his waistcoat and breeches. She'd never seen a man dressed in such finery, his cravat tied in a perfect arrangement and lace at his wrists.

He stood as she imagined he might have done while on the bow of his ship, feet spread shoulders' width apart, hands locked behind his back. His demeanor was one of strength and power, a man capable of taking on the world.

And he'd wanted to take her on, instead.

The vicar's words jumbled together. Not a prayer. He spoke of days of judgment and impediments. Were there impediments? Was she an impediment? And then he addressed Cameron.

"My Lord, Captain Cameron Samuel Benjamin Denning, wilt thou have this woman to thy wedded wife, to live together after God's ordinance in the holy estate of matrimony? Wilt thou love her, comfort her, honor, and keep her in sickness and in health; and, forsaking all others, keep thee only unto her, so long as ye both shall live?"

"I will." His words rang out confident and strong.

But that she could absorb some of his confidence.

Who was she to marry such a man?

A nobody. A girl who, behind her looks, hid ugliness and shame. And then it was her turn.

"Louella Rose Redfield, wilt thou have this man to thy wedded husband, to live together after God's ordinance in the holy estate of matrimony? Wilt thou obey him, and serve him, love, honor and keep him in sickness and in health; and, forsaking all others, keep thee only unto him, so long as ye both shall live?"

"I will." Was that her voice?

"Who giveth this woman to be married to this man?"

"I do," her father answered and removed her hand from his arm.

She did not float away. For when her father released her, Cameron tucked her hand into the crook of his arm and then patted it comfortingly and leaned down. "You look beautiful," he whispered.

She wanted to say something witty, something perfect to her husband-to-be.

"So do you," she mumbled.

One side of his mouth lifted in a half smile. And then he turned as the vicar began to speak.

So do you? She chastised herself for such an inane comment. *So do you?*

Stop thinking about it. Listen to the vicar. She didn't want to mess this up, this beautiful ceremony, by missing her cue to recite her vows.

Her hand was warm, tucked between the sleeve of Cameron's jacket and the silk of their gloves.

Without letting go, Cameron took her right hand in his and repeated words read to him by the vicar. She focused intently upon his injured hand. He was not perfect. Nobody was perfect.

She wished she could touch him without her gloves. She wished his bare hand rested on hers.

He squeezed her fingers, as though reading her mind.

And suddenly, the thundering sounds of her heartbeat retreated somewhat.

She inhaled deeply.

This close, his familiar scent reassured her. His voice vibrated through her as he recited the solemn vows. She squeezed his hand back.

And she listened.

"I, Cameron Samuel Benjamin Stanton take thee Louella

Rose Redfield to my wedded wife. To have and to hold from this day forward. For better for worse, for richer for poorer. In sickness and in health. To love and to cherish. Till death do us part, according to God's holy ordinance. And thereto I plight thee my troth."

The vicar then took her hand and placed it atop Cameron's. She recited the same words to him.

They meant something, didn't they? In sickness and in health? Till death do us part? Could two people love and cherish one another *from this day forward*?

Oh, she hoped so! She would do her best! She did not want to let him down as she had so many others in her life.

And then she removed her glove, and Cameron slid the ring onto her finger.

And they kneeled.

And prayed.

She no longer floated above herself. She was not alone in front of all these people.

She was married.

Good God! She was Lady Captain Cameron Samuel Benjamin Denning, the Marchioness of Stanton!

CHAPTER SIXTEEN

THE PRELUDE

"*J*ust my banyan." Cameron toggled his eyebrows in his valet's direction. He hoped to find his bride well rested. He and Louella had bidden farewell to the remaining guests, following the rather lengthy breakfast, over an hour ago.

This suite, separate from the rest of the household, had been utilized by his father and grandfather before him. More an apartment than a set of bedchambers, it had been designed specifically for their purpose. If they'd been in London, he'd have obtained a hotel suite for them. He'd rather not have the shadow of his father lurking in the room on his wedding night. As soon as the thought crept into his mind, he dismissed it. He wasn't a suspicious man. He'd build his own future, his own legacy.

Along with his bride.

He'd left Louella alone with her maid to change out of her bridal gown into… something more comfortable. He'd also ordered a small meal sent up for the two of them. In spite of all the food laid out, he'd not had a chance to eat earlier. He didn't think Louella had either.

A sitting room adjoined their chambers, and he wondered, as he strode through it, which room they would settle upon. He did not intend upon utilizing two chambers as husband and wife.

Arriving at her door, he rapped twice and then waited.

"Come in."

Cameron licked his lips and turned the knob. The early evening light filtered through the windows, illuminating his bride who sat waiting for him.

Fully clothed. Dressed as though she were expecting the highest of sticklers to show up and partake of low tea. At this moment, he realized that although he'd kissed her, and they'd pledged the remainder of their lives to one another, they'd spent what would barely amount to less than twenty-four hours in one another's company.

He determined to remedy the circumstance as his gaze traveled around the room. A tray sat beside her, the meal he'd ordered, and she looked up at him expectantly. And then her eyes widened in surprise.

She looked so adorably taken aback that, even dismayed, he couldn't help but laugh. He'd make the best of this, anyhow. In fact, he rather enjoyed removing a lady's garments for her.

"I'm afraid I'm a little underdressed for this occasion," he teased. His banyan stopped at his calves and tied loosely, exposed more of his chest than he supposed she'd ever seen on any man.

She blushed prettily. "I thought—"

"What culinary delights have been provided?" He shushed her and lifted a few covers from the plates to reveal an assortment of cheeses, meats, and bread. There was also wine and fruit. "Much like our picnic at the mine."

She nodded. "It seems so long ago." Her voice sounded a little thin. She was nervous. Of course, she would be.

He pulled a chair up beside her and poured wine into the

glasses provided. She filled a plate for him, all of his favorites, and placed it in front of him.

Not exactly what he'd had in mind, but it was a good enough start anyway. He held up his glass. "To the end of a wedding and the beginning of a marriage." She lifted hers with a smile and then drank with him.

"Did you think of that yourself? It's rather poetic." Her sense of humor had reappeared. This was a very good thing. She'd seemed tightly wound all day.

He lightly pounded a fist over his heart. "You wound me, my lady. Of course, I composed it myself. You've not married a plagiarist."

A giggle escaped her. She glanced up at him from under her lashes. "Did you see Mrs. Faragoat's hat? I've never seen so many feathers in one place."

Cameron chewed his food before answering. "How many birds are running around naked so that she could wear that monstrosity, do you suppose?"

"Five... no, more than that! At least ten!"

"Poor birds," he returned. "I can think of a better use for a feather."

At first, she looked confused, but as understanding dawned, she narrowed her eyes at him.

He pulled his chair closer to hers. "Are you ticklish?"

More laughter from her. "You wouldn't dare!"

But their eyes held, and she knew he would.

Later.

They joked and flirted throughout the meal until finally, they both sat back, sated and satisfied. The wine was gone, and his sweet Louella looked considerably more relaxed as the sun dropped below the horizon. Although heavy shadows had replaced the early light, he could still see enough of her to appreciate what was to come.

Cameron rose and extended his hand.

Curling her tiny fingers around his, her grasp felt tentative at first. But as he rubbed his thumb along her wrist, she tightened her hold somewhat trustingly.

He was surprised that he not only found himself excited but nervous as well.

He didn't get nervous. But he supposed this was his wedding night and although he'd taken his fair share of pleasure throughout his bachelorhood, he'd never bedded a virgin —or a wife for that matter. And she excited him. He'd need to keep himself in check so that he wouldn't frighten her.

He led her to the canopied bed, a gigantic piece of furniture with thick posts and a headboard that nearly covered the entire wall. Three steps were set out from it so that one could embark upon a night's sleep without having to resort to gymnastics.

He grinned. A few gymnastics *in the bed* were something he'd consider for later on.

An adjacent window overlooked the woods to the west of the house and a full moon shone in the indigo sky. Stars would be twinkling soon. Although it was still early in the evening, it was time. There would be no more delay.

Now, to remove the lady's apparel.

Raising her hand to his lips, he kissed each of her fingers, opening his mouth by the time he kissed the smallest of them. As she watched him, her lips parted. The pulse just above her collarbone quickened. Simply touching her like this, and he was fully aroused.

And then he did something he'd wanted to do since the day they'd met. With one flick of his hand, he untied the knot of the bow around her wrist.

A tremor ran through her as he held her gaze.

And then with a heartfelt sigh, she closed her eyes and swayed toward him. Sweet, floral woman greeted his senses as he pressed himself against her. They had all the time in the world today. They had all night. They had tomorrow. They had their wedding trip.

They had a lifetime.

The soft skin of woman unlike any he'd ever touched before. Perhaps it was her youth or her innocence. Perhaps she affected him because she was now his wife.

Or perhaps she was simply Louella.

He touched his lips to her pulse and tugged at the bow again so that it relaxed around her arm. And then, like the tail end of a firework, it cascaded to the floor.

He watched it fall with passion-clouded eyes. He would see her gown fall in a similar fashion.

And then he slid his hand up the inside of her wrist. Except...

It was not smooth unblemished skin he found beneath his fingertips but ridges of lines.

Geometrical scars, crisscrossing flesh that ought to be as soft as a butterfly's wings.

He opened his eyes and glanced down. She moaned a little and reached her other arm around his neck. Not wanting to bring any sort of halt to where this was headed, he placed his mouth upon her shoulder and viewed the carnage of her forearm in the quickly diminishing light.

Hundreds of white raised scars lined up perfectly, the uniformity of them only marred by the variances of thickness and length. He swallowed and then trailed his mouth back to her throat. She liked it when he did this. She purred for him when he touched her here.

What had happened to her? Obviously, that was the reason for the ubiquitous ribbons. It had not been done as a fashion statement. She'd never gone without the ribbons or long sleeves as far as he could recall.

Those scars were not from one particular injury.

They'd been inflicted over an extended period of time, but by who? Her parents? Her sister? A governess or teacher?

He wanted to demand that she tell him right now. Blood roared in his ears as his imagination provided other horrifying scenarios. He needed answers so that he could punish whoever had done such a heinous thing to her.

But he was standing here with a warm willing woman in his arms. A timid but excited woman whose hands this very second were drawing lazy circles down his breastbone. On a hiss, he inhaled when those fingers worked their way lower.

Hooks?

No. He would unfasten her buttons. As he located the fasteners on her dress, he chastised himself for not assessing these earlier.

But he'd been hungry for her kiss—hungry for *her*.

He'd assumed the marriage bed couldn't hold a great deal of excitement. But since meeting Louella, his bride...

He caught her mouth with his and delighted as warm lips parted in anticipation. Velvety and tender flesh. He groaned and imagined other velvety skin he'd find on her person. Only a small amount of blood must remain in his brain.

With her gown now unfastened, he pushed the loosened fabric down her arms until it dropped to the floor.

Beneath it, her corset and wrinkled chemise tantalized him to be closer.

She mewed a little beneath his mouth. God in heaven, but this was killing him. He ought to just lift the chemise and bury himself inside of her. He could explore her sweet naked curves afterward.

One of her hands continued exploring his chest, his abdomen, waist, back, and on a few teasing strokes, the indent where his thigh met his torso. She was curious, too, apparently.

Her other hand clutched at his hair and the back of his neck.

In one swift move, he swung her into his arms and tossed her up and onto the massive mattress, causing her to squeal and then giggle. Not wasting any time, using just one of the steps, he vaulted himself up beside her and rolled her onto her front.

The corset was tied in the back.

Which, he decided as his fingers worked to unlace the damn undergarment, gave him an enticing view he'd not considered. After unknotting the lace, he swiped it out from under her. All that was left was the thin chemise.

Before she could roll onto her back again, he covered her with his entire body and pressed his erection against the soft pillows of her pert derriere.

"Are you trying to go somewhere, Lady Stanton?" he growled into her neck. And then he kissed her there. Just because he liked kissing her.

"Nowhere, Cameron," she sighed and then pressed her bottom upward. She both surprised and pleased him with a little wiggle.

Praise the heavens she wasn't frightened at all. She was as aroused as he was, and she was very, *very* curious.

Cameron trailed one hand down to the hem of her chemise and drew it upward. He would watch her legs come into sight.

He'd always found himself unusually excited by a woman's legs. Who wouldn't be? They led a man to the greatest treasure on earth.

Stockings!

And a garter! She would make him work even harder than he'd thought.

His enthusiasm flagged when he caught sight of the scabs on the bottom of her feet. He could ignore these for now. He'd not wonder if she'd truly been caught by thorns. Later.

He'd investigate later.

Because for now, most of his blood had traveled away from his brain and she lay pliant and willing beneath him.

He'd go so far as to believe she was a little wanton.

If possible, he hardened even further as he unfastened her hose from the garter. If he were to push her chemise up a few more inches…

Sweet, rounded pale buttocks.

"Cameron?"

He was going too slow apparently. He curved his hand around her and squeezed and then gave her a resounding pat. "Too many garments, my lady." He pushed himself to all fours and, with her assistance, removed the chemise and tossed it off the bed.

There were so many things he wanted to do just then, but he decided he'd best ease her into them incrementally. "Sweet, sweet Louella Rose."

She slowly turned to face him. It was at that moment that she seemed to realize he could see all of her. She raised her hands and covered her breasts.

Seeing the bow on the wrist he'd not unbound, he swallowed hard.

The lines on her abdomen could possibly have been from the stays, but they resembled the markings on her wrist too closely.

He forced himself to keep the questions from showing in his eyes. She was being brave. She was forcing inhibitions away that would have been ingrained for all of her life.

He would investigate later. For now, he was going to make love to his wife.

CHAPTER SEVENTEEN

CONSUMMATION

*I*f it weren't for the hunger in his eyes, she would have died, absolutely died of embarrassment. No candles had been lit but the room was not yet engulfed in darkness. She could see him well enough. She could see hunger in his expression and his lips glistened from kissing her.

But his eyes...

His eyes devoured her. And his hands trailed a path of desire, exploring, caressing, daring...

And now, as he hovered above her, her body ached to feel the texture of his rougher, hairy skin rubbing along her own. She pushed away his banyan and arched upward.

"God, yes, Louella. God, yes," Giving in to her demand, he relaxed his arms and pressed her into the mattress with his weight. She cradled him between her thighs, urging his member closer to her sex. She wanted him there. Short rapid breaths rushed past her lips and into his mouth as she waited, impatient and yet scared.

And then she felt it. An intrusion, a pause, and then a harsh thrust.

Her core throbbed. She'd torn! She was certain something

inside of her had torn! Her mama had said "a twinge." And the book had said it would be over quickly. Surely, this was not what they'd all been referring to?

This wasn't at all what she'd imagined.

As much as she grieved to disappoint him, she tensed and attempted to pull away.

But he followed her, remaining inside. She'd thought she wanted this, but—"Stop! Wait! Cameron!"

He retreated for a moment and then thrust again, his eyes fogged with desire.

"Please, oh, please!" she gasped.

His mouth covered hers. He was lost in his passion. But it hurt!

She twisted her head. "Stop!" she cried out finally. "Stop!"

At last, he stilled. "Louella. Oh, shite, I'm sorry. Damn me to hell, Louella!" He started to move off, but she tightened her legs.

"Just... hold still... a moment." She'd wrapped her arms around his neck and held him tightly. Despite the raw sensations inside, she didn't want him to leave her!

He froze, and she could barely make out the recriminations behind his gaze, the shadows even darker now. His brows furrowed but he held himself still, exactly as she'd asked. As a few moments passed, her muscles gradually relaxed. "I just need a second, please." His breathing sounded loud by her ear. "But don't leave me."

And then his lips were on her cheeks, her nose, her forehead, and her eyes. "Sweet love, I'm sorry. I forgot myself. I'm a brute." He spoke the words between kisses.

"You're not a brute."

He looked into her eyes. "I am."

"No." She removed one arm from around him and placed it along the side of his face. "Nobody calls my husband a brute."

This was marital intimacy. She'd never felt so exposed to

one person as long as she'd lived. Not only was she married to him, she belonged to him—legally, yes—but in a more carnal way. She'd willingly opened her body to him.

And in that instant, his body surrounded hers. He belonged to her, as well. She could touch him, stroke him, *love him* freely.

"What do you want me to do?" he whispered. He'd not moved for over a minute now. He was inside of her, fully inside of her, and the throbbing was much less intense now.

"Wait just a moment." She moved her hand from his cheek to run one finger along his mouth.

Such a lovely mouth. His skin had appeared smoother in the morning, in the church. Tiny stubble was now barely visible, making it delightfully coarse.

"What would you like me to do while I'm waiting, oh, wife of mine?" And then he caught her finger with his teeth.

His mouth fascinated her. She'd never considered knowing anyone's teeth but her own. Sharp, pointy, and white. He held tight to her finger, exerting enough pressure that she could not escape, and yet not so much pressure as to cause pain.

"You could try kissing me again."

And then her finger was free. And his mouth was on hers.

How did one go for so long and not experience the taste of another person like this? His tongue danced with hers, and explored, and then... thrust deeper inside. The sensation sent heat swirling to where they were joined.

And suddenly the fullness, the stretching... felt...

Wonderful.

She slid her hands down to his waist and around his backside and then wiggled her hips. "I'm fine now."

He knew. He must, for he began moving again, mimicking the rhythm he'd started with his mouth. He'd slide back, making her want to cry out for him, and then he'd come back to her, deeper, fuller, more demanding.

And then he'd do it again, as though torturing her to intensify her pleasure.

As his pace increased, he buried his face against her chest, creating more sensations as his stubble scratched her breasts. She was fascinated to see his shoulders and neck straining and tense as he held his weight above her.

He drove deeper, faster. She wanted it that way. She felt he was conquering her inhibitions, seeking to know all the secrets of her body.

As a man would.

As a man and woman were meant to do.

Why else would they be created this way? Created so that his body could stroke hers into a frenzy of delightful hysteria?

"Yes, oh, yes!" she demanded. He ground deeper. "Please! Please!"

From that point, she was lost in the frantic passion of their need. As was he. There was violence in love, in this sharing.

How wonderful!

How absolutely wonderful!

* * *

When it was over, her husband—ah, yes, her husband—collapsed atop her. She'd felt his release, the heat of his seed, in the end, and relished in the thought that he could plant a life within her.

Her legs still wrapped around him, she barely had the strength to stroke the back of his head with her hand.

Was this love? Did she love him?

And then, in one of the most significantly poignant moments of her life, as she lay exposed and dreamy, the door to their chamber flew open violently.

CHAPTER EIGHTEEN

INTRUSION

"*G*od damn you, Stanton!"

Was this madman really the duke! In their chamber? Louella struggled to believe her own eyes and ears.

Cameron whipped the sheet up and over her.

What on earth? This could not be happening. Horror-stricken, all she could do was shake her head slightly.

"I'll snap your fool neck! How dare you change the contracts without my consent?" Snarling and cursing, he did not care that he was interrupting their wedding night. With a guttural sound ripping from his throat, he set aside the candle he carried, grabbed a nearby vase and spiked it into the wall. The glass shattered, and fragments flew across the room. Seething hatred shot from narrowed eyes set in his ruddy-colored face. "You've betrayed this family again, and by God, I'll not abide by it!"

In a cold voice, she hoped would never be directed at her, Cameron's words chilled her through and through. "Get out of this chamber before I remove you myself."

The duke merely shook his head with narrowed eyes. "I

did it for you! I specifically wrote those contracts so you could go an entire lifetime without fear of empty coffers! Why have you put so much effort into the mines when you have no intention of carrying out your duty? Have you been so befuddled with lust for this little twat that you've forgotten where your loyalty lies?" He gestured wildly before settling his gaze upon Louella.

At these words, her sweet, loving, *naked* husband snarled something fierce and flew across the room in a rage. Chairs tipped over, and the contents of her vanity went flying when he launched himself at his father.

Wrapping the sheet around her, Louella crouched on the bed, feeling utterly helpless. Was Cameron going to kill his own father? "Stop!" she managed to scream although her mouth had gone dry. "You're going to kill one another." And when neither of them took any heed of her protests, she bellowed even louder, "Help me! Somebody stop them!"

The duke was an older man, but he was also fit and strong. He pulled back one arm and then threw it into Cameron's jaw. She felt the cracking sound in her own stomach. And then there was a low thud and a simultaneous grunt from the duke. She couldn't watch. The blows continued and after one particularly ruthless blow, blood splattered on the wall.

"Stop it!" she screamed at the top of her lungs.

Cameron paused to look at her as though he'd suddenly recalled where he was, that his wife looked on in horror, but when he did so, the duke saw his opportunity.

Thwack!

Her husband's head spun around and then his body collapsed.

"No! No! No, no, no!" Clutching the sheets still, she jumped off the bed, nearly falling over herself, and crouched down on the floor.

"He'll be fine," his father scoffed. "Selfish bastard. Sold out his own family. I should have known when he left before. Cares more about himself then his duty."

Cradling Cameron's head in her lap, she looked up at her new father-in-law. By this point, she seethed with her own indignant rage and confusion. "What kind of man are you?" She choked on a sob, frightened by Cameron's lifelessness. "What is the meaning of this? Call for a physician, Your Grace! If you've killed my husband, by God, I'll—I'll—" She sputtered and gulped. She was screaming at the Duke of Crawford, barely covered by a bedsheet—and her husband might very well be dead. "Call for a physician." She buried her head. "Call for a physician." This time, she begged.

She heard the door close but did not look up to assure herself that he'd left.

Not thirty seconds later, the door opened again and Jane and Cameron's valet rushed inside. Jane threw a dressing gown over Louella's shoulders and Mr. Longley crouched down, holding a small vial beneath Cameron's nose.

"He'll be fine, my lady." His attempt to reassure her drew even more tears. "Navy man. Tough as they come."

And then Jane was tugging at her. "Let Mr. Longley do cover him, miss... my lady. Come with me into the dressing room while this mess is cleaned up."

A few footmen and three housemaids hovered at the door.

Cameron jerked his head and then brushed Mr. Longley's hands. Relief washed through Louella.

"I don't know what happened." Louella began trembling. "I don't know why...But the duke! We were just... And then he burst in on us!" And that was it.

Tears and a few dismayed sobs weren't enough. She collapsed into Jane's arms, weeping as though the world had ended.

Because it kind of felt as though it had.

* * *

The first thing Cameron saw when he opened his eyes was a man in spectacles with bushy gray eyebrows hovering over him. "Wake up, my lord. Let's get you to your chamber."

What the hell? Why in the feathering tarnation was he lying on the floor? And where in the blazes was he?

And then it all came roaring back. He'd been with his wife, *in the Biblical way*, and his blasted devil for a father had barged into the room.

Crawford had disgraced her, called her a twat! And yes, he remembered then lurching from the bed and attacking his plague of a father with rage he'd kept pent up for decades.

But why was Cameron the one lying flat on the floor?

"Her ladyship is near hysterical."

Ah, yes. Her ladyship had been screaming at the top of her lungs for them to stop.

Cameron had done as she asked. The devil who'd supposedly sired him had not.

And damn, but his head pounded something fierce. Sitting up was not pleasant. As Longley assisted him to his feet, Cameron surmised standing to be even worse.

Leaning upon his valet more heavily than he'd prefer, Cameron allowed Longley to assist him back to his own chamber.

Crawford obviously had read through and then been none too pleased with Cameron's contractual amendments. If only the blighter had waited one day longer to read them over. Bleeding bollocks, but this was a tangle.

Louella would need reassurances.

In all of his life, Cam had never heard of such a disastrous wedding night. He winced at the memory. Likely, it would haunt both of them far into the future.

He needed to talk to Louella.

Oh, hell but his head hurt.

Cam grabbed hold of the bureau as the room swam before him. Damned if he hadn't been walloped by an old man.

Longley chuckled as he dabbed a warm cloth at Cameron's face. "Poor Lady Stanton. She like as thought you were dead. I told her, of course, that you would be fine. Tough as nails, I told her you were."

Cam didn't feel so tough presently.

He ought to track Crawford to ground and call him out. Tonight.

But it was his blasted wedding night! He ought to be partaking of those gymnastics he'd had in mind. Or tangled in the sheets, basking in the afterglow of swiving his wife.

Longley took hold of his arm when Cameron swayed unsteadily and led him toward the bed. Apparently, he wasn't as resilient as the valet had boasted.

"My fault. Damn Crawford." he murmured as he collapsed upon the mattress. Just a moment. He'd only rest for a moment and then return to Louella's chamber.

He'd be damned if he'd spend his wedding night alone.

She'd been incredible, so trusting and willing. He'd not had to coax her into letting go of her inhibitions; she'd wanted everything he'd wanted to give her.

The scars though. The memory of the faded white lines, some still a little pink, were a matter he'd have to deal with. Because whoever had done something like that to a young girl deserved to hang.

Had she been tortured? Contemplating it now, without having to attend to a raging erection, the horror of what she'd endured haunted him.

She would tell him everything. He'd not leave her be until she told him who the perpetrator was. Because she was his wife now, a part of him, and he would protect her.

He ought to be with her this very moment.

Sitting up again caused his head to pound. That last hit had come like an anvil. He'd not known the old man had it in him. Gaining his bearings, Cameron slid off the bed and found his footing. Not so bad.

He would go to her.

* * *

Louella had no idea how long she'd sat huddled on the large chair in the dressing room. She'd shivered, Jane had thrown a quilt around her, and the two of them had sat listening while servants cleaned up glass and furniture on the other side of the large oak door. Finally, when the sounds ceased, covered from head to toe in nightshift and dressing gown, Louella tentatively followed Jane back into her bedchamber.

"What kind of household is this?" The doubts uttered by her maid echoed her own. "That a person would interrupt a couple in their marriage bed." Jane blushed profusely. "And then get into fisticuffs in a lady's chamber?"

Jane's words summoned images Louella would banish from her mind forever if only she could; worst, by far, seeing that final blow the duke had landed. Hearing the crack of bone meeting bone.

She glanced around the room. Her vanity had been righted, but several of the perfume bottles were now absent. Strong aromatic odors hung in the air. The glass could be cleaned, but the remnants of spilled perfume would persist for some time.

The pictures the men had bounced off of had been set to rights, as had a chair that had been knocked over. And the left-over trays from their dinner had been removed. Even her bed was made up again.

The servants' efficiency impressed her. Perhaps they were used to this sort of thing.

"You'll be wanting to rest now, love." Jane fluffed up a pillow. "I've a pinch of some draught, if you need something to sleep?"

A habit of her mother's. Should she? Louella shivered, glancing around the unfamiliar setting. "I'm fine." A lie? Louella couldn't know, but she'd rather lie awake restlessly than subject herself to unconsciousness in this inhospitable place.

As much as she hated what the duke had done, seeing Cameron fly into such a rage equally unnerved her.

His anger had been understandable, entirely within reason, but the violence in which he attacked his very own father chilled her. Where was he now? Should she go to him? Did she *want* to go to him?

Jane patted her shoulder comfortingly and then bid goodnight. "Everything will look better in the morning, dear."

Louella wasn't so sure about that. She wasn't sure about anything.

Everything had changed in the matter of a few hours. Yesterday she'd been Louella Redfield. Today she was a wife. A marchioness. She no longer belonged to her father but to a man she didn't know nearly as well as she'd thought she had.

Her sewing box rested on the floor, beside the bed.

Sitting in that dressing room, Louella had cried and then told Jane she wanted to go home. She could never face the duke again. After he'd been so rude, so violent and insulting.

And then, her new husband, her kind, gentle-mannered husband, the man who'd considered her feelings so thoughtfully, had been transformed by a violent rage.

Was this how the inhabitants of Ashton Acres lived?

Jane had insisted she could not return home. Her papa, Jane explained, would force her to return to her husband. Louella would be turned away. For a flash of an instant, she imagined running to Olivia's cottage where the two of them could hide away forever.

And what had brought on the duke's attack? What had her husband done to invoke it?

You've betrayed this family again and by God, I'll not abide by it!

Had Cameron betrayed his family? And how? Oh, God, this must have something to do with that dratted mine! The duke had first shouted something about contracts. He had to have meant the *marriage contracts.*

He'd called her a twat. And although she had never heard the word and didn't know the exact meaning, the manner in which he'd used the word did not bode well for its definition.

She wanted to go home.

But Jane had told her she was a married lady and this place was to be her home. She would not be welcomed by her parents.

Which left her sitting in this very unfamiliar chamber with memories of embarrassing pleasures and then horrifying violence. A few of her belongings had been set about. Some of her books, her jewelry box, and escritoire.

Her sewing box. Merely seeing it solaced her. It represented relief, pain… comfort. And her mama was not here to take it away again.

She rose from the chair and padded across the carpet in bare feet. The cuts on her feet were already healing from the salve Cameron had applied.

Guilt sliced through her at the thought of the lie she'd told him. But this was *her body.* She wasn't hurting anyone!

She crouched to the floor and opened the basket. Thread, a thimble, the unfinished gown, and ah, yes. Three needles.

Louella withdrew her favorite. It had a finer tip and was sharper than the others.

She made herself comfortable against the bed and rolled up one sleeve.

She would only cut once... maybe twice.

She always had her wrist bows. Cameron hadn't even noticed the lines on her arms when they'd made love. If he had, they hadn't bothered him. It seemed her mother's fears had been misplaced, for she was certain he'd not be sending her off to Bedlam.

She located a slim patch between the faded white scars and drew a perfectly parallel line. Watching the seeping red liquid appear on her skin, she inhaled deeply. A strange peace entered her lungs along with the air.

The duke had accused Cameron of changing the contracts, of putting his own wants above the dukedom. Which made no sense. He'd come home to fulfill his obligations to his family, to take on the burdens of his title. Even she knew he'd not have offered her marriage if he hadn't felt some responsibility to his father, his family, the title.

What had he done?

So much about him that she didn't really know.

Except he was her husband now—in every sense of the word.

They'd consummated their vows, and she was no longer ignorant as to what happened in the marriage bed. Besides the pain, which presumably was to be a singular occurrence, the activities he'd introduced her to had been... incredible, enthralling... addicting! She'd felt a worth, a completion, unlike anything she ever could have imagined. Did all married couples experience this? Had it been something special between herself and Cameron? Would it ever happen again?

Cameron's skills came from years of experience. Experience she'd benefitted from.

She didn't know what to think. Conflicting emotions trolled her brain, disorienting her further.

What had he done to anger his father to such an extent?

When Cameron had held her, she'd basked in his tenderness. She'd gone so far as to wonder if she loved him. She'd been certain those sensations resulted from more than lust. His body could not have merged with hers, surely, in such a way without emotion. Only she had heard differently on more than one occasion. Cameron had lived his life as a bachelor. Was it possible she'd credited him with more character than he was due?

She'd been terrified the two men would murder one another in front of her eyes.

The edges of her vision dimmed to black, the room crushing in around her. She drew another line, deeper, deeper... and longer. Closing her eyes, she inhaled. She would be fine. She would figure everything out.

And then a voice jolted her from her meditations.

"You do this to yourself?"

* * *

Cameron could hardly believe his eyes after staggering through their adjoining sitting room. He'd imagined himself stealing into her chamber and climbing into her bed. He'd planned on waking her with kisses and exploring hands.

Instead, he discovered her mutilating herself!

All the horrific images he'd conjured up of some dastardly villain torturing her had been grossly wrong. *She'd given herself all of those scars.*

As he watched her calmly drag the needle into her flesh, the reality of it stunned him.

He rubbed his eyes to be certain he wasn't seeing things. He'd taken a hearty blow to the head perhaps... But no, his eyes did not deceive.

Instead of finding his lovely young wife curled up in bed, he came upon a stranger performing some repellant ritual, sitting on the floor. This was not his Louella.

"You cut yourself?" He couldn't help repeat the words as the impossibility of what he discovered overwhelmed him.

Upon first hearing him, she'd met his eyes almost defiantly. But then the light in her eyes flickered, and she dropped her gaze. Her shoulders slumped, and she curled her knees up to her chest. It was as though she physically shrank before his eyes.

He slammed a fist into his other hand. And then he turned and punched the wooden bedpost, causing the entire bed to shudder.

How could she do this? Bile rose in his throat, and his eyes stung at the thought of all those scars. Why would anybody do such a thing? He'd thought somebody had tortured her. He'd imagined pummeling the perpetrator, and now...

Before he could say a word, she turned away from him. "Go away!"

"Louella." He took one step toward her.

"Leave me alone!"

A pox on all of this. He'd travel to London alone! Or perhaps he'd head down to Dover. Leave her and such insanity here with his hell-breathing father. God's bleeding balls, what had he gotten himself into?

He needed to leave before he said something he'd regret. He needed to leave before he *did* something he'd regret.

With a pivot, he strode out of the room, through the foyer and down the stairs. Blinding anger drove him. He took note of nothing as he marched out the door and into the darkness.

With only the moon for illumination, he set to hiking a path he'd often traversed as a child. It climbed the hills and circled a distant lake. Depending upon which branches of it he stayed to, he could walk for hours and remain upon the estate.

He pushed off with his heels and ran.

And ran.

The pounding of his steps eventually settled into an even pace. The steady rhythm calmed his heart rate, his breathing. And the calm that washed over him settled his rage and eventually began to clear his thoughts.

He'd believed he knew her. She was his perfect debutante, the perfect wife. Throughout the dukedom, she was considered an incomparable.

Even his sisters had mimicked her fashion and flair.

It had all been a lie.

He forced himself to recall the image of her sitting on the floor with a needle poised over the translucent skin of her wrist.

Why?

And when he'd caught her, she'd crumpled. In shame? In fear? In submission? When had he observed such a look on her face before? Not when he'd first proposed, not when they'd been together in the garden.

Louella was not who she seemed. Was she some sort of lunatic? No sane person would do such a thing, would they?

This was the same woman who'd insisted he apologize for hurting her sister's feelings a decade ago. He paused at an overlook, breathing heavily, and stared into the vast darkness.

She was hurting herself. Did she need to be protected from herself? Would she ever hurt anybody else or did she limit the damage to her own person?

She'd enraptured him earlier this evening. Seduced him with her bold and yet timid sensuality. They had laughed and joked and flirted. And she'd even charmed his sisters over the past weeks.

So why would she do something so horrific? He turned and continued climbing the path, pushing his body in hopes he could summon the answers he needed. The moon provided enough light that he could see the footpath just clearly enough.

It cannot be something she elects to do. He'd heard of people who found euphoria in pain. Could her actions be related to this phenomenon?

What could have triggered such a need in her? Their betrothal? The wedding? The ball?

Had she done it because she'd found his lovemaking repulsive?

Good God in heaven! Those wounds on her feet hadn't been from thorns! She'd put them there herself!

The revelation had him slowing his footsteps to a walk and then bending over his knees, breathing heavily. He'd not discover the answers he needed here, nor in London, nor by escaping to a tavern.

He needed to return to the manor.

He needed to discover what was going on in his wife's pretty little head.

CHAPTER NINETEEN

*L*ouella's shivered. Her feet felt like ice, and her arms and legs would likely cramp when she moved. How long had she been sitting here?

His words. *"You do this to yourself?"* The look in his eyes. Disbelief. Confusion.

And then disgust.

She could not remain. In spite of their wedding, in spite of what had transpired in this bed, she could not stay at Ashton Acres with Cameron as his wife. There had been loathing in his eyes. Loathing and horror. No doubt, he'd be happy to find her gone when he returned.

If he returned.

And if her parents would not take her back, then she would go to Olivia. Olivia would never send her away.

Jane could remain here if she wished.

Forcing her cramped limbs to move, Louella scampered off the floor. She would leave. There had been no question of staying the moment his gaze landed on the blood glistening on her arm.

She'd told him to leave her alone. He wasn't supposed to see her that way! Ever. But he had and now everything was ruined.

He wouldn't understand. Nobody did.

And how could she make him understand when she didn't herself?

A portmanteau had been packed for travel to London tomorrow, along with a trunk and several hatboxes, so she had no need to go rifling through the wardrobe. But she did need to get herself dressed.

She was going to require Jane's assistance after all.

She drew the bell pull and then located a serviceable gown that had not been packed. It was an older, dull-colored frock but she didn't care.

When Jane appeared, she seemed to know exactly what Louella was up to. Before the maid could speak, however, Louella sent her a glance curtailing any argument. "Help me dress. We're leaving."

When Jane merely stood in the doorway twisting her hands, Louella pulled the gown on over her night rail without the maid's help and presented the back to be fastened.

"Tonight," she added.

"But, my lady—"

"Tonight." Louella would not be convinced otherwise.

"You cannot wear that dress over your night rail. I'll help you, but I won't have you going out looking like anything less than the lady you are."

Louella contemplated telling Jane that Stanton had discovered her with the needle, but she couldn't bring herself to speak the words out loud. Both physical and emotional exhaustion tugged at her now, and she'd require all her strength for their departure.

Jane fussed and argued, clucked her tongue when she saw the fresh cuts, but after what seemed like forever, eventually had Louella tied up and fastened enough so that she could emerge from her bedchamber.

"But how will we get there?" Jane asked when Louella grasped the portmanteau by the handle. "It's after midnight!"

Running away with a fussy maid drained some of Louella's urgency. "Wake the butler!" she ordered. "We must... We can... Well, Jane, cannot a footman order a carriage brought round?"

It was dark outside. Likely everyone in the household was abed. What with all the work that had been required of them earlier in the day—for the breakfast and a house full of guests.

Jane twisted her hands anxiously again. Louella supposed this wasn't a convenient set of circumstances for her. They'd barely arrived, and now her poor maid's mistress was demanding she awaken a virtual stranger.

"Then we shall walk!" Louella decided.

"In the middle of the night? But it isn't safe, miss!"

"Enough!" Louella threw her arms into the air in frustration. She must leave tonight! If she were to stay, she'd have to address the duchess with explanations, as well as Cameron's sisters, and any other guest who happened to be about.

Oh, God, and the duke.

And her husband.

And what if Cameron failed to return? Everyone would know she'd angered him. They might think any number of unseemly thoughts regarding her wedding night. They'd think she'd not satisfied him, which she supposed was better than the truth, but still...

Oh, she couldn't stay! She simply could not!

"You decide, Jane. Either order a carriage or we walk." She could not be moved in this matter.

"A carriage, then. But it might take some time. You wait here while I find one of the footmen. One of them must be awake, in such a grand place as this, wouldn't one think?" Jane spurred into motion as she settled Louella into the sofa. "Wait right here, dearie. Don't go trying to walk alone. I'll arrange for a carriage if I have to wake the butler himself."

And so, Louella waited.

And waited some more.

As she glanced toward the mantel where the clock revealed her maid had been gone for over forty minutes, she bit her lip. What was taking so long? Had Jane had to go in search of the stable master herself? Or was Jane still trying to keep her from leaving?

The latter was most likely the cause of her absence.

Jane was delaying them from leaving in hopes that Louella might fall asleep. Or change her mind.

Although she had nearly nodded off a time or two, Louella had most certainly not changed her mind.

Dawn couldn't be far off. Deciding she could waste not a minute more, Louella located her belongings and tiptoed downstairs. When she arrived in the front foyer, it was just as she thought.

Jane had nodded off, sitting on a long-cushioned bench at the bottom of the stairs.

She would send for Jane later.

Peering outside, she nearly changed her mind at the thought of walking alone in the darkness, but she forced herself out the door. She would walk to Olivia's home. It was only a few miles, as the crow flew. Perhaps a little longer if she stayed to the road.

Hmm… The drive appeared dark and lonely, but the fields represented a sea of the unknown. She couldn't be sure she would be going in the proper direction. Oh, bonnets and whiskers, she'd have to take the road.

She ought to have left her case behind, she realized, as the handle dug into her hand.

She ought to have donned a coat. She wrapped her free arm around herself and shivered.

How many hours had passed since she'd last slept?

Drat her maid for making her wait so long! She could have been at Olivia's already if she hadn't wasted time waiting for the carriage that her maid had not summoned. With heavy lids and weighted feet, Louella adjusted her grip on the case and forced herself onward.

Past the gardens, past the stable block.

She stopped.

Something was in her slipper. And now her feet *were* hurting again. She should have worn her half boots. Probably all part of Jane's diabolical plan.

With a groan, Louella made a seat out of her case, lowered her bum, and emptied the pebble from her slipper.

"Going somewhere?" Cameron called out to her from the darkness.

"Stop sneaking up on me like that. It doesn't show very good manners," she said without looking to see where he was. She would not give him the satisfaction. He'd caught her at her worst, but he was not without fault either.

He'd been disgusted by her. She'd seen it in his eyes.

Still, she didn't understand the duke's attack. And no one had bothered to explain anything to her.

The crunching of steps on the gravel spurred her to replace the slipper and resume walking again toward the main road. If only her luggage didn't feel as though she were carrying stones. And, of course, now she would limp. The pebble hadn't dislodged itself; it had merely moved to an even more uncomfortable spot.

"Louella." The footsteps behind her had quickened and were louder now. And then she felt him behind her, his hand covering hers on the handle of the portmanteau. "Louella."

This was too much. She was tired, angry, frustrated, and...

"You don't want to stay married to me. I don't blame you. Just please let me leave..."

An arm wrapped around her waist, and she felt his breath on her neck. "Why wouldn't I wish to stay married to you?"

But he knew. And she knew that he knew.

"Because." She tried to shrug him off while at the same time wanting to burrow into his warmth. "Because... you know. You know why."

And then his hands located her wrists and slid her sleeve upward. His fingers skimmed along the ridges of her scars. "Because of these?"

She nodded.

No one else had ever touched them. Not her mother, not even Jane.

He didn't say anything right away, but he pulled her closer and buried his face in her neck. She wished she could see his expression.

She thought he hated her and now...

He was here, treating her tenderly, sharing his warmth. Reassuring her that he was not repulsed by the scars on her body.

"I can't pretend to tell you I understand it, nor that it doesn't make me angry. But we're married, Louella, and tomorrow the two of us are leaving on our wedding trip."

Could it all be as simple as that?

"I don't want to see your father," she insisted, still willing to return to her home if need be.

He squeezed her. "Then we'll leave tonight."

She couldn't help but twist around to look at him. "Really? But what about..." She had no objection to the idea. "Right now?"

He raised his brows.

"I don't want to go back into that house," she persisted.

His shadowed eyes narrowed, and before she could utter a word of protest, her breath swooshed out of her, and she was dangling over his shoulder. With her bum in the air, she kicked a few times to no avail. He merely gathered her case in one hand and began marching back in the direction of the house.

"I'm not letting you out of my sight." He acted as though carrying her was a perfectly reasonable solution. "You'll wait with me in the stables."

Hanging upside down made it difficult for a lady to hold onto her dignity. "Put me down, you barbarian! I can walk, I'll have you know! Just because you married me doesn't mean you can haul me around like a sack of flour!"

A sharp swat landed on her bottom.

"This cannot be happening," she mumbled into his back.

"What's that?" His hand had settled warm upon her backside, and she presumed he was itching to swat her again.

"You don't have to be carrying me!" She spoke louder into his jacket. And then, spying his own backside, she landed a swat of her own. "Put." Slap. "Me." Slap. "Down!" Slap.

And then his hand was no longer on her backside but sliding up her leg. To her thigh and even higher.

"Do you really think you can win this game, Louella?" His voice sounded huskier than usual as his hand lodged itself between her legs.

This could not be normal for married couples. But for the life of her, with his hand on her leg, everything they'd done earlier that night sent a hot needy feeling coursing through her. The urges he'd awakened came to life again. The most unlady-like urge to spread her legs for him right there on the dark road had her heart racing. The thought was an embarrassing one, to say the least. Anyone could come upon them outside.

In front of his father's house.

And so, she wrapped her arms around him instead and searched about for the falls on his breeches. In response, he inched his hand higher between her legs.

His walk had slowed, and she could sense his altered purpose. They were barely even moving now.

Still hanging upside down, she clutched at the fabric of his shirt and tugged until his shirttails no longer presented an obstacle. Blast and fiddlesticks! A man's shirt was nearly as long as her dress! Oh, but she was to be rewarded for her persistence.

The skin on his stomach was hot, slick from sweat, tight. His muscles jumped when she ran her hands around his navel. A trace of hair curled beneath her fingers.

He stopped and craned his head as though looking for something. When he started walking again, she noticed he was no longer carrying her along the graveled road. Larger rocks and grass replaced the groomed surface of the drive. A few tall weeds bounced and flew past quickly as he strode along with her in the upside-down position.

Even with her hands in his falls, she couldn't quite reach what she sought.

What had come over her?

"Let go, Louella." He'd crouched down and was setting her back on her feet. And then his hands roamed over the front of her dress, pressing her up against a tree.

"You aren't leaving me anytime soon. Do you understand?" Emotion seemed to catch in his voice.

He moaned then, and his mouth covered hers as he hitched one of her legs around his waist. His arousal thrust at her apex.

She, in turn, allowed her own hands to roam his person. Locating his falls again, she fumbled with the buttons. "I won't," she gasped against his mouth. "I do."

She wouldn't think about the operations at the mine or his father or the look he'd given her when he'd caught her with the needle. She wouldn't think about the house nearby, filled with guests who'd attended her wedding, or Olivia, or William, or anyone else in the world.

She could only think about this moment. This craving to be with him. To be a part of him.

His falls opened and for the second time in her life, she joined with a man.

This time outside. Under the trees and sky.

Words she'd hardly ever thought, let alone thought to speak, tumbled past her lips. Words of longing, depravity, and passion. She clutched at him. She devoured him with her mouth.

Crying out, not in pain, but in satisfaction, she relished in his strength as he pumped and ground into her, lost in this tumultuous storm.

He wanted her.

Whatever his reasons were for marrying her, he needed this as badly as she. For once he'd spent himself, his breathing labored and sweat beading above his lip, he kissed her softly on the brow. "You're not leaving me, Louella," he reminded her.

"No," she agreed.

But was this enough?

CHAPTER TWENTY

FOUNDLINGS

"*Y*ou were returning to your parents' home, I presume?"

Louella tensed in his arms as the carriage bumped along the road to London. Could she feign sleep? Would he have other questions? Questions she could never answer? At the thought of having to give him an accounting of why she did what she did, and when it started and how it helped her, her heart raced.

"Don't ever do that again. I'd have gone out of my mind if I'd discovered your chamber empty."

She wanted to bury her face in his shirt but was already beginning to think she'd acted cowardly. "If they wouldn't take me in, I was going to go to Olivia's."

He exhaled a deep breath. She knew he wanted more from her, but she couldn't think what else to say. Not about what he wanted to hear.

But then he completely surprised her. "Would you prefer to see the Tower or Vauxhall first?"

What? It took her all of thirty seconds to register his question. He was not going to demand explanations? *This man.*

Just when she thought she had him figured out, he surprised her.

"Do you like the opera?"

"I was only in London for a short time and didn't see much, let alone an opera, so I wouldn't know." She nearly laughed out loud in relief. "I think the Tower in the daytime and Vauxhall at night... when they have fireworks."

"There will be numerous invitations already delivered to Crawford House, what with the Season in full swing now. Perhaps we can make it to a few balls."

Louella turned in her seat to stare at him. Was he jesting?

His eyes were sincere, and his mouth had twisted into a painful-looking grin.

"I didn't think gentlemen liked attending balls. That's what my father says, anyhow."

A grimace. "It doesn't matter if I like them or not. Would *you* like to attend a London ball? If I'm to understand correctly, as my stepsisters explained to me, marriage to me has robbed you of your Season."

"I think that would be absolutely lovely." And then she added, "But only if you'll dance with me."

"Just try and stop me." He adjusted his arm behind her head. "Are you comfortable?"

She turned on the bench to lie against him. He brought one leg up beside her and braced them both with his other on the floor. "Umm," she murmured. "Now I am."

* * *

Cameron ought to have known she'd try to flee. Stupid of him, really, to imagine she'd do anything else. His father had accosted them in their wedding bed and then Cameron had abandoned her abruptly upon discovering her secret.

A cold streak of something he'd rather not analyze swept through him at the thought of her traipsing along the road in the dark by herself. Thank God he'd seen her lone figure before she'd made it any farther.

Her hair tickled him beneath his chin, but he could tell by the even rhythm of her breathing that she'd fallen asleep.

God, what a night.

She'd looked so forlorn, almost ghostlike with the moon reflecting off her hair. At that moment, she'd touched his soul.

He'd considered her perfect. In fact, he remembered thinking it on more than one occasion. He'd taken in her perfectly placed features, glossy hair, and cream-colored complexion and not bothered to dig any deeper. Stupid of him. She was human, of course. She was flawed. And perhaps even more than that.

This girl, so beautiful and charismatic, was *tortured*.

Oh, not physically. The cuts, the scars, they were merely a symptom. No, she was tortured in her mind.

Why else would she...? He hated even thinking about it. Those haunting eyes when he'd caught her. Her blood, like ink, rolling around on her skin. And now she'd taken it upon herself to think to leave him in the middle of the night—on foot, no less.

He'd called out her name, but she hadn't stopped. In fact, she'd increased her pace.

He didn't want her to run from him, to be afraid of him. He wanted to make her happy.

There was no way he was letting her get away.

He'd taken hold of her from behind and done his best to calm her, to allow her to absorb some of his... strength? His warmth?

Love? He dismissed the notion.

He dared not guess at what compelled him, but he'd wanted to give her whatever she needed just then. He'd wanted her to feel confident and beautiful again.

And then afterward… by the tree. He couldn't bear to think about that right now, or his arousal would awaken her, and she needed sleep.

But, oh, good God in heaven, he'd never imagined he'd experience this sort of passion within his marriage. If they spent as much time doing bed sport as he had in mind and took in all the sights she had in mind, this wedding trip could prove to be… exhausting.

She made a soft humming sound and turned onto her side, drawing her hands up to rest beneath her cheek. As she did so, she revealed some of her wrist.

She would not have dressed them with the bows for her midnight getaway. He ought to have suspected something. He was surprised nobody else ever had.

Most of the lines were white, but some of them were pink and more raised than the others. And there was a fresh cut, one she'd made tonight. All the lines were precise and equally spaced.

He swallowed around the lump that had formed in his throat and hugged her closer.

* * *

Louella awoke when the driver passed them over what must have been a large rut, nearly bouncing her off the bench. The previous night's events rushed at her unapologetically, both the good and the bad.

She'd fallen asleep using Cameron for her pillow. Although

this sounded lovely and romantic, the reality left a serious crick in her neck.

Cautiously sitting up, so as not to awaken him, she crossed to the other bench and stretched as much as one could while riding inside of an enclosed carriage. She then opened one of the drapes and peered outside.

London wasn't at all as she remembered from just a few weeks ago. Not the outskirts, anyhow. She recalled that her mother had made a face and then pulled the curtains closed before. Louella hadn't thought much about it, but she couldn't help wondering if her mother had done so in order to protect her from seeing such poverty. With the coverings pulled back from the window, she was not protected from noticing the makeshift dwellings and hovels that exuded dismal living conditions, filth, an essence of hopelessness.

She opened the window and then quickly shut it again. Outside wafted a foul stench, unlike anything she'd experienced before. The air was dense with soot, and dogs and chickens ran wild through the streets.

And children.

Most of the structures they passed appeared as though they would not hold themselves up against a stiff wind. A few two- and three-storied brick buildings had been erected amongst numerous other ramshackle dwellings.

And the road could hardly be referred to as a road. She preferred to contemplate that most of it was mud, but the smell belied such an assumption.

"It gets better."

She tore her eyes from the dilapidated scene outside at her husband's comment. He'd not moved at all, reclining still in the position she'd left him. His clothes were wrinkled, his hair a bit on end, and his face dark with the beginnings of a beard, all causing her heart to jump, nonetheless.

She turned to look outside again. "Why are those children

in the street all alone? Where are their parents?" She imagined they'd been there when she'd traveled a few weeks ago. She'd been too intent upon her own situation to even consider the different villages they'd passed through.

Cameron dropped his other foot to the floor and leaned forward to see where she was pointing. "Foundlings," he said. "Their parents cannot afford to keep them at home, and so they are forced to make their own way." His voice sounded casual, but the look in his eyes was sad.

"But they're so young!" Louella was shocked. "How can their own parents put them out?" She turned back to look outside, astonished at such a cruel place as this. Some of them looked to be barely six years old…

"Too many mouths to feed."

All the little mouths in Luke Smith's family came to mind.

"Is their existence as wretched as it looks?" The children were not only filthy but woefully thin. "Don't their parents care about them?"

Cameron continued peering out the window. "If they have parents. How can a mother support her children when she cannot support herself?" He sighed heavily and sat back. "Reform is needed. For some, the workhouse is a death sentence. Children can sometimes find work elsewhere but often in deplorable conditions."

"Why has there not been reform, then?" Surely, the government knew about these children's circumstances. "But what can be done? There are so many of them! Parliament should act!"

Cameron grinned. "A proposed bill is making the rounds now, you'll be happy to know."

"Will it pass?" There was no reason it should not, was there?

Her husband raised his shoulders. "One would hope." And then he stared out the window again.

"You are involved," she guessed.

"I'm doing what I can." He did not contradict her.

"Is that what angered your father?" Maybe it wasn't the mine after all. Maybe it had nothing to do with her.

Cameron's eyes turned cold. She hadn't wanted to bring any of that up. She preferred to imagine everything was perfectly normal as they rode away for their wedding trip.

"I must look a fright," she blurted.

His gaze softened again and then lazily traveled over her. "Beautiful as always."

And for some reason, this made her feel a little like crying. She was not beautiful. She didn't deserve somebody like him. "Thank you."

She turned again and watched out the window as the buildings became taller and closer together and the streets more crowded with humanity. Summer was upon them. The air had been crisper just a few weeks before. It seemed thicker now, stifling even.

"It's better when the wind blows," Cameron explained.

"Is it always like this? So many people crowded into one place. Of course, that makes for hundreds of stoves, thousands of chimneys!" She frowned. "Is there a place they can go? For food? To sleep at night?"

She couldn't stop thinking about the children. They'd reminded her so much of William, only they had no homes! And they wore clothing that was ill-used and soiled. What if one of them were to become sick as Will had?

"There are orphanages, and some form gangs and learn to take care of their own. But it is not a good life, Louella. I'll not lie to you."

She wiped a tear. "I'm sorry... I just wasn't expecting to see..." And then she smiled tremulously at him. He was bringing her here for a *holiday*! "Are we far from Crawford House?"

"Don't apologize for feeling compassion." He reached for her. "Come back here, I've yet to kiss you today."

Moving into his arms seemed the most natural thing in the world. He placed one hand along her jaw and kissed her full upon the mouth. "Much better. And no, Crawford House isn't far now. It's in the center of Mayfair. Thirty minutes, less if we can avoid heavy traffic."

Why was he *so good* to her? He'd seen what she did! And he'd been angry—she'd not been mistaken.

"Mayfair is a different world." She remembered the vast lawns at the garden party. The clean streets, governesses and nurses with every child.

"Very."

He'd been to so many places, and she'd been tucked away at home but for the few days she'd spent here a month ago. What else had she missed? She peppered him with questions about London and then different lands he'd been to. Before she knew it, the landscape had indeed changed. The buildings took on more majestic facades, and the houses became ornamental and sturdy looking. Iron fences surrounded some of them, and they passed the large park that resembled the countryside.

"Hyde Park." She'd meant to visit, but they'd left before she'd had a chance. So much natural splendor in the middle of the city. It made no sense, setting as it was amidst the hustle and bustle of everything else.

"We shall walk in it this evening."

Louella glanced down at her dress. It was so old, brown, and ugly! And now she had slept in it and done... other unmentionable things in it. She was sticky and dirty and... "Not today. I'm a mess!" And then she grinned at him. "Tomorrow though, for certain. And I want to try the ices and go to the Temple of the Muses! I still cannot imagine so many books in one place."

He chuckled. "And don't forget Rundell and Bridge's."

"What's that?"

"A jeweler. Don't you think a new bride deserves a few baubles?"

But she did not want him to spend money on jewelry for her. "A book, my lord, all I need is a book."

"Than a book, it shall be." An indulgent smile danced upon his lips, and for the first time, she noticed the bruising around his eyes and the shadows beneath them. Such an inauspicious beginning to their marriage. It could only get better!

CHAPTER TWENTY-ONE

AN OFFERING

The suite prepared at Crawford House for the newly married couple was even more elaborate than the one they'd been given at Ashton Acres. Jane oohed and ahhed for all of ten minutes over the high bed with burgundy lace drapes and a padded bench at the foot before settling down to begin unpacking Louella's belongings.

And the bathing areas! Such a dream. The white tile surrounding a huge tub with shining brass spigots gleamed. Servants were not required to lug heavy buckets upstairs, for the water came directly into the house through a pipe! Louella didn't understand exactly how all of it worked, but Jane had exclaimed that she must have died and gone to heaven.

Louella wondered if Cameron would come to her again tonight. He would, wouldn't he? She'd told him she was tired. Exhausted, actually. And yet, after eating and changing into a night rail, she had no desire to sleep.

She'd been so angry with him last night, but even worse, she'd been embarrassed and afraid that her mother had been right. But he'd hardly mentioned her secret at all. *"I can't pretend to tell you I understand it, nor that it doesn't make me angry.*

But we're married, Louella, and tomorrow the two of us are leaving on our wedding trip."

He'd not ordered her to cease. He'd not demanded she hand over all items she owned that were sharp. He'd done none of those things.

No, instead, he'd made love to her again.

Outside.

Against a tree.

Emboldened by an unexpected sensual awareness, she entered the adjoining sitting room and then knocked upon his door. Was this something a wife ought to do? Her mother had omitted such details, and Olivia's book hadn't really addressed such, but then again, neither had it mentioned what one could do while pressed up against a tree...

Biting her bottom lip, she listened for sounds from the other side.

She didn't think she had the courage to enter his chamber if he'd already gone to bed and so breathed a sigh of relief when creaking footsteps grew louder.

Her worry was in vain.

When he opened the door, all oxygen swooshed out of her lungs. He wore black breeches, a linen shirt that emphasized every muscle on his chest and arms, and stockings.

And that was all. Louella licked suddenly dry lips. The nature of his dress seemed almost more intimate than the banyan he'd worn the night before.

His unbuttoned shirt revealed the smattering of hair that trailed down to his waist and the purplish bruises left by his father. She met his gaze boldly.

"I couldn't sleep," she told him.

"I wasn't going to let you," he returned.

She recognized the look in his eye. Last night he brandished the same one before he'd swooped her over his shoulder.

As he moved to within inches of her, she licked her lips

again. Then she reached out and trailed her fingers down the length of his chest. "Oh, really?"

He stood perfectly still. Then *he* licked *his* lips and grasped her hand and settled it on the bulge below his waist. "Really," he answered.

Tonight would be different. How many ways could two people do this? She had ideas, depraved ideas that had come over her on the other two occasions, but she dared not utter them.

So instead, she unfastened his falls and released his sex. His throat worked as he seemed to swallow hard. Afraid of losing her courage, she dropped her gaze to just below his waist.

This time, it was she who swallowed hard. She'd not had a chance to examine it before and was shocked at what it actually looked like. Red, almost purple, angry, and bold.

He put it inside of me.

Liquid heat settled between her legs.

Cameron wrapped her hand around it and groaned. With an innate knowledge older than time, Louella knew he liked her touching him this way.

The skin was hot and silky, and a tiny amount of fluid escaped from the tip.

"Is this what you had in mind?" Her voice came out low and throaty.

She captured the droplet with her thumb and swirled it around. His pupils had dilated so much that she could hardly see the green in his eyes. His breaths seemed to come quicker, and his hand tensed as it covered hers.

"One scenario, yes," he responded. He hesitated a moment. "Sometimes, a woman uses her mouth."

Oh, really?

"I don't expect you to. I'm just letting you know... I would never presume—"

She dropped to her knees.

Cameron braced one hand on the doorframe, his other moving to her hair. "God's holy breath, Louella." His voice was strained. When she looked up at him, his manhood by her lips, his eyes were half closed.

She'd never felt so powerful in all her life.

He did not close his eyes all the way, heavy with desire though they were. She leaned forward and ran her tongue along his length. His hand clutched at her hair. Using both of her hands, she positioned him more conveniently and wrapped her lips around the head.

She knew what he wanted. It was the same. The same as the other.

Only different.

And just as she was hungry for him below, she wanted to capture as much of him in her mouth. Breathing through her nose, she slid him past her teeth and wrapped an arm around his thigh. His muscles were tense as she slid her tongue along his length. She sensed his need increasing with her speed.

She *was* depraved.

But he was moving with her, clutching her head and thrusting with his hips. He moaned, a few expletives escaped his mouth, and then he went to jerk himself away, only she would not allow it.

He shuddered and released himself in the back of her throat.

Salty, hot, excitement.

Louella couldn't help but recall her mother's advice on the eve of her wedding.

Her mother had gotten this all wrong.

* * *

Alone in his large bed, where they'd eventually moved their activities, she stretched and yawned. He'd worn her out quite thoroughly.

Over the past twenty-four hours, Louella had learned that her new husband quite appreciated her depravity. Not that everything they did was depraved, per se, but even thinking about some of it brought a wicked smile to her lips.

And he had assured her that this sort of activity was expected of a newly married couple. Although she suspected he exaggerated slightly.

She couldn't imagine, no, she *refused to imagine* any of the married couples she'd been familiar with partaking of the delights she'd recently learned about. She preferred, instead, to believe she and her husband—her lover—were the only two people in the world to have discovered such pleasures.

Dark curtains had been drawn, closing out the world, and Louella had lost all track of time. Cameron had dressed and slipped out a short while ago. She vaguely remembered him kissing her and promising to return soon. He'd not said where he was going. She wouldn't have remembered had he done so.

But she could not lie in his bed all day. After searching through some sheets and under the bed, she eventually located her night rail on a sturdy chair. Ah, yes, the chair. She tingled at the memory and slipped the garment over her head.

She then returned to her own chamber and found Jane hanging some of her dresses. "I wondered when you would rejoin the living," her maid teased her with a twinkle in her eyes. "Decided he's not so bad after all?"

But it was all too new for her to discuss with even Jane. "He'll do." But a grin tugged at the corners of her mouth. The clock on a tall bureau read half past four. Louella pulled open the windows and allowed the bright sun to caress her skin.

She wished now that she'd asked Cameron where he was

going—when he was returning—and if she should plan on going out tonight. After all, this was her wedding holiday!

Jane closed the now empty trunk and brushed her hands. "I'll go downstairs and scrounge up some rations. Such a lovely kitchen, and the cook is as sweet as they come. I have to admit, if you don't mind me saying, that I far prefer the staff here than at Ashton Acres."

Louella could not disagree. Not that she knew anything about the staff, but she was happy to be anywhere where she wouldn't have to see her father-in-law again.

"Do you think you could bring me some tea as well?" Suddenly, she was famished as well as thirsty. She had aches in places she'd not considered before. Her arms, her thighs… and other places.

Jane nodded knowingly, chuckled, and slipped out the door.

These feelings were enough to overwhelm anybody. Elation. Despair. Questioning. And then elation again.

Louella sat at the vanity and stared into the looking glass. She somehow expected that she ought to look different. Being with Cameron, being a wife, had changed something inside of her. At first, the thought felt silly, but it was as though she'd gone through a rite of passage.

She drew the brush downward, smoothing her hair instinctively. She'd shared her body in unimaginable ways and explored the most intimate places of her husband's.

Her musings were interrupted by a knock at the door.

"Come in!"

His eyes met hers in the mirror as he stood at the threshold. He did not step in right away, however. "Are you… occupied?"

Am I occupied? What did he think she was—? Oh, heavens! He thought she might be using the needle! "Oh, no!" She turned on the stool and faced him. His face was freshly shaven, and he was dressed in black breeches, a dark green waistcoat, and a brown jacket. He wore a fabulously tied cravat, and his hair had been slicked back with pomade. Forrest green eyes gleamed from what was fast becoming her very favorite face in the entire world.

He held what looked like some sort of a cigar box. Had he gone to Rundell and Bridge's without her? But it was not a jewelry box. With a sheepish grimace, he handed it over.

"What is it?" She took the box in wonderment.

He just shook his head. "Open it."

She untied the leather string and opened the lid. The contents made no sense to her at first. Some ointment, several folded linen cloths, some paper packets of willow bark… and a small envelope containing several needles.

She shook her head. "I don't understand."

"I don't want it to make you ill. I don't like it. In fact, it scares the hell out of me, but I don't want you cutting your feet with thorns or ever going without healing ointments. There's always the possibility that they'd putrefy. Throw the needles away after you've used them a few times. Let me know when you need newer ones, or if these aren't sharp enough." He stopped talking and looked down at the floor. "I'll not try to stop you, though."

He'd rendered her speechless. This…gift of his, this… acceptance. She blinked a few times and then set the box on the table.

She didn't want to cry. "Thank you," she finally managed.

He strode toward the window and stared down toward the street. "I'd like to understand. I'd like for you to explain it to me when you feel ready. But I'll not send you away. I wanted you to have my reassurance."

Nothing had prepared her for this. Better than any smile. Better than any kiss. Better than making love.

"I'm at a loss for words." For what he'd done for her. For what he'd given her. She wished she could give him what he wanted in return. An explanation. A cause. Some logical reason for why she did what she did.

"And I'll not enter your room without your permission. I imagine you expect some privacy while you're doing it."

What could she offer in return? She'd be honest with him. Always. She'd give him that at least. "I don't always have a need for it." She forced herself to add, "For the blood—something to do with the blood—and the pain. I've seen gentlemen, and ladies sometimes, either take some snuff or a shot of brandy. And an expression appears on their face."

It sounded so nonsensical when she said the words out loud.

"That is what I feel when I open the skin. And watching the blood, it makes the world stop spinning sometimes. I can think. I can breathe." There, she'd done it. She'd told him something of her madness.

He flicked his eyes back toward her. "It brings you calm." He nodded in understanding.

She'd not really thought about it, but yes. That was exactly what it did.

The repercussions of it, unfortunately, brought her more grief. The shame. The fear of discovery, that one of the cuts would begin bleeding in public and her secret would be exposed.

The pain she'd felt for weeks now, whenever walking any distance at all because of the flesh she'd opened on the soles of her feet.

"Some." She lifted a hand and indicated the box. "This— offering." Yes, it was some sort of offering on his part. A truce. "It helps. Thank you."

He seemed to be mulling her response in his mind before nodding. "Good then." And then a tight smile. This was not comfortable for him. "I've some tickets for the opera this evening."

But she could not leave him standing there alone. By his expression, he'd been uncertain of how she would respond to his thoughtfulness and generosity.

It was the most natural thing in the world for her to walk into his arms. Pressing her cheek against the fabric of his jacket, she hugged him tight. "The opera sounds lovely, Cameron. Absolutely lovely."

CHAPTER TWENTY-TWO

THE HONEYMOON

The next week flew past in a whirl. Together, they visited all the places he'd promised to take her and more. And he spoiled her at every turn. Not one but three flavors of ice at Gunter's. And not just a diamond pendant necklace but a matching broach and a ring and barrette. A Chinese fan from this vendor, a bonnet from another. He insisted at every turn.

He'd even made a large donation to some genteel ladies collecting funds for a foundling home at her request.

Oh, but the nights.

During the night, he breathed new life into her.

And the wedding trip was not to be over when they finished in London! He had arranged for them to catch a packet to Brussels, and then to Paris! He told her they'd only return to Ashton Acres when she was ready. Perhaps they'd not return at all if that was what she'd like.

They could live in London. He'd rent them their own townhouse.

It was a special time, unlike anything she'd ever known. Anything she'd ever expected.

Of course, it could not go on forever.

The evening before they were to travel down to Dover, after a drive on Rotton Row, they decided upon a quiet evening at home.

Doing all the things one wanted was so very tiring, after all, she joked with him. But just as the first course of their dinner was served, Mr. Longley peeked into the dining room and hesitated at the door.

"What is it, Longley?" Cameron gestured for his man to enter.

"A courier is here from Ashton Acres with two letters. One for her ladyship, and one for you, my lord."

With a frown, Cameron held out his hand. "Good man, good man. We'll read through these now. You can offer the courier some supper as well. We'll provide responses within the hour, if necessary."

Longley, looking uncomfortable to have interrupted their meal, bowed and backed out of the room.

Cameron handed one missive to her. It was in Olivia's handwriting. He set the other one down beside his plate. "Good news, I hope?" he encouraged as she broke the seal and withdrew the letter.

"It's from Olivia." She couldn't help but smile as tears threatened to spill past her lashes. "She says she misses me." And suddenly, the excitement of leaving the country seemed somewhat less wonderful than it had initially. Louella had married, discovered new heights of passion, and even hoped to have an affectionate relationship with her husband, all the while Olivia remained alone in her cottage.

Cameron reached across with his handkerchief, and she used it to dab at her eyes while reading through the remainder of the letter. "She writes that she's assisted with the Smith infant." Perhaps he'd not heard of the tragedy last month. "Mrs. Smith died in childbirth a little while ago. Leaving her sons without a mother. She says she'd like me to come with her to visit them when I return. Wonders if I—if *we*—might be able to do something to help them."

But he was nodding. "I did hear, actually. The father, Luke Smith, is working at the mine."

She swallowed hard at the look on Cameron's face. The mine, it seemed, might always be a sore spot between the two of them. Despite what he'd told her.

"I suppose we could postpone Paris." But he didn't look all that happy about it. "And it wouldn't hurt for me to inspect the new construction."

Oh, she felt it. She felt the bubble burst with those words.

She didn't want to think about the mine, or his father, not even of the young boys awaiting family to help care for their new little brother. "I suppose we could." And then she glanced at his letter, innocently resting alongside his plate. "Is that business?"

He seemed to have forgotten all about the second letter. "It's from the duchess. I presume she wants to attempt to repair matters between Crawford and myself." He ripped off the seal and opened the parchment.

She watched as the light diminished from behind his gaze. He turned the letter over as though looking for more, and then reread the front one more time.

All the while, Louella sensed something was very, very wrong.

"The mine's collapsed." His features seemed frozen. "Three bodies have been recovered." His eyes glazed over as he added, "Along with Crawford."

Three bodies? But wait, Crawford?

"Your father?" The duke? Of course, who else would he mean?

He nodded.

Louella reached across the table to place her hand over his.

"We must return right away. I'm so sorry, Cam. The duchess will have need of you. As will your sisters." Fiend though he was, Crawford had not only been a duke, but he'd been a husband, a stepfather… and a father.

Cam nodded again.

She squeezed his hand, but it remained motionless beneath hers.

Suddenly, she wished more than anything they'd left for Dover yesterday. In less than five minutes, the fragile joy they'd been existing in vanished. Was the closeness they'd shared so delicate that it could not hold up to life's realities? But no, she would not believe that!

And then it occurred to her that the last time Cameron had seen his father, they'd fought bitterly with one another.

"Cameron." She willed him back to her, but no words came to mind. Everything she thought to say felt cliché and meaningless.

She didn't even know if he'd loved his father! Cameron had abandoned his family for nearly ten years. He'd returned out of duty; she remembered him mentioning that. But what had their relationship been like? And what had caused that horrid argument?

The duke had called him selfish. He'd told him he'd shirked his responsibilities to his family, to the dukedom.

The last time he'd laid eyes upon his father, the man had thrown a fist to his face, though the bruise around his eye was now barely noticeable. "Shall we leave for Ashton Acres this evening?"

Finally, he pulled himself out of his trance. He seemed almost startled to see her still there. "I suppose we must. For Her Grace—and the girls."

They'd barely begun their meal before Longley had interrupted them. She could hardly eat now.

Cameron picked up his fork once again and went to take a bite. "You should eat though. Before we leave. It's a long drive."

He could not have been unaffected by the news. And yet he ate heartily while she picked at each course. He'd sent instructions to the servants to prepare for their departure but otherwise continued with the meal as though nothing had happened.

"A shame to cut our trip short, Louella, but we'll go to the continent another time."

"Of course." She was uncertain of his mood. He continued eating, but she couldn't even look at the food. It was as though he felt nothing.

She had not seen this side of him, and seeing it now left her feeling as though the floor beneath her might disappear—as though she could any moment fall into a black pit of emptiness.

Why was he not showing any grief? Had he hated the man so very thoroughly?

She willed him to talk to her. She wanted to know what he was thinking, what he was feeling, and yet, he'd respected her privacy in her matters. Would he resent her for not doing the same?

She could not endure the uncertainty a moment longer. "I'll check on Jane."

He stood when she rose from her chair and bowed slightly.

"Very well then." He kept silent, waiting for her to leave, intent upon eating his meal.

"I'm so sorry." She spoke hesitantly, as though he'd ask her to remain with him.

She wanted to offer him something more. Something concrete, meaningful. Something he could trust.

Her love.

Would he even want it?

A strong urge to wrap him in her arms, to soothe him, stilled her. She wanted him to look at her with those green eyes of his again, in the manner that usually left her tingling. But he remained stiff, withdrawn.

"Is there anything I can do for you?" She made another effort.

"Be ready to depart in an hour's time." And then he lowered himself into the high-backed dining chair once again. Dismissive, lost in his own thoughts.

She paused, hoping he'd look at her again, but to no avail. Exiting the room, a sob nearly escaped, but she would not allow it.

She could not, however, do anything about the tears that welled up in her eyes.

* * *

Crawford had probably done it on purpose. Made it a point to get himself killed while Cameron was enjoying his bride on their wedding trip—the very bride the devil had found for him.

Staring across the empty table, his vision blurred.

What had Louella expected? That he should burst into tears? Crawford had accused him of betraying his family. He'd accused him of disloyalty. Hadn't she heard the last words he'd spoken to him?

Cameron ran a hand through his hair, immediately regretting his thoughts. She'd done nothing to deserve his ire.

But God damn Crawford to hell.

Cameron fought the urge to send his glass of brandy crashing into the window. And his plate. Hell, the entire contents of the room.

Three men had perished along with the duke. There were likely more bodies trapped inside.

Workers *he* had contracted and for whom *he* was responsible. Having begun the project, Cameron never should have walked away from it.

Hell, from the very beginning he should have heeded his instincts and objected to the entire agreement. There had been too many unknown variables. Even Kingsley had expressed concerns. Why hadn't Cameron listened?

The engineers had been operating off of too many far-reaching assumptions.

Cameron had ignored his conscience, convincing himself the engineers wouldn't take unnecessary risks. But they'd been employed by his father. Of course, they'd tell Crawford what he'd wanted to hear.

Cameron's gaze drifted to Louella's empty seat.

She hadn't touched her food. It irritated him that she'd not done as he asked. Although it shouldn't. He didn't understand why he felt annoyed with her right now.

Perhaps because he'd done everything he could to be understanding, and yet she'd worn a silk ribbon on her arm this morning.

When had she found time to do it? She would have had to extricate herself from his arms in the middle of the night and then crept out of the room to light a flint.

He wanted to understand her. He wanted his affection to "fix" her.

His fist slamming onto the table echoed throughout the room.

All he'd done hadn't been enough.

The clearing of a throat jolted him from his thoughts. Louella hadn't closed the door and now Longley stood tentatively at the threshold. "It is true? My lord? His Grace is no longer with us?"

Ah. Yes. Others must be informed. Announcements sent to the papers. Funeral arrangements. Legal matters.

"If I'm to believe the letter from Her Grace, it is. You've been informed, I hope, that we're to depart within the hour?"

"I have, *Your Grace*, I simply wanted to look in on you. I heard a crashing sound..." He looked around, apparently surprised when he didn't see any of the carnage Cameron had been tempted to wreak.

If Crawford was dead then Cameron was now His Grace... Crawford, damn him.

"Very well, then." He dismissed the man with a nod.

He wanted to be alone. Hell, if Louella weren't so anxious to see her sister, he'd probably leave her to return at her leisure. Except something squashed this idea. Not just his baser urges, but an ache that tapped at his heart.

Striding to the sideboard, he poured himself a full glass from the open bottle and then downed nearly half of it in one swallow. Liquid heat burned his throat, his chest, and finally, his gut. The second time caused only half as much sensation.

Duty.

Loyalty.

The words burned more than any spirit ever could. He'd known the time would come but always suspected it to be decades away. Crawford had been built like a pile of bricks. Stronger and heartier than any man his age ought to have been.

Not that it had protected him from the tons of earth and rock that collapsed on top of him.

In his mind, Cameron recalled a few of the workers' names that had been written on the missive. Luke Smith had been one, along with others he could barely match a face to, but he'd been the cause of their demise.

They wouldn't be the first who'd died while under his watch. But, God, how he hoped it was the last.

In all his years on the seas, he'd lost eight men throughout his tenure. Dangers lurked within the ocean, as well as on the ship itself. Cameron had done his best to protect his men but there had been calamities he'd had no power over.

With one stroke of the pen, he'd now lost eleven. Twelve if one were to account for his dear, loving papa.

He poured another glass.

Why had she done it? Why had she needed to draw blood last night? Was she unhappy with him? Was she missing home, her family? She'd tried to explain some of it, how it made her feel. He'd heard her words with his head, but deep down, they hadn't made any sense.

He wanted to protect her, remove everything that was sharp, and force her to cease the cutting. How did one protect a person from herself? Restrain her? Have her watched?

She'd hate him for it.

She'd bloody hate him and likely do it all the more.

CHAPTER TWENTY-THREE

HOME

The city was bathed in darkness when they finally departed the manor. But for a few street lamps and lanterns held by drivers, there wasn't much to see this time as Louella gazed out the carriage windows. No animals, no venders... no foundlings.

Her heart squeezed at the thought of small children left to their own devices in such a cold and heartless manner. She shivered.

Cameron sat beside her, but on the opposite side of the bench. He hadn't said much since they'd departed. It was going to be a long and uncomfortable ride if this were to continue.

She didn't want to force him to hold her if he didn't want to.

It was his voice, gravelly, strained, that finally broke the uncomfortable silence.

"Why do you do it?"

She placed one hand over her wrist. He had noticed.

She'd not meant to. She hadn't understood it herself. It was almost as though she'd known something was going to happen to interrupt their paradise.

"I don't know."

He made a disparaging noise and turned his head back to the window.

He needed something from her. Did she have it to give?

She forced herself to remember her thoughts from the night before. "A sound, something from the street, woke me. I don't know what it was." She'd been tucked beside him, his arm beneath her neck. "But after I woke up, I couldn't get back to sleep. I listened to you breathing. I felt the beating of your heart beneath my hand. And then it came."

They must have traveled nearly half a mile before he responded. "What came, Louella?" He didn't sound hurt. His voice gave away frustration... confusion.

"I imagined your heart not beating. That something could happen to you. It was far reaching, I know, but once the thought came it wouldn't go away. It's always worse in the darkness, the spinning. The tightness. I didn't want to wake you."

"You did not think I could help you? You'd prefer to turn to your needles? Did you think I would stop you? Is that why you wanted to hide it from me?"

Surprised that he would lash out, she shook her head. "I don't know. It was foolish. I didn't want to wake you is all..."

Again, that disappointed sound grumbled in his throat.

"What would you have me do?" she asked, resentment building. She'd done her best to be understanding of his pain. Why was he so angry with her? He'd been supportive until now. His gift... Had he only been playing with her?

He folded his arms across his chest and stared out the window blankly. Frustration exploded inside of her. "You would have preferred that I light the candle, pull out the needle, and do it right there in front of you?"

He shrugged, almost dismissively. She wished she could see his face, but the moonlight wasn't bright enough.

"Why not? You aren't shy with anything else."

He might as well have slapped her across the face.

Or punched her in the gut.

She'd trusted him implicitly. She'd shared her body with him wholeheartedly.

Reaching below the seat, she withdrew her reticule and opened the string at the tip. She always had one with her. She'd not have to go searching. And then she pushed up her sleeve and held out her wrist. He wanted her to do it in front of him? He wanted to understand what drove her to cut her own skin? Did he think she liked that she had to hide her scars? That she was afraid of being caught?

Not thinking, in a violent and angry motion, she drew one long line from the bottom of her palm to the crease of her elbow, intersecting all her other cuts.

White hot searing pain, unlike any she'd inflicted while cutting before, speared along her arm. "There you see! Is this what you wanted?" As blood began spurting from her arm, the awfulness of what she'd just done had the edges of her vision turning black.

She stared at her arm in horror. *What had she done?* She'd not meant to cut herself so violently. Her arm burned, and blood was dripping onto the skirt of her dress and even onto the floor.

This was not why she'd ever cut. Shame and remorse swept through her.

"Holy hell, Louella!" He'd burst to life in order to take hold of her arm. His other hand worked at his cravat and then whipped it into his lap. "You're going to be the death of me! I swear," he muttered under his breath, alternating between curse words and endearments as he wrapped the white cloth around her arm. By the time he'd tied it off, she was awash in embarrassment.

She wanted to bury her face in his chest, forget any of this had happened.

What had she done?

He'd just lost his father, and she'd gone and done this. And why? All because he wanted to understand her better. Because he was concerned.

And yet it hadn't felt like concern at the time. He'd wanted what her mother had always wanted. Reasons. And then promises. Promises she didn't know how to make. Promises she knew she couldn't keep.

Had she already ruined her marriage?

She'd wanted to hurt him and knew somehow that by hurting herself she could do this.

She was evil! She deserved to be sent to Bedlam, just as her mother said.

"I'm sorry." Her voice caught, quickly followed by a choked sob. Was there anything else to be said? Could he be any more disgusted with her than she was with herself?

"No, Louella. You aren't." He released her arm and leaned back into the cushioned bench, fatigue evident in his posture.

His words stung.

She was sorrier than he'd ever know. She moved to the opposite bench, unwilling, unable to even sit beside him. First, he'd insulted her brazenness in their bed, and now he presumed to know her thoughts! He'd refused her apology.

And then he stared at her across the carriage through narrowed eyes. "Do you want to die, Louella? Just tell me if that is the case." He watched her closely as her own eyes flew open wide.

"No! Of course not! I'd never!" She shook her head in adamant denial. "It has nothing to do with that. It just helps me somehow. And I *am* sorry." She stared at the crisp white linen he'd bound her stupidity with. "I am." She could not make him believe her, just as she couldn't make him understand why she did what she did.

This marriage business was too complicated. How could he make her feel so wonderful one moment and then so awful in the next? Furthermore, how could she wish herself a thousand miles away from him and yet ache for the comfort of his arms at the same time?

Noticing the tension in the tightening of his jaw and the tiredness around his eyes, she was beginning to suspect he felt much the same.

She curled her feet beneath her, closed her eyes, and leaned against the side of the carriage. If she could make herself disappear at that moment, she would. She was tired of being sorry.

He turned his head to stare out the window, dismissing her.

"Fine, then," she muttered beneath her breath.

They had a long drive ahead, and she didn't think she'd be able to sleep. She was too wound up, on edge with him tonight.

He shifted in his seat and leaned against the opposite wall. Within minutes, his deep even breaths told her *he'd* fallen asleep! Although arguing with him had been almost intolerable, the loneliness she experienced now was even worse.

* * *

"We're nearly there, Louella."

At first, she thought to smile, to stretch and reach for her lover. He'd spoiled her over the last several days now with whispered endearments and early morning lovemaking.

"Nearly where?" she mumbled sleepily. But she wasn't in a comfortable bed! They were moving along in a carriage. She didn't want to remember what had transpired the night before. She wished she could take it all back.

He must hate me now!

A weight of despair crushed her quickly enough. He'd placed one hand upon her shoulder, like a stranger almost.

No warm lips nuzzling her neck this morning. No hands exploring beneath the covers.

She squeezed back tears before opening her eyes. She would not beg for his attention, despite her traitorous heart.

Her whole body ached from being bent up and jostled all the night through. And her arm throbbed.

Familiar landmarks proved Ashton Acres not far ahead. "Will you instruct the driver to drop me at Thistle Park? That way I won't have to return later."

At her words, his eyes snapped quickly enough in her direction. That couldn't have been panic hidden in his expression. "As my wife, you'll reside at Ashton Acres with me. You will not be running home to your family."

Surely, he didn't want her with him, intruding on his family's grief. He'd not indicated that he would anyhow. And yet she was his wife...

"I thought you wouldn't want me to come home with you."

"You're the duchess now. You have a duty to return with me. You'll assist my stepmother in the necessary planning and..." He swallowed. "I'd appreciate it if you would comfort my sisters. They've viewed Crawford as a father for most of their lives."

Of course, she would be there for his sisters. She was less certain of her ability to assist the duchess.

"Why was he so angry?" She'd not intended to blurt the question out. "When he stormed into our chamber. He said you had betrayed him. It had something to do with the mine, didn't it?" When she'd brought the subject up before, he'd managed to evade giving her a straight answer.

His jaw clenched. He stared out the window silently before finally answering, "I amended the wedding contract."

Louella contemplated what that might mean. When her father had shown her the contract with Cameron's full name on it, she hadn't even considered reading the details. She wished she had. She ought to be able to. It involved the rest of her life, for heaven's sake! But what had he done to anger Crawford to such an extent?

"He called you selfish."

* * *

Had it been selfish of Cameron to put his honor before the title? His father would have seen it that way. Selfish of him to treat his future father-in-law fairly, to refuse to rob him of what could have proven to be hundreds of thousands of pounds.

Although she hadn't asked him *why* his father had called him selfish, the look on her face held a myriad of questions. Questions he did not want to answer.

He simply wanted her to trust him. It irked that she would even have to ask.

"Do you agree with him?" he returned and immediately felt remorseful. What had happened to his resolve to be understanding of her? To be patient? Everything had been damn near blissful between the two of them until those damn letters had arrived from Ashton Acres.

Eyes wide, confusion crossed her features. "Of course not! You're the most generous person I know!"

Damn his eyes. He had no idea how to get past this. He dipped his chin, somehow acknowledging her opinion.

But perhaps she was wrong.

He'd only showered her with gifts for his own benefit. To make her smile. To ensure her gratitude?

And he wanted all of her. He hated that she'd hidden anything from him.

He also wanted to be her hero. He wanted to save her from herself. Save her for him.

"How did you amend them? What made him so angry?"

He'd done what was right. Period. Not simply what would be best for the dukedom. "I changed the settlement so your father's estate maintained one-half of the mineral rights."

He did not look at her as she mulled over his statement.

"Without informing the duke." So, yes, now she would understand.

"Without informing him." Cameron's jaw clenched.

Just then, they pulled into the drive.

So much had changed since they'd driven away, not quite a fortnight ago.

How could he believe Crawford was dead? The man had seemed indestructible. But it would not be a joke. It would not be a mistake. He hated that his heart skipped a beat at the thought.

As they slowed in front of the entrance, the large doors of the manor opened, and the duchess emerged. Martha, Cora, and Lillian huddled behind her.

Cameron didn't wait for a footman to open the door. Instead, he swung it open himself and jumped to the ground without a step. Martha ran into his arms.

The duchess wore all black, her face shrouded in a veil. Cora smiled at him tremulously, and Lillian held herself back, arms crossed.

He was aware that the footman had assisted Louella out of the carriage, and she'd crept up behind him. "Your Grace." Her voice broke through the sounds of Martha's gentle sobs. "I am so sorry. So very sorry."

She'd taken one of the duchess' hands in both of hers in a warm clasp.

Her Grace acknowledged the sentiment with a nod.

Cora's eyes were suspiciously shiny, but Lillian's eyes were dry. She did not join her sisters and mother, choosing instead to wait atop the steps.

Cameron placed a kiss on Martha's head and led them inside. With Crawford dead, Cameron would have innumerable tasks ahead of him. Death was an unpleasant business at best. If he were to assume his father's responsibilities, he'd best begin now.

He was Crawford now.

The thought chilled him, and not for the first time.

"I've sent notices to the papers and informed the House of Lords, but I'm uncertain as to what else must be done. Perhaps the solicitors…" The duchess seemed more concerned with the continued running of the estate and other matters than with the fact that she'd lost her husband. It was her way. He knew she would consider it a weakness to be overly emotional. She'd always shown more dignity than his father had.

She calmly informed him that his father's body was laid out in one of the front drawing rooms as they made their way into the duke's study.

The letter had stated that only three of the workers' bodies had been recovered so far. He needed to go to the mine and ensure that those involved in the recovery effort were not putting themselves in harm's way. He'd be expected to meet with the families.

Cameron did his best to follow along as the duchess listed a litany of details she considered vital to Crawford's services and final resting place. All the while, the thought of his father's lifeless body only steps away disturbed him.

Lowering himself into the large chair behind Crawford's desk, unbidden memories crowded out their last moments together. How many times had he looked across the smooth mahogany while that man wielded his power over all of them?

One time, in particular, pressed itself into his thoughts.

The day, so long ago, when Crawford presented him with the commission he'd purchased. Yes, it had been a devil's bargain, and yes, it had been done grudgingly, but the duke had understood Cameron better than Cam had understood himself. He'd known Cam would have left the country regardless and had used his influence and money to protect his heir.

Whether Cam had wanted it or not.

It had been done to protect the dukedom, but he'd done it, nonetheless.

And, God's truth, but Crawford had led him to Louella. Again, it had been done for financial gain, but had he not, Cam wondered if he would have found her on his own.

Louella.

In spite of their falling out last night, his heart swelled at the thought of her. Hell's bells, but she was not the simple debutante he'd imagined.

Cam had contemplated calling Crawford out for dishonoring her so blatantly. It had been unacceptable! Would he have done so upon their return, if Crawford had lived? Cameron had relished the thought of meeting the fiend on a field of honor on more than one occasion.

When Crawford had burst into their chamber, he'd referred to Louella by a word that oughtn't have ever been spoken in her presence. He'd shown no respect for her as a gentlewoman, let alone Cameron's wife.

Cameron clenched his fist, resisting the urge to pound on his father's desk. With Crawford dead, Cam would be denied any vengeance.

He wished he could hate him. If only it were that simple.

"Is Kingsley at the mine?"

The duchess nodded "As far as I know."

"I need to meet with him to discover exactly what happened. We had security measures in place. It doesn't make sense." He also needed to address the deceased men's next of kin.

"My understanding is that recovery efforts have been slow." His stepmother's voice, again, was matter-of-fact.

Cold, black culpability settled in his gut. He'd meet with the families as soon as possible. Arrange for burials and set up some sort of payments. It was the least they could do.

The measures he'd taken had not been enough.

"I'll leave now, then." He had never been close to his father's second wife. In reality, he barely knew her. And although he knew the girls slightly more, he ought to have been a better brother to them. Hopefully, he could make up for that in the future.

He thought he should say something else. *I'm sorry for your loss?* But it was his loss as well, wasn't it? "Thank you for informing me so promptly. I regret that I wasn't here when it happened." He could have somehow prevented it, couldn't he? If he'd been here?

The duchess bowed her head. "He was obsessed with the gold—believed it to be the cure to all his problems. He's watched other peers fall into debt and vowed he'd not allow it to happen to this title under his watch."

Always the title. Always the dukedom.

Crawford had been fixated with it. If only Cam had spoken to him about the contracts before the wedding, explained his reasoning. Would it have made any difference? Was there any way he could have stayed Crawford from hurrying operations?

Because damned if there wasn't a fortune locked in that mine. More than enough gold for both Hallewell and the Crawford dukedom to profit for generations. And with his marriage to Louella, most of it would eventually pass to his own son, God help him, another Crawford heir.

But Cam hadn't faced Crawford when he should have. And now it was too late.

He would summon Crawford's steward and look over the books later.

"If you'll excuse me then, Your Grace." He waited for her to rise. "I'll try to return for the evening meal, but don't hold it for me if I'm absent."

"Of course."

He ought to find Louella, tell her where he was going. For the past several days, they'd lived in one another's pockets. And yet it hadn't bothered him. No, in fact, he'd rather enjoyed it.

Considering the current state of their marriage, this disturbed him.

Instead of searching her out, not bothering to change out of his traveling clothes, Cameron headed out to the stable block to have his horse readied. He'd deal with the grim realities of the mine first.

He'd try figuring Louella out later.

CHAPTER TWENTY-FOUR

A HOUSEHOLD IN MOURNING

*H*e changed the contracts to benefit my father.

Louella had no time to contemplate Cameron's explanation, but she tucked the information away, to remind her of his character. To remind her of the sort of man she'd married.

An honorable one. She blinked away tears at the memory of her selfish act last night.

To this fair-minded man. She wished she could take it back, be strong and comforting to him instead of acting like a spoiled child.

She hoped she hadn't ruined everything.

But for now, she needed to find her composure. They had a household of mourning to face.

Louella hadn't realized Cameron's sisters had held their father in such affection. Even before he'd invaded her bedchamber, she'd thought the duke somewhat cold. While Cameron had disappeared into Crawford's study with the duchess, Louella remained in the drawing room with his sisters.

Although she would have wished to clean up first, Louella

didn't relish the thought of returning to the suite they'd abandoned a week ago. When Lady Lillian called for tea, she readily agreed. She wasn't hungry but tea was always a good idea.

It was Lady Martha who spoke up first. "Why did you and Stanton leave without saying goodbye?"

Ah, a delicate matter.

"They wanted to begin their wedding trip as soon as possible, Martha," Lady Cora saved her from answering.

Louella simply nodded. "How is your mother?" she asked instead, directing her inquiry to the eldest of the girls.

"She has barely spoken a word of it to us. She told us about the cave-in and then began speaking about arrangements."

"I don't even think she's cried," sixteen-year-old Cora inserted.

Louella wondered if the duchess had been close to her husband.

"It is the end of an era." Lady Cora's words were laced with despair.

Louella glanced over at the windows, all darkened with black cloth. It was as though the rules of mourning, rather than allowing one to grieve naturally, stifled any sort of release. The heavily shadowed room certainly wasn't doing anything to lift her own spirits.

She considered all the times she'd cried at William's grave. She'd found relief from sitting beneath an open sky, listening to the leaves rustle in the wind, knowing that the sun would continue to rise each morning and set each night.

Something elusive stirred in her heart.

"My sister lives nearby and we've never been away from one another this long before. I miss her dreadfully." She didn't know these girls very well but hated seeing them dwelling in this cold and heartless room. "Since she is family, I think it would be permissible to visit her this afternoon—that is if you'd like to join me?"

Perhaps they'd resent her offer. Louella was taking a chance by inviting them. She might have just as well offended them with such a suggestion, if they were sticklers, that was.

Young Lady Martha snapped her head up from the embroidery she had been working on. "I'd like nothing more than to go outside... but Mama..."

"Louella is family now, however." Lady Cora glanced questioningly toward the eldest, Lady Lillian.

Lady Lillian glanced around the room and then sighed heavily. "Perhaps if it is only a very short visit. Mama would not be averse to all of us taking some exercise..."

Lady Martha's foot was bouncing on the ornate rug beneath it, as though she were ready to burst from the room that very moment.

"Olivia lives on the edge of my father's property, so it isn't far at all." Well, perhaps a half an hour, Louella guessed.

"Your sister does not live with your parents? I thought she was unmarried." Lady Cora narrowed her eyes a tad suspiciously. Louella did not fault her for such a question. Olivia's living circumstances were unusual.

"My parents don't expect her to marry." If they hadn't heard stories about Olivia, then Louella was not going to make any explanations. Obviously, they'd not been introduced to her at either of the wedding events then.

"How odd," Lady Lillian added her opinion.

"Would you care to join me, then?" Louella would allow them to meet Olivia without any bias. "I need to freshen up, of course. But I can be ready within the hour." Jane would be unpacking her trunks again... in that room... where Crawford had... "Or perhaps within a half an hour."

Lady Cora met Lady Lillian's gaze and then shrugged. "It's only one in the afternoon. We have an entire year of mourning ahead of us."

With a shrug of her own, Lady Lillian conceded. They

would all meet in the foyer in forty-five minutes with the explanation that they were going for a solemn walk about the property.

And Louella could present her sister to them, finally. Perhaps dwelling at Ashton Acres wasn't going to be such a trial after all.

If only she could fix matters with her husband as easily.

* * *

As it was, the girls required all of forty-five minutes to arrive at the drive leading up to Olivia's small cottage. And just as they turned onto it, they could see that Olivia herself was walking home along the dirt road dressed in an older day dress and bonnet.

"Olivia!" Louella shouted.

Upon glancing back and seeing who was calling her, Olivia dropped her basket and came running back to swing Louella into an exuberant embrace. Inhaling the familiar scent of her older sister, unexpected tears filled Louella's eyes.

"Oh, I've missed you. Such a tragedy! Mary's brother, and Mr. Smith. So many men! And it needn't have happened. The engineer had halted work." Not taking Louella's companions into consideration, Olivia continued, "And from what Miss Cline has told me, the duke flew into a rage. He demanded the work continue and led those poor workers back into the mine himself. Luke Smith was one of the workers who has perished. The children... I was with them this morning."

"Mr. Smith?" Louella couldn't help but be horrified. "Where are the children now? What will become of them?" Louella's heart sunk. She couldn't help but recall the foundlings she'd seen in London.

"Miss Cline is staying with them temporarily. The eldest is eight and will be sent to a workhouse. Unless some family can be located who is willing to take them in, the others will end up in an orphanage or foundling home."

"How old are the little ones?"

Olivia pursed her lips. "There's the baby, of course, and then a set of twins, about four years old now. And the oldest, Luke Jr, is eight."

At that moment, the three girls Louella had practically forgotten stepped forward.

"Didn't the family just lose their mother?" Lady Lillian frowned.

Louella nodded. "Yes, Mrs. Smith died in childbirth a few months ago. Please, pardon me for not introducing all of you to my sister. Ladies Lillian, Cora, and Martha, I'd like to present Miss Olivia Redfield, my sister. Olivia, Cameron's sisters."

They all curtsied in the most genteel manner but then quickly turned their attention back to the village's tragic newest orphans. Louella couldn't help but dwell upon the fact that the mine had been on her father's property; that it would not have been opened again but for her marriage. And now these motherless children had lost their father too. How must Cameron feel? If she was feeling culpable, surely, he felt a million times worse.

And she'd acted horribly with him when he'd asked about the new cuts. She'd been aware that he must grieve his father somewhat but hadn't considered the weight he most surely experienced for the workers.

"Mama told His Grace it wasn't a good idea," Lady Martha said, drawing a warning glance from her older sister. "Well, it's true," she persisted.

"The children will be separated then?" Lady Lillian turned toward Olivia, who frowned. Louella noted for the first time the dark circles etched beneath her sister's eyes. Olivia seemed... less herself. This horrific tragedy would leave none of them unscathed.

"If no family member comes forward. It's unlikely anyone would be willing to take on four small children." Olivia sighed. "They are a handful."

Lady Cora was watching Olivia closely. "I've never seen eyes the color of yours. Violet? Stunning, really. Why does one move by itself?"

"Don't be rude!" Lady Lillian again tried to shush one of her sisters, but, although Louella bit her lip, Olivia merely laughed.

"They are violet. My grandmother's eyes were the same color. And the one moves by itself simply because it can."

"Can you see out of it?" Lady Cora asked.

"But of course."

At that moment, Louella could hardly have been prouder of her sister. Olivia was gracious in ways her parents had never been able to see. They had been short-sighted about both of their daughters, choosing to see Louella as perfect and Olivia as flawed. It was as though William's death changed their perception of the world. Had that been it?

She struggled to remember if they'd treated Olivia differently before...

"We've lost our father, but we haven't lost our world," Lady Lillian said softly.

And the truth of her words moved Louella. Yes, they were privileged. That didn't give them permission to ignore the plight of others. Her mother had drawn the curtains closed while driving to London, but that didn't mean poverty did not exist.

Foundlings, Cameron had called them. Alone, with no safe place to sleep, never knowing where they might find a meal.

"We must do something for those children." Louella swallowed hard. It was one matter to drive past the abandoned children along the road, quite another to ignore the orphaned children in their own village.

Olivia made some suggestions of families who'd expressed an interest in the eldest boy, but this had Louella shaking her head. The brothers would need one another. They were all each other had.

"No matter what's ever happened, Olivia, I have had you. And Lady Lillian, Cora, Martha, you have had one another. We need to find a family who will take all of them in. I'll ask Lord Stanton."

"Crawford," Lady Lillian reminded her. "He is Crawford now."

Which meant …. She winced at the thought.

She wasn't ready to acknowledge the change in her own status.

Louella swallowed the lump that had suddenly formed in her throat. "Of course."

* * *

After partaking of the tea Olivia so cordially had her maid serve, they bid one another goodbye and set out to make the hike back to the manor at Ashton Acres.

Martha spoke more freely than she had earlier, asking questions the elder girls would not. Why had Olivia not been presented to them earlier? Why did she live in a separate residence?

Louella answered in as much a manner as possible so as to not paint her parents into a terribly bad light, but she was pleased to hear how easily these young women had taken to her sister.

Olivia could be presented in London. She could be given every opportunity she deserved.

Overall, the outing had been a good one. And that made Louella happy. But she couldn't stop thinking about the Smith children. Somebody needed to do something! She would go and visit them. Perhaps take over a basket...

* * *

Nobody commented upon Cameron's absence at dinner that night. Except for the duchess, who barely mentioned that he'd gone up to the mine and had told her he might not make it back on time.

Why hadn't he told Louella?

She simply nodded, as though she'd been apprised as well. Perhaps he hadn't wanted to interrupt her time with her new sisters-in-law. More likely, he had felt an urgency that precluded him from searching her out.

Or perhaps he was done with her.

He'd spoken to her in such a lifeless tone—when he'd said he did not believe she was sorry.

But oh, she was. Dreadfully so. It had been a stupid and immature thing for her to do. If she could take it back, she would in a heartbeat...

Sitting in her chamber that night, a different suite than before, in the main branch of the house, Louella waited for sounds of his return.

And waited.

Jane had long since helped her change into her nightdress and left to go to her own bed when Louella finally heard shuffling sounds next door.

There was a door adjoining their suites, and since returning from London, they'd grown lax in requesting permission to enter one another's bedchamber.

But tonight was different.

And yet she knew that if matters were to improve between the two of them it was up to her. She padded across the room and took a deep breath for courage.

Lifting her hand, she knocked, oh, so softly.

Nothing.

Another deep breath and then without waiting for an answer, she pushed the door open.

Cameron was just handing Mr. Longley his waistcoat when she stepped in.

Irritation flared in his gaze, but she noticed something else in his eyes as well. It was this "something else" that gave her the courage to enter.

"That will be all, Longley." Cam's words were unusually sharp.

Louella nodded and sent a timid smile in the valet's direction.

An unusual silence fell between them after the door closed.

She'd never seen Cameron looking so... tight... nor fatigued. He seemed anguished, even, as he tossed his cravat onto the nearby wardrobe.

"Has it been stabilized?" She'd known he would be concerned for the wellbeing of the recovery workers. She was afraid to ask anything else. His countenance reminded her of a string on a violin that was stretched too tightly.

He ran one hand through his hair. "That's what we've been trying to decide. I don't want any more men going in until we're certain."

"And the engineers are not."

"No." He lifted his hands to unbutton his shirt but fumbled with it. That was when she noticed the blisters on his palms.

Not even stopping to think, she stepped forward and

pushed his hands away. "It's best to wait, then." She focused on the buttons but as she worked her way down, revealing his hair-smattered chest, her eyes drank in his skin and her breathing quickened. His nearness would always affect her this way.

She unfastened the last button and then ran one hand across his chest, over his shoulder, before lifting the material up and over his head.

He'd yet to send her away.

When she leaned in and placed her mouth near his throat, he groaned. It shocked her, how much she needed this. How much she needed him.

And then he tilted her head back and ground his mouth into hers. It wasn't in anger; she could tell the difference. He seemed as desperate as she.

His arms clamped around her and he was moving her toward the bed, but when she went to climb onto it, he stopped her. He'd somehow managed to lift her gown and unfasten his falls in the same motion. Using his feet, he spread her legs and pressed into her from behind.

It shocked her. At first. In all their time in London, they'd not been together like this. She fell forward, burying her head into the mattress as he worked himself frantically.

His passion was raw, desperate. The sounds of his body slamming against hers caused primitive sensations to grow, basic urges to blossom. As he clutched her waist with his hands, she clutched at him from within.

But despite reaching her own completion in a spiraling, dizzying freefall, she nearly gave in to an urge to weep.

He still seemed lost to her, distant this way. She lay almost passively on the mattress as he quickened and thrust into her one last time. Neither of them had spoken a word throughout this encounter. No reassuring endearments, no exclamations of passion. Nothing.

When he was done, he collapsed atop her. His hot breath upon her neck seemed more intimate than the act itself had.

"I'm sorry, Louella. I just… I don't know why."

She was tempted, oh, so tempted to answer him as he'd done in the carriage earlier that day. But she was a married woman now, and she wanted to repair things between them. "I'm sorry, too."

Apparently, those were the words he needed to hear. For something in him broke.

And her words had been sincere. She was sorry they'd argued. Sorry for cutting herself so stupidly in the carriage. Sorry for cutting at all.

Sorry for trying to hide it from him.

She was sorry she'd hurt him.

His hands wrapped around her, and he nipped at her neck. Every kiss, every lick, and tender bite whispered his remorse.

Sometimes, she thought as she curled up beside him later that night, people spoke more honestly with their bodies than they could with words.

CHAPTER TWENTY-FIVE

FOUR SMALL BOYS

*C*ameron had intended to tell her he was tired.

He'd intended to put matters off with her. He didn't understand his feelings where Louella was concerned, and the overwhelming tragedy he'd dealt with that afternoon had left him little mental energy to fathom how to proceed with his wife.

And then she'd touched him. All he'd known at that moment was need. Would any woman have been able to meet it? But no.

He'd needed to bury himself inside of her, almost as much as he needed to breathe. As he'd stood there, pumping his body into hers, he'd felt her confusion and hurt. But he'd done it anyway.

He'd taken her, *almost* as though she were a common whore, and felt like shite afterward.

Why did people hurt those closest to them? Because they were hurting, themselves? Maybe Louella wasn't so alone in her cutting. Maybe she simply did it in a physical way while most people used other, less visible methods to hurt themselves.

"Are you awake?" Her small voice surprised him. He'd thought she was asleep.

He had wrapped both arms around her from behind and her hair tickled his chin. "I'm awake," he mumbled softly.

"Do you remember that I had a younger brother? William?"

He couldn't help but kiss the top of her head at her question. "I remember."

"He was often sick. And as a result, terribly spoiled."

"That makes sense." William Redfield had been the viscount's only son. Cameron understood that dynamic all too well. He wondered where Louella was going with her train of thought.

"He could be terribly demanding at times, and there were days when I wanted to knock his block off."

Cameron chuckled at this but allowed her to continue. She must have a point to her narrative.

"And then, one day, he asked me to read him a story. I wanted to play outside but Olivia had sent me to the nursery to keep him company. He'd fallen into the lake earlier that week and was sick again.

"When I got up there, I decided I was going to read my own book, to myself. I tried ignoring him... But Willie kept whining and crying until I could stand it no longer." She obviously wasn't comfortable talking about this. He could hear it in the tightness of her voice. "I took the book and jumped onto his bed. I told him he wasn't really sick! He was a fraud! And as I jumped on his bed, I tore page after page out of his favorite book. It was a book of limericks. Anyway, the nurse came in, and I was walloped and sent to my room and the next day... William died."

Oh, Christ!

But now he understood why she was relaying this story to him. "It's hardly the same, Louella. You were a child. And the timing was coincidental."

"I've told myself that a thousand times, Cameron, but... how does one convince one's soul of something like that? What if I'd read him a few limericks that night instead? What if he hadn't had reason to be upset and carry on? Surely, the stress of his sister pouncing upon him cannot have been good for his health?"

Cameron squeezed her from behind as she continued, "William had been ill for a very long time, and now I know that he was even worse after he fell into the water. My head knows this. But knowing with my heart is something altogether different. And thinking about Crawford, and the last words exchanged between the two of you... Well, it reminded me. And I wanted to tell you that I might understand just a little, how you might be feeling. Confused. Guilty. I cannot even fathom what you're thinking about the workers who perished. If I hadn't consented to the marriage, would the mine have been opened up again? We can't figure all of it out at once. It's going to take a long while before our hearts catch up." She turned around and buried her face in his chest.

Fiend seize it, he understood guilt all too well. And he understood resentment. He didn't want to think about this.

Molding his hands to her body, he decided to make up for earlier. She would not object. Moaning sleepily, she parted her legs and flicked her tongue over his chest. This lovemaking was slow, lazy, and tender in every way. He slanted his mouth over hers and reveled in her familiar taste. Like coming home felt for others, she was a special balm to him.

* * *

Each day Louella wondered more and more about the relationship her husband had had with his own father, a man he seemed at times to have hated.

And she wondered if Crawford had hated his son. This wasn't an unreasonable idea, when she remembered how he'd come flying into their wedding chamber.

A few nights later, her head resting on Cameron's arm after a warm bout of lovemaking, she sighed softly and dove in. "I've been wondering about two things for a while now."

"You should be sleeping." He rubbed his hand along her thigh. "Have I not worn you out adequately?"

But she would not be shushed. "When you left Ashton Acres to join the navy, you said you were full of vigor and wanting to sow your oats, but most young men did this in London. Especially the only son of a duke. Why were you so adamant about leaving England? Did you hate your father even then?"

He'd stiffened beside her when she first voiced the question. And she wondered if he would give her any answer at all.

And then he let a long breath out. "If you'd come to know Crawford at all, you would have learned the type of man he was." He paused, but Louella didn't wish to interrupt. "He valued three things in life. And in this order; the dukedom, funds, and then family. My mother understood this. I understood this, and anyone who knew him understood this. His decisions regarding his priorities could be ruthless.

"You do not agree, then?" She knew the answer to this but couldn't help considering that he might have altered his opinion recently.

He was Crawford now.

"No. And God help me, I never will." He moaned a little and then buried his mouth on her shoulder. "You really wish to discuss this now?"

"Yes." Very simple. She needed to understand him better.

"My father had only one heir: me. He never trusted me. I was a wild one. It seemed the more he pressed my responsibilities upon me, the more I resisted. As I got older, he determined he needed a spare. I watched my mother suffer through more failed pregnancies than I can remember. His crusade eventually killed her."

"How old were you, when she died?"

"She died during my last term at school. When I returned, he'd already remarried. That was my last summer at home."

"He'd already replaced her, then," Louella surmised.

Cameron squeezed Louella from behind. "He didn't bring me home for her funeral. I simply returned to find a different woman living my mother's life. And a trio of little girls running about."

No wonder Cameron had been so unruly that summer.

"And the irony was that his second wife couldn't provide a spare either."

"But Crawford purchased your commission." This made no sense at all, if his father was already concerned about the succession of the dukedom. Did such an unorthodox decision show love for his son?

"I think he was certain his second wife would be prolific. Purchasing my commission merely ensured I wouldn't be on the front line. Something of an insurance policy, really."

Louella covered Cameron's arms with hers and snuggled closer. "And then you returned. And you were willing to marry your father's choice of a bride. Had you forgiven him by then? Is that why you came home?"

Silence, again. She simply waited.

"I promised I would marry the woman of his choice in exchange for the commission. If I were still alive in ten years. If I managed to make it back. I'd given him my word."

So, he'd not had any choice, really. Would he simply have married whomever his father wanted? She didn't want to ask him such a question. What if the answer wasn't what she wanted to hear?

"Did you hate your father? Do you have no fond memories of him?" Surely, he must! Surely, Crawford hadn't always been so manipulative and controlling?

"I don't know, Louella. It was a long time ago." His voice wasn't so patient anymore.

She would wait.

* * *

The duke's funeral was held in the same church where Louella and Cameron had wed. Crawford had been a powerful member of the House of Lords. His death was a loss to some and a boon to others. Regardless, several peers traveled from London and others from their own country manors in order to pay their respects. The caravan of carriages and horses following the elaborate coffin to the family plot at the edge of the estate was going to be remembered and remarked upon for years to come.

It was also on this day that people had begun to address Louella as "Your Grace." At first, she'd turn to look behind her. It seemed a mistake. She'd spent so many hours with the *real* duchess that she'd hardly considered it to be her role. It sat heavy upon her shoulders, made her feel an imposter.

New responsibilities she'd not expected to take on for years, decades even, rained down on her in a matter of days. She'd been called upon to assist in many of the finer details surrounding the funeral despite the fact that she, nor the duchess, nor any of Cameron's stepsisters could attend. That would have been considered gauche.

When the dowager duchess wasn't making decisions, she'd disappear for hours into her chamber, leaving Louella to take on many of her normal duties. Louella spent a good deal of time with Ladies Lillian, Cora and Martha. The sisters seemed to seek her out for company. They'd ask her questions about London, marriage, and fashion. Louella was gratified that she could bring them some comfort.

And throughout it all, she made certain to keep apprised of the Smith children's situation.

A modiste had been called in to take orders and measurements so that they would all have fashionable black wardrobes. Even Cameron wore all black in addition to the requisite armband. She believed he did it more for the workers than his father. There was no question that the house would be in official mourning for the full year.

Despite all of this, Louella had decided to focus first and foremost upon her husband. He moved through the day like a man possessed. Traveling to and from the mine and then spending late hours locked away in his study, sometimes with stewards from various Crawford estates. He'd mentioned once that he'd avoided his father's attempts to introduce him to such matters before. He'd always thought there would be more than enough time.

And she worried. She knew only too well how guilt could eat a person up.

The only time he was the tender-hearted man she'd originally married was during the nighttime hours, in bed. Sometimes, he managed to tell her a little about what was happening at the mine. He informed her each time another body was recovered.

And although it was frowned upon for her to do so, she made a point to attend each funeral with him.

Those days were the worst.

To each family, he made his formal apologies, always looking stoic and locking any emotions away. She knew he blamed himself. He hardly ate and dark circles had formed beneath his eyes. She'd be speaking to him, only to have him glance up, not having heard a word. The emotion behind his gaze was all too familiar.

His conscience was eating away at him like a poison.

If not for the nights, she would have felt hopeless. But in the darkness, he seemed to allow himself to forget.

Then came the day of Luke Smith's funeral. Along with a small cluster of town's people gathered around the simple wooden coffin, Louella could not help but watch the newly orphaned children to the right of the vicar. Miss Cline jostled the infant while doing what she could to keep the others silent.

The oldest boy appeared sullen and angry. The twins had difficulty standing still, pushing and nudging one another. At their young age, they didn't understand the significance of the day's events.

Louella had wanted to assist in their care, but the dowager had insisted she allow others to do so. After the ceremony, Cameron turned away from her to greet a few gentlemen nearby, giving her a moment to approach the children.

She'd met the vicar's sister, Miss Cline, on a few occasions, and greeted her first. A spinster, in her late thirties, she looked to be more than a little overwhelmed by her charges. Holding the infant, the woman dipped into a shallow curtsey when Louella stood before her. "Your Grace," she murmured.

"Miss Cline," Louella murmured as she leaned in to peer at the baby. So tiny and helpless. All the breath seemed to swoosh out of her lungs.

"May I hold him?"

Raising her brows, the lady shifted the child and then handed him over.

"He seems so small for his age." Louella observed as his weight settled in her arms. The air was warm and the sun high in the sky, but the baby was swathed in a rough woolen blanket.

"Not yet two months. He's small for his age, I believe—a poor eater."

Louella gathered him against her so that she could see him better. The tiny face was flushed, and dark eyes peered up at her.

He'd not cried once throughout the short ceremony.

In his gaze, Louella saw all the hopelessness of his future. But then he reached a tiny hand up and tugged at one of her curls, as if to tell her not to give up on him yet.

She blinked away the surprising tears that threatened and covered his hand with hers. So tiny! And yet his grasp of her hair was nearly painful in its intensity. "What's your name, little one?"

"He's Harvey," said one of the ragamuffin twins dancing about them. Her heart broke all over again at the innocent unknowing smile on his face.

"And what's your name?"

Before he could answer, Miss Cline pulled him forward. "You'll make your bow to the duchess, Marcus." She then grabbed the other, identical child and ordered him to do the same.

The oldest sneered in their direction and drifted to the edge of the gathering.

Louella learned that Marcus was the more rambunctious of the twin boys and Michael the quieter one. Marcus informed her that their older brother's name was Luke. Like their dad. But their dad had gone to heaven to be with their mama.

"No family members have yet come forth?" She'd known the answer to this as of two days ago but hoped...

Miss Cline did not answer until after the twins hopped away to bother their older brother.

"Not a one." Her lips pinched. "And the church has already provided care for over a week now. I have other chores to attend to. We might be able to find a home for the baby. Young enough as to still be manageable. My brother has made inquiries at a foundling house a few villages over, for the middle ones and it'll be a workhouse for the oldest."

No!

Without thought, without pause, Louella tucked little Harvey's head beneath her chin. "His Grace and I will take them in. We'll take them home with us this afternoon, if possible."

Miss Cline laughed. "You oughtn't to joke about such matters, Your Grace."

But Louella wasn't joking, and it only took a moment for the vicar's sister to realize this. As the sincerity of Louella's assertion settled upon her, a look of interest lit the woman's eyes. "Why, then, Your Grace, you're more than welcome to take the boys with you now. My brother can do up some guardianship papers and we'll send what few belongings they have to Ashton Acres later today." She narrowed her eyes. "They're a handful, though. I'll have you know. Haven't had much discipline in their lives before I got ahold of them."

"We've more than enough hands. I've no doubt we can manage."

And then she caught sight of Cameron, who was eying her curiously. Louella flinched, realizing what she'd done without consulting him, and then bit her lip.

"If you'll excuse me a moment, Miss Cross." Louella turned away from the spinster and met her husband as he approached.

He looked very ducal today dressed in a black waistcoat, jacket and perfectly tied cravat. He raised one eyebrow at her, glancing at the baby in her arms.

"I'm keeping them." She lifted her chin. She couldn't send them away. It was because of the ridiculous mine that they'd lost their father. She could not ignore the hopelessness of their futures.

Both of his brows raised. "Smith's sons?" He had not said no to her outright. Rather he glanced over to watch the other boys. The twins were punching one another while the oldest kicked at a nearby headstone. "Vicar's yet to have located any family, I take it."

She'd discussed her concern only briefly with him shortly after they'd returned to Ashton Acres. She'd not wanted to pile more cares upon him. But seeing the children, hearing the prospect of their futures...

"Nobody is claiming them." Louella placed one hand atop the baby's head. It felt warm, and soft, evoking ethereal memories of William as an infant. "I can't let them be torn apart, Cameron. I simply cannot." She dug into her position, preparing for a fight.

Cameron reached up and tugged at his chin. "Very well."

CHAPTER TWENTY-SIX

ADJUSTING

*O*ddly enough, Louella's announcement following the burial service had not surprised Cameron. What *did* surprise him was the strange sense of relief he felt knowing he could do something worthwhile.

He'd known about the boys' situation. He'd sent out multiple notices himself in search of any family who might step forward, and he'd felt increasingly ill at ease each time the vicar hinted that his sister was running out of patience.

And now, upon hearing Louella's determined little voice declare she was bringing them home with her, a part of him was able to breathe.

"I imagine we can advertise for a governess." He wasn't completely certain how his sisters would react, nor the dowager duchess, but with such limitless accommodations, he imagined they could keep the children well out of their way if necessary.

"I want to raise them as family. I don't want them delegated to servants' quarters." Her chin lifted again, her small hand rubbing the infant's head protectively.

His wife had asked for very little since returning from

London. She'd not asked anything of him since she'd requested the trip to Vauxhall. In fact, she'd only given.

She'd opened her heart when his sisters or the duchess had need. But more than that, she'd given of herself freely to him. He'd been stoic, morose… something of a brute, he knew, and yet she'd welcomed him each night in their bed.

He could do nothing to squash her innate ability to put others first. He could not resist her quiet giving. It revealed more character than he'd credited her with. Her heart rivaled the beauty of her face.

He remembered wondering if someday he would be on the receiving end of her loyalty, her dedication. Astonishingly enough, he wondered no more. Her strength lessened the significance of the scars decorating the various battlegrounds of her body.

How could he deny her anything?

"There's an entire nursery upstairs that hasn't been used since the girls have grown. Won't take much to have it aired out and stocked for four boys."

He could tell by the look on her face that she'd been expecting an argument. She'd been expecting him to be difficult.

Christ, but he'd been a brute these past few weeks. The worst of it was, he didn't like himself. Perhaps he could make some amends today. Their driver was just coming around with the carriage to collect them. "Let's get you and the baby situated, and then I'll round up the other boys." They'd ridden in a closed black coach.

At his easy acquiescence, Louella nodded. "Of course." But her eyes were shining. From what Lillian had told him, his wife had been worrying over these children for weeks. Perhaps she felt the same relief he did.

As she moved to climb in, Cameron stepped forward to assist her from behind. She sent him a grateful smile, and like an ambush, his heart nearly burst. She was so precious to him, and they'd yet to have resolved all of their differences.

Physically, yes. He'd found solace in her body every night. And he believed she found comfort with him as well. But it hadn't been the same as it had been in London.

They'd not shared one another's thoughts in the daylight hours. He'd hardly dined with her except for a few occasions. The only outings he'd included her in had been the funerals. He'd not shared *himself* with her, and he'd encroached upon her trust that first night, when he'd taken her from behind.

He'd done it in frustration. Without thought of her.

God, but he reminded himself of Crawford. This scared him more than anything. He'd hated Crawford, hadn't he? And yet, now he understood some of the weight his father had carried upon his shoulders. The dukedom contained a vast collection of properties, ventures, and tenant families. Hundreds depended upon it and were anxious for their futures.

Still, he'd not put it before his wife and children.

For now, he placed his hands around her waist and supported her as she climbed into the carriage. She bent over slightly, holding the babe, and scuttled to the end of the bench.

Now to collect the other boys.

Surprise flitted across their faces as he addressed them by name.

He had no trouble with Marcus. This urchin was happy to take a ride on a tall gentleman's shoulders, but Michael held back, holding tight to Miss Cross. Luke, the oldest boy, watched them suspiciously as they piled in with Louella.

Taking casual steps toward the child who already considered himself a man, Cameron kicked at the dirt near where young Luke shuffled about. Perhaps he ought to have discussed his wife's plan with the boy beforehand. "It's been one hell of a week, hasn't it, Luke?" He'd not pretend the boy's life hadn't just been turned upside down.

The boy looked at him sideways, not answering.

"I'm Crawford. I knew your father. He was a good man. A hard worker." Cameron extended one hand toward the boy.

"I know who you are. Yer the duke now." The boy didn't take his hand but nodded. "My pa got killed in yer mine. The other duke didn't care if they all died."

The child had not pulled his punches. Cameron couldn't address any of this now. After all, the child was not wrong. "The thing is, Luke, we haven't been able to locate any family to take you and your brothers in."

"I heard. I know that. We ain't got no family. That's why. Not nobody that wants us."

"Well, that's where you're wrong." Cameron crouched down and then pointed toward the carriage awaiting them. "I'm sure you couldn't help but notice that pretty lady over there. That's my wife, the Duchess of Crawford, and she'd like nothing more than to take care of you and your brothers. If some family shows up, some family you'd rather go with, then you'll be welcome to go with them. But for now, we've got a home, and a room, and lots of food and toys and books for you and your brothers."

Young Luke seemed relieved for just a moment but then crossed his arms in front of him. "What if we don't like it there? I can take care of my brothers. We don't need nobody."

This one could prove to be more difficult than his wife had bargained for. "How about you give it a chance first? Do you like chocolate?"

This did the trick. "If I come, you'll give me some chocolate?"

Cameron needed to maintain some semblance of control. "After the evening meal. Now is it a deal?" He held his hand out again.

This time, young Luke shook it. "My name's a lot like yours," he said as they began walking toward the coach.

Cameron had no idea what the child was talking about.

"You know," Luke explained as though it was obvious. "Luke, Duke...practically the same."

Cameron laughed and nodded. "Right you are, lad, right you are."

* * *

Watching Cameron negotiate with little Luke cracked something inside of Louella's heart. This was the man she had fallen in love with. Yes, at last, she could admit to herself that she loved him. She loved the man who now wielded his charm on a sullen little boy. He had crouched down to the boy's size and was gesturing toward her.

The eight-year-old looked so lost—and angry—but as Cameron spoke, something splintered a little. He perked up, took her husband's hand, and approached the carriage.

Marcus chattered away, as though he was the spokesperson for both himself and his brother. And Michael nodded and agreed with everything his twin said.

When Luke climbed into the carriage, he ordered Marcus to sit still. He then, with narrowed eyes, warned Louella that the baby cried almost all the time. "He doesn't like to eat."

Louella wondered at how a child would not like to eat. Surely, the boy was mistaken.

Cameron climbed in last and signaled for the driver to move out. The boys rode on the back-facing bench, while Louella held the baby, facing front beside Cameron.

Her husband sent her a questioning look, as though to ascertain that she was *sure* she knew the responsibility she took on. She could change her mind, she knew. Nobody would blame her. But it felt right. Even when a damp warmth permeated the front of her gown just before arriving home.

They were only four small children. How difficult could it be?

* * *

Following the last of the funerals, Cameron's focus at the mine turned from recovery to feasibility once again. It seemed to require all of his attention as he'd leave the manor before sunrise on some days, not returning until well after the evening meal had been served many nights.

During the day, Louella spent all of her time with Baby Harvey, the twins, and young Luke. She had help from one of the housemaids, and Martha, Cora, and even Lillian entered the nursery on occasion.

Cameron had advertised for a wet nurse to no avail, and the nanny being sent by the agency would not arrive until the end of the week.

At first, Louella had assumed the housemaid could manage the baby easily enough, but halfway through the first night, she realized that was not the case.

Not with this child, anyhow.

She'd been unable to lay abed with the sounds of the crying baby coming from upstairs, and so she'd donned her dressing gown and joined the maid in the nursery. Even with both of them caring for little Harvey, the task was more than she'd ever expected.

Luke had shown her how to use the glass bottle filled with goat's milk. A piece of leather was jammed into the opening and baby Harvey occasionally, when he really wanted to, would suck the milk out through it.

But the leather was old and musty. Louella tried other methods to control the amount of liquid flowing into the baby's mouth, but nothing seemed to function very efficiently.

What the baby needed was a wet nurse, of course.

"Drink up, little Harvey," Louella coaxed while the maid folded the freshly laundered clouts on the bureau. This was the third time she'd tried feeding him that night. How could the child live if he did not eat? She dabbed the cloth at the end of the bottle along his lips, but he merely pinched them together and then, when he did open them up, let out a blood-curdling cry.

He stopped breathing for a moment. He'd done this before, and so Louella didn't panic this time. Because eventually, he gulped in some air and let out another wail. It was almost as though he was in pain.

She forced back the tears that threatened. "Hush, darling, hush." He couldn't cry forever. Surely, he would tire soon.

Louella hopped out of the rocker and began pacing the floor again. Sometimes, if she bounced and patted him just right, he'd go silent for a few moments. On a few rare occasions, he'd fall asleep when she did this.

On the morning following the fourth night, exhausted and confused, Louella sent for her sister. Olivia had spent some time with the children before their father passed. Perhaps she knew something that might appease the baby. Besides, Louella missed her.

Olivia's appearance reminded Louella of the world she'd seemingly left behind by marrying and now taking on this responsibility that was perhaps more than she'd bargained for.

Olivia, her loving and compassionate sister, took one look at Louella and, smothering a laugh, shook her head. Louella knew most of her hair had escaped the chignon Jane had tied earlier and dark circles had taken permanent residence beneath her eyes.

Realizing her mirth wasn't appreciated, her sister sobered sympathetically. "When Miss Cline told me you'd taken them in, I wondered how you were faring. Which one got to you? The baby? Or was it the twins? You goose. You've always been so much more sensitive than me." She took hold of little Harvey and bounced him in her arms. "This one is still being difficult, I take it? He was a fussy eater when I sat with him last month. I imagine he misses his papa. Why didn't you send for me sooner?"

"Honestly, I haven't had a single silent moment to think about anything other than locating a wet-nurse." Olivia was cooing at the infant, so Louella continued, "And it was all of them. I couldn't walk away from them, Livvy. But now... I don't know what I'm doing. I can't get little Harvey to eat, the twins seem to speak their own language, and Luke Jr. hates me." She burst into tears.

Tiredness overwhelmed her to the point that she could hardly think straight. Tiredness and frustration and fear. But she needed to do this. There was no question of her doing this.

Memories of the children she'd seen lining the road to London came to mind, mixed in with that last day with William. "They are alone in the world, Livvy. But for now, I simply need this one to eat. Will you try? You've always been so good with children, and I'm at my wits' end." She explained how much the baby cried and the lack of success they'd had with their efforts.

Before she could finish her explanation of what they'd tried, her sister was examining the device they'd been trying to feed him with. "I think the puncture is too small. Let me open it up more. Do you have a needle on you?"

Her last question sent a wave of shame rolling through Louella.

Yes, Louella had a needle. She always had a needle. Not that she'd found a moment to put it to use since taking the children in, but she'd wanted to. Dear God, she'd wanted to.

Without saying a word, she slipped the shining tool out of her ribbon and handed it over.

Olivia stared at her knowingly before taking it in exchange for Harvey.

He'd quieted and rested his head on her shoulder. Relishing in such a peaceful moment from him, Louella patted the baby's head and watched as Olivia poked at the leather device.

"I wondered if you would keep doing it after you married. What does your husband say? Surely, he has seen the scars by now."

Ah, yes, he had. Baby Harvey buried his face into Louella's neck and amazingly fell asleep on her shoulder.

Louella chewed at the flesh inside her lip. "He has." Before Olivia could comment, Louella pressed on. "And he has no intention of sending me to Bedlam, as Mama predicted. He's been... mostly understanding. But..."

"It's not an easy thing to understand. You know I hate that you do it."

Olivia had known about this habit since the first week Louella had made cuts. After demanding Louella cease doing it, unsuccessfully of course, and then meeting only with frustrations when trying to understand why, Olivia had eventually given up. Aside from the occasional disapproving glance, she hadn't brought the subject up again.

But Louella wished Olivia, of all people, could understand somehow. "I hate how Mama and Papa treat you," she blurted, surprising herself. She wasn't sure why she would come out with this now.

The cutting had begun shortly after her mother insisted Olivia move out of the manor. They'd insisted it would be better for Louella. Prospective suitors, they'd said, might be put off if they discovered she had such a flawed sister.

Olivia glanced at her sharply. "Please tell me that is not why you do it."

It wasn't. Of course, it wasn't. She shook her head in denial. "It's about me." Again, her own words surprised her.

Perhaps she made the admission out of exhaustion. She hadn't slept much more than a few hours per day since taking the children in. In addition to fearing her inadequacy where they were concerned, she hated the gulf that seemed to be widening between her and Cameron.

"And what does His Grace think of all of this? Is he happy to have all these urchins underfoot?" Olivia gestured to where the twins sat on the floor playing.

He'd supported her decision to take them in. He'd even seemed to approve. But with their nights interrupted now, she barely saw him at all.

"Happy? I don't think any of us are happy right now," she admitted. "But he seems to feel the same as I do. We simply need a nursemaid so that..." Frustration washed through her. "A few women have applied but they looked... well, I couldn't trust that one of them wouldn't transfer some deadly disease in her milk. None of these ladies looked to be in good health. It's all just so terrifying, to be responsible for other little human beings."

"I'm certain a suitable wet nurse will present herself soon enough, and then perhaps you can resume your wedding trip..." Olivia's words trailed off doubtfully. "You can change your mind, you know."

Louella would not.

Little Harvey's vulnerable cries had wrapped themselves around her heart. He was not her own child. Neither was Michael nor Marcus. And she knew that Luke would likely have found his way had he been sent to a workhouse. He was a fighter, that one. So very different than William had been.

She couldn't help comparing the two boys. The oldest brother was the same age William had been when he'd passed. Nonetheless, Luke Smith needed them.

He'd taken a liking to her husband. Often sullen and contrary with Louella and the maids, he perked up as soon as Cameron appeared in the nursery.

He never smiled though.

So many wounds. So much need.

And not just the children.

She glanced at the scars peeking out from beneath the ribbon she'd tied around her wrist that morning and remembered the first time she'd drawn her own blood.

She'd used her fingernails. The deeper she dug them into her skin, the greater relief she experienced.

She remembered how empty the manor had felt in Olivia's absence. Nothing could fill the empty bedchamber. Not the new dresses Mama had ordered made up for Louella, nor the planning for her debut.

That had made for two empty bedchambers down the hallway from Louella's elegant chamber. Williams. And then Olivia's.

"They sent you away because of me." She gasped as the words tore past her throat. "Because of me." Louella dropped into the chair behind her, afraid her knees might buckle.

Olivia knelt on the floor before her. "Oh, Louella. No. They sent me away because of my affliction. And because of their own fears, their own insecurities. It had nothing to do with you."

By now, though, Louella couldn't halt the tears. "But it did."

She was barely aware of Olivia removing the sleeping infant from her lap and sending him away with the maid. Olivia's arms wrapped around her and Louella melted into her comfort.

Sweet, kind Olivia. So much the better person than herself. "Hush. Hush." Olivia squeezed her tight. "You could do nothing about it. You did not take any satisfaction in my being sent away. You are a wonderful sister. The best I ever could have had. Perfect even."

"No, not perfect," Louella adamantly denied. "I was sad that you went away. But Mama went on and on about... she was unwavering, and Papa didn't argue with her. I believed them for a while. I'm horrid, Olivia. You deserve so much more than me." Shame washed over Louella but so did relief. Relief that she could finally admit her failings.

"Hush. I suppose you are right. None of us is perfect. What a ridiculous word to apply to any person. You are not perfect. I am not perfect."

"And her husband is most certainly not perfect." Cameron's voice drew both of their gazes to the now-opened doorway.

He was leaning against the doorframe, his eyes tired, and his clothes dusty. He'd left for the mine before sunup. What had caused him to return?

Louella pulled out of her sister's arms and brushed at her eyes. She wondered how much he'd overheard. He already knew many of her failings. In the short time they'd been married, he'd seen her at her worst.

Even so, she struggled with the ugliness inside of her.

"Hello, Olivia." He pushed himself away from the frame of the door and sauntered into the room, looking more handsome than the day they'd married. A wayward lock of hair hung along his chin and the tiredness in his eyes lent him even greater appeal. "I'm afraid I'm going to have to order my wife to bed before she makes herself ill."

"But you can't do that! What of little Harvey? He has yet to have eaten," Louella protested as Olivia nodded in agreement and rose from the floor.

"I can and I will. A wet-nurse, one I'm certain your sister will approve of, is waiting downstairs. Would you be willing to assess her suitability for the babe?" Cameron asked Olivia.

"I'll apply my utmost discernment to the decision," Olivia responded, smoothing her skirts.

Louella continued sitting, more exhausted than she had been a moment ago, and met Cameron's stern gaze. "She is healthy then? The woman?" She would be certain of this matter first.

"If she is not, I shall send her away," Olivia reassured her. "You do as your husband says. Take some rest. You'll need it for tomorrow and the day after. If you intend to keep these little monsters, anyhow."

Cameron crossed to the chair Louella had dropped into and stood beside her almost protectively. "Thank you," he told Olivia.

Olivia's violet eyes flicked between the two of them. And then, as though coming to a decision, she nodded. "You're most welcome."

* * *

Cameron had overheard the two sisters discussing "perfection." It was not the first time Louella had visited the concept. When had she brought it up before?

And then he remembered.

Upon his second proposal. He'd been thinking of her as the "perfect" debutante. He'd made a joke of it. *Are you trying to tell me you have some bad habits, Louella? That you are not the perfect debutante, after all?*

"*I am not perfect. I am so very far from perfect. And I just wanted you to know...*"

And they'd been interrupted. What had she wanted him to know? Had she been going to show him her scars? Convince him that she, too, had flaws?

He crouched beside where she sat. "Louella."

She dropped her head against the back of the chair, eyes closed. "I'm sorry."

He ought to be the one to apologize. He'd left her to her own devices far more than he ought as her new husband. Rather than face her humanness, her imperfections, his own imperfections, he'd chosen to work himself to exhaustion in his father's study.

He gulped. *His* study now. And at the mine. And visiting next of kin. Anything to avoid facing the realities he'd discovered about himself and his new wife.

He was quite good at that. Avoiding conflict, that was.

He'd chosen not to confront his father, before the wedding, with the changes he'd made to the marriage contracts. He'd hidden his actions. He'd been wrong to do so.

Between his own inadequacies and the knowledge that at any time she might be drawing blood for some unknown reason, he'd lost his normal optimism.

She was not happy with him.

He hadn't been fair. He'd hidden as much from her as she had from him. His faults didn't leave visible scars but would affect them both, nonetheless.

He'd told her he might come to love her someday. Had he simply told her what she wanted to hear?

He'd run from his family for so long. He'd disconnected whenever another person attempted to draw close to him, knowing it wouldn't last. They'd want more eventually.

And now he'd essentially done the same to her.

Despite the responsibilities that nagged at him, despite all the annoyances that he knew he must attend to before the day drew to a close, he simply wanted to be with his wife. Although the familiar urge to keep himself private, to keep his feelings private, lurked in his mind, he wanted her company.

Needed it.

"Would you mind if we went for a walk?" Her voice shook him out of his reverie. "I'm dreadfully tired, but I don't think I can fall asleep."

Deep shadows etched themselves beneath her eyes, making her appear more beautiful to him than she'd been at their wedding. Several tendrils of raven hair escaped her coiffure and a stain of some sort soiled the front of her gown.

"I don't mind at all."

He assisted her to her feet. She would not need a wrap. The weather had grown warm as of late. Was it already the end of June? He shook his head at the thought that he'd lost nearly an entire month.

When had his life become so complicated?

Upon reaching the foyer, they waited for Cogsworth to fetch her bonnet. When her fingers fumbled with the ribbon, he brushed them aside and tied the bow himself. And then he took hold of her hand and pressed a kiss against her palm.

When had she become so precious to him?

As they descended the steps outside, he wanted to ask her questions. If she were to remove the bow tied around her wrist, would he discover fresh wounds? Or was she happier with him gone most of the time? Did she enjoy more contentment with his absence?

A myriad of questions and doubts swirled around his mind. He would not question her, though. He'd told her he wouldn't tell her to stop, and it might make her defensive.

So instead, he offered his arm and led them toward one of the more well-tended paths. And as they walked, the sun melted the barriers between them. Of course, the breeze, rustling leaves, and wispy clouds lent some assistance. He walked in a comfortable rhythm with his wife, content to enjoy her presence.

Neither of them spoke until they'd climbed a small rise overlooking the tops of the trees growing in one of the lower valleys on the estate.

"Do you think heaven feels as peaceful as this?" Her question drew a chuckle from him, for indeed, despite the responsibilities awaiting them both, he hadn't felt this serene since... well, since he'd returned to England.

He slid his hand down her arm and wrapped it around hers. "I cannot imagine it being any more so," he answered, giving her a gentle squeeze.

A melodic breeze stirred the air, and he felt her take a deep breath beside him.

"I'm going to quit. I don't know how. But I want you to know."

She spoke the words in a rush, and Cameron nodded silently. He wasn't sure how to feel about her declaration. Did she want to because of him? Or because she feared the rest of his family discovering the scars?

"Why?" He met her gaze, continuing to experience the peace of their surroundings. He would not put high expectations on her resolve. Somehow, he knew that would work to her detriment.

Staring up at him, she bit her lip and winced. "It hurts others." She turned to stare across the valley. "The pain. The cuts and the blood. They are a way to cope with feelings that I haven't ever really understood. I want to understand those feelings better, so that I can... move beyond them."

Cameron considered the bottles of scotch he'd emptied on his own since they'd returned from London. The soothing effects of the alcohol numbed the raw emotions he'd been determined to avoid. He certainly hadn't coped with his own confusion, inadequacy, and hatred since his father's death.

"Guilt." The word floated from her mouth almost as though he'd summoned it. She made that little wince again, with her eyes, and then faced him with a shrug. "I'm sorry I've hurt you, if I have. I just want you to know."

Warmth spread through his chest and softened the space around his heart. "I'm sorry if I've hurt *you*."

It was a beginning for them. A beginning that wasn't driven by anything other than the desire to strengthen the tenuous connection they'd begun together since that first day he'd proposed. A desire to build trust on both sides so that they could have an emotionally satisfying marriage. So that they could stand together, support one another.

It was a beginning.

CHAPTER TWENTY-SEVEN

UNDERSTANDING

A few days later, while searching for the ever-elusive housekeeper, Mrs. Bee, Louella wished she could have bottled up the contentment she'd experienced with Cameron on their impulsive walk. Life at Ashton Acres, rather than settling down, had become even more demanding.

Louella had never imagined she would become a duchess so quickly. Her mama and governess had taught her the basics of home management, but to suddenly find herself in the position of managing such a massive household would have been a steep challenge by itself. Add to that, the responsibility of the children? She'd too quickly become Her Grace—and now *Mama?*—to the Smith children, and at times, she felt as though she were drowning.

And Mrs. Bee, although pleasant and welcoming, seemed resentful when Louella made any attempts at participating in household decisions. Her loyalty to the dowager was commendable.

The woman had declined all of Louella's suggestions regarding the gardens and essentially dismissed any input

Louella attempted to make regarding menus or servant schedules.

Her own mother had visited on a few occasions and told her she needed to begin as she intended to carry on. She went so far as to warn her that if she didn't establish herself immediately, she'd never become the mistress of her own household.

Which was what she was trying to do at that moment, if only she could locate the long-time retainer!

But it wasn't that simple. Louella knew this. Mrs. Bee merely wished to comfort the dowager, who was hurting in a way that Louella hoped to not understand for years and years. And so, Louella stepped lightly.

Baby Harvey had not, in fact, taken all that well to Mrs. Littlefield, the woman Cameron had brought back to be hired as a wet nurse. Thank heavens for Olivia, however, who had reworked the feeding device. At last, the little cherub was feeding heartily.

Such a relief!

There was nothing in the world like a crying baby to make it feel as though the sky was crashing down.

Except now these other tasks pressed in.

Cameron, too, seemed to be more in demand than ever. Not only with the horrid mine but managing decisions regarding other estates, as well as investigating details surrounding a reform bill he'd gotten behind. The latter fascinated Louella, and she wished she could discuss it with him more than in passing. It involved workhouses and placing limits on child labor. She knew so little about it and would have enjoyed hearing his position.

For now, she would have to endure all these demands and hope their relationship could endure as well. They'd drifted miles apart, which was sad, really, considering they'd been married for only a few months.

Unable to share their nights now, was he losing interest in

her? Had she only imagined his affection? Was all the magic she'd experienced before gone?

Giving up on her search, for now, Louella climbed the stairs and, without thinking, drifted toward her own chamber. At this time of day, she could be alone, as Jane would be busying herself below stairs.

Louella had not made love with her husband for nearly two weeks now. He'd sent her a few smoldering glances, at first, but even these had grown far and few between.

Her husband had always shown her respect and every courtesy. He could be inordinately charming. But never overly effusive with his emotions. Not knowing his thoughts gave rise to conflicting sensations inside of her. Uncertainty being the worst.

He'd told her he could perhaps someday come to love her.

He'd said perhaps.

He'd given her no promises.

But he'd shown her well enough that he cared. He'd shown her great affection throughout their engagement and during their time in London.

And on their wedding night. Before they'd been interrupted.

Did he only feel lust for her?

Those horrible moments in the carriage during their journey back from London persisted in filling her with more doubts. They gnawed at any peace she could find.

Why were the bad things so much easier to recall than the good?

Louella sat on the tall-backed, velvet chair in the lady's chamber that adjoined her husband's. Her gaze trailed around the room. No longer did she display the dolls from her childhood, nor ribbons and bows. No, the nature of her belongings was changing from that of a girl to that of a woman, a lady. A duchess? A mother?

A cluster of toys she'd purchased for the boys sat in the corner that had before been decorated with a large floral arrangement. She didn't wish to give any to the boys until Cameron could join them.

Where once only perfumes and jewelry had cluttered her vanity, ideas she had for the children's meal service were scrawled on scattered sheets of foolscap. On the table beside her bed, a feeding bottle had been forgotten and was growing rancid.

Louella was changing. It was good, was it not? She shivered. Because at that moment, she wasn't sure who she was.

One item remained, virtually untouched since they'd returned from London. Drawing her gaze with the force of the tide, her sewing basket rested innocently beneath the bedside table.

The sight of it sent relief sweeping through her.

* * *

Cameron folded the letter and slipped it back into its envelope.

The necessity of his presence in London could not have come at a more inopportune time. Several reform bills he'd been following were being put together for the fall session and all those behind them were being called upon to assist in garnering support for the upcoming vote. Kingsley's presence would be demanded as well.

Cameron would have to order work at the mine halted until he could return, but he could charge Mr. Compton to cope with any issues that might arise in his absence.

What troubled him most was the thought of leaving

Louella. She needed him. The four little boys they'd impulsively taken on were not proving to be an easy lot.

Not that he regretted the decision to provide a home for the Smith children. And Louella seemed to love them already. They'd given her a purpose she'd lacked before. And for him, in taking on this responsibility, he sensed an odd feeling of absolution, forgiveness even.

Not that he deserved it.

But he could not put off this journey, and he needed to inform her right away.

Resigned, and not looking forward to disappointing her, Cameron climbed the steps to the third floor. Over the past week, she'd spent nearly every waking hour in the nursery. Even the nights, when he'd prefer to have her in his bed.

He wondered if she missed their lovemaking. He'd prefer to imagine that she did.

He missed the comfort that came with holding her, with bringing her to arousal and then burying himself in her wet warmth. He missed her curious hands, exploring and at the same time seeking new ways to pleasure him.

When he returned, they would talk again. She ought not to be so overwhelmed.

He needed her. She needed him.

Surprisingly, he found the nursery quiet. One of the recently hired nurses informed him that the baby was asleep, and a maid had taken the other children outside for some sunshine.

"The duchess was going to find Miss Bee, but also mentioned she needed to change her gown. I imagine she's in her chamber by now, Your Grace."

Cameron thanked the woman and turned in the direction of the stairs, his purpose sharpening. If Louella was in her chamber alone, perhaps he'd delay his departure by an hour.

Perhaps two.

He'd not miss such an opportune moment.

* * *

Louella wanted to change—in the worst way. She wanted to fulfill the promise she'd made to Cameron during their hillside walk, and yet, she feared the loss of something that had brought her comfort—great comfort—heady comfort.

Without thinking, she slid off the elegant chair, lifted her skirt, and dropped onto her knees.

One last time. She could experience it one last time. She'd hardly used the needles since she'd made that stupid slash on her arm in the carriage.

Her breathing grew shallow, and her heart raced as she crept on her knees across the rug.

Almost as though she was watching someone else perform the ritual, she removed the basket, unclasped the latch, and withdrew one of the unused needles Cameron had given her.

A sharp reflection blinded her momentarily, as the silver metal caught the evening sunlight. She untied the bow and carefully set it aside.

And then... ah. Ah, yes.

She gulped. Some relief but also... regret?

She blinked in confusion as the sight of the blood failed to invigorate or relax her as she desired. It achieved some of its usual effect but something else was happening. She slanted the needle so that it cut deeper and then dragged it slowly beside the other crimson line she'd drawn. A slight sense of euphoria, but also pain. Shame. Understanding?

Her antidote for calm was not an antidote at all. It was a distraction. An imposter.

She blinked her eyes again in confusion and tears filled her eyes.

The blood was just… blood.

She imagined how she might feel if Martha or Cora discovered her practice. What if they mimicked it as they had the wrist ribbons?

Louella shivered. What if young Luke cut himself?

An overpowering sense of wrongness filled the room. Not peace. Not comfort. The smallest amount of relief, but not enough. Not enough to make it worth it.

She'd hurt her parents. Olivia. Jane. Cameron.

Louella swiped one of the folded pieces of muslin from the box and pressed it against the wounds. They weren't nearly as deep as she'd cut in the past. The blood would stop quickly. She turned the white cloth and bit her lip at the angry red lines standing out alongside the white and pink ones that had healed over time.

"I wondered."

Louella jumped guiltily at his voice.

Cameron. She hated that he would witness this again. He didn't look angry or resigned. He looked sad.

"It's not what you think." The urge to reassure him had her jumping to her feet. She needed to tell him. That she'd had an epiphany? That she'd realized how selfish she'd been?

That she just might be able to quit? She'd told him she was going to try and yet, her sewing basket sat opened on the floor.

"You are so very unhappy? All of this is not enough? The children? A home?" His voice broke on the last word.

Of course not!

She removed the cloth and shoved her arm toward him. "I haven't done it since the children arrived… Such horrible timing, of course, that you would find me here today." She hated how she sounded, as though she were defending herself or making excuses.

In a deflated motion, he waved her arm away from him and

strode toward the window. "It's of no matter, Louella. I don't want to hear excuses." His shoulders sagged in a defeated posture she'd not seen before. "I won't command you to halt this behavior of yours, this cutting... whatever it is that you call it."

"But—"

"The reform bill has hit a snag, and the committee chair has called an emergency meeting. I'm leaving for London within the hour." He spoke without any emotion. It was as though he had no feelings either way regarding his pending departure.

With a sharp jerk, he turned to face her. "I do not know when I shall return. I may travel to Bell Heights for a week or two. Look in on the estates there. So damned much to do..." He shook his head but then strode toward her. "Mr. Compton will know how to contact me if necessary."

And then, taking her hand, he bowed over it formally, meeting her gaze, oh, so briefly. A hint of remaining emotion lurked in the back of his eyes, but he'd shuttered most of it.

"I—" She needed to tell him what she'd discovered but checked herself. His eyes glinted coldly as they seemed to look right through her.

His demeanor was meant to put off any explanations she might try to make.

"I'll miss you, Cameron." A tremor danced in her voice. She wanted to force him to listen to her. She wanted to wrap her arms around him. Keep him from leaving until they resolved this misunderstanding, but he'd not welcome her touch. He was treating her like a stranger.

She lifted her other hand, as though to touch his face, but when she did so, the line of blood she'd drawn came into view for both of them.

He tightened his lips. "Take care, Louella." He seemed to struggle with those words.

And then he was gone.

CHAPTER TWENTY-EIGHT

CONFESSIONS

Kingsley rode alongside Cameron as they began the day-long journey to London upon their mounts. His friend admitted to having put off his own duties for far too long now. Although the Season had concluded over a month ago, his fiancée, he'd been informed, could be found in London with one of her aunts.

Cameron clenched his jaw, feeling sick inside. Catching her at it again, carving into her pale, tender skin, invoked a memory that didn't make much sense. Like an uncomfortable itch he couldn't reach. He rode for a while before recognition gradually dawned.

He remembered a day that had nothing to do with his wife or marriage. Of his father, shouting at his mother in the same chamber he'd discovered Louella cutting herself.

Memories of conversations, shouting matches, rather, that he'd overheard years ago flooded his thoughts. The worst of them arose vividly, so much that he remembered that the wooden molding along the long corridor had recently been polished, smelling of oil and lemons. The sun had filtered through the windows, and he'd been able to see little particles of dust dancing in the air.

His father had never hidden his dissatisfaction. Cameron had known it existed but denied what it meant. Until that day.

"I cannot depend upon him as my only heir! I cannot count on him not to do something stupid!"

Of course, his father had been speaking about Cameron. Knowing he'd hear nothing good, he'd halted outside his parents' chamber and eavesdropped, nonetheless.

"He's soft, too easily swayed by others. The Crawford heir must be stronger than that boy, by God. He shows no fortitude at all." His father had never budged on this.

"He is the eldest—your firstborn. As long as he lives, he will inherit. You can do nothing to change that."

"If he lives."

Cameron had been confused by such a comment. Of course, he would live; he was barely ten and two!

"And as for the other, so says you. I'll never know for certain." At the time, Cameron hadn't realized the magnitude of his father's words. His innocence had protected him. It had taken weeks of turning them over in his mind to understand why his father seemed to hate him so.

But worse remained. His mother's tears, her pleas that followed. "He is healthy. He is strong. I have tried to provide a spare for you." Cameron could never quite forget the sound of his mother crying. "I have no more strength, Crawford. You're going to kill me."

And then he'd thought he'd heard the sound of flesh striking flesh. Cameron had done nothing. He'd been afraid of his father's temper. More than once, he'd been on the receiving end of it himself.

"He's rebellious. He's weak minded and lacks intelligence. I don't give a damn if you die trying; you will provide me with my spare."

"And then what?"

Cameron had covered his ears at that point, afraid but paralyzed by the sounds coming from his mother's chamber. As he'd grown older, he'd done his best to ignore the truth of what he'd overheard, but he'd failed.

God, how he'd failed.

Had Crawford purchased Cameron his commission in the hopes that he would not return? He'd not hidden his desire to sire more sons with his new wife. Bile churned in his gut whenever this question taunted him.

What in the hell did all of this have to do with Louella?

Cameron urged his mount along in a futile attempt to purge the memories from his mind. He'd been on the road for barely an hour, only recently passing through the local village. Already he experienced misgivings at abandoning her so harshly and guilt for refusing to give his wife the comfort she'd sought. Why had he given her the tools, the blades, and bandages, to continue her habit when they'd been in London if he'd not expected she would use them?

Had he been so deluded as to believe that his affection and attention could ever be enough?

Cameron removed the flask from his pocket and poured the harsh liquid into his mouth.

Burning. Hot. Familiar.

Relief.

"Hand it over, *Your Grace*. If you're starting early, I might as well, too." Cameron had practically forgotten Kingsley riding beside him. He plugged the opening and tossed it to his friend.

After tilting the drink into his mouth and then wiping his lips along the sleeve of his jacket, Kingsley again broke the silence. "I cannot imagine Her Grace was thrilled at your departure."

Cameron scowled, initially imagining his stepmother's response.

Ah, but no. *Louella.*

Damn him, but he'd refused to hear her explanation. What had she been trying to tell him? He wouldn't put much stock in any promises. How could he?

And yet, she'd seemed so earnest.

Discomfort gnawed in his gut.

"Whether or not she was thrilled has no bearing upon the necessity of this journey." Cameron didn't feel at all himself. He was never short with acquaintances and friends. He'd never imagined speaking so disdainfully to his wife. It reminded him too much of his father.

Cameron felt Kingsley's curious stare and shrugged. He wouldn't discuss Louella with anyone. Theirs was a private matter.

Kingsley laughed. "Already wanting to slip the harness, eh?" He tossed the flask across to Cameron again.

He did not wish to *slip the harness.* But something was missing between himself and his wife.

Trust?

Acceptance?

Love?

Was he wanting these from her?

He shook his head, afraid to contemplate the emotions he experienced where his wife was concerned.

Cameron could not embark upon such a discussion while sober. He ought not to embark upon it at all. But Kingsley, despite his own attitude toward marriage, possessed an honorable character and seemed to be his only friend.

"She's not happy with me, Kings." The moment he spoke the words, he wondered if they were true. God, he sounded like a petulant and spoiled child.

"In bed?" Kingsley would ask such a question first and foremost.

"Hell, no. Matters in bed are more than... I'll not discuss

this with you, damn your eyes." Cameron swallowed more of the whiskey.

"Ah, so what doesn't she like about you, my friend? Your good looks? Your lowly title? Your diligence in caring for your responsibilities? The friendly and respectful manner in which you treat those around you?"

The questions held more than a little sarcasm, and yet they gave Cameron pause. What about him did not make Louella happy? She'd never expressed finding any particular fault with him. He'd apologized for his egregious behavior toward her sister. And she'd been adamant that she'd put that in the past.

He'd frightened her on their wedding night when he'd pummeled his father. And then on their return journey from London. But she'd forgiven him both times, hadn't she?

Cameron shook his head, unable to pinpoint what he'd done or hadn't done that would cause her to fail to be satisfied with him.

"Did you ask her?"

The question rocked him. He hadn't.

Cameron glanced over his shoulder. They were an hour away by now. He really could not go back. The first meeting was to commence tomorrow morning. Already, they would be riding past sundown.

If he returned to Ashton Acres now, took the time to hash all of this out with Louella, he'd have to travel through the night to uphold his promise.

"She'll be there when you return," Kingsley reminded him.

Cameron rolled his shoulders in an effort to release the tension gripping him. He'd shared too much. "Of course, she will." And yet a dark memory taunted him.

He'd gone away to school assuming all would be the same when he returned, only to be horribly disillusioned. His mother had died. His father had remarried.

Ridiculous for him to draw comparisons between then and

now. He would listen to her explanation upon his return. Surely, she knew this? And she would forgive him, of course.

Wouldn't she?

"Hell and damnation," he said without thinking. Ten years ago, he'd walked away from his responsibilities. Nay, he'd run.

Duty beckoned. The situation between Louella and himself must wait. He straightened his spine with purpose. "Let's go over our game plan again."

Kingsley nodded, amenable to the change of subject.

Nothing Cameron could do now.

He grimaced, feeling empty inside.

* * *

Louella stared at the unoccupied doorway for several minutes after her husband departed. The silence, which had been comforting before, was deafening now. Her heart gaped in emptiness.

But no tears came.

She did not hate him. She could never hate him. His words swirled around in her head though.

He'd been angry with her. Disgusted to think she had been at it again. But he already knew about it.

There had been something else. Almost as though, in truth, he'd been angrier with someone else. His father?

Himself?

You are so very unhappy? All of this is not enough? The children? A home? But the words she suspected he truly meant to say taunted her. Had he been asking her instead if *he was not enough?*

He was everything she ever could have dreamed of. Yes,

things had been difficult between them recently. But their marriage showed promise. Or it had, anyhow.

"Your Grace?"

Louella jerked when a small voice interrupted her thoughts from behind the room divider.

Luke!

She stilled and then flinched. Had the boy been there the entire time? Had he seen her drawing her own blood? Heard the argument?

"Come out, Luke." Her voice emerged harsh. He ought not to have been in her chamber. But with whom was she the most angry? The child who'd been hiding in her room? Or herself for doing something he ought not to have seen? Or Cameron for refusing to listen to what she'd discovered?

She closed her eyes in an attempt to calm herself and then softened her tone. "I won't punish you, Luke. But I want you to come here."

First, those pale blue eyes of his peeked out, and then, upon seeing that she did not appear to be ready to thrash him, the rest of him moved into view.

This child. So brave. Small for his age. Lost in a world completely unfamiliar to him. Afraid to trust anything new, already having had so much torn away.

"You should not have come into my chamber without permission." She must make this clear. "And you ought not to have remained hidden."

He nodded with a grimace. "I'm sorry, Your Grace."

Louella found it difficult to meet his knowing gaze.

"I wish you hadn't heard all that—seen any of that." Dear God, she'd likely ruined this child for life. What should she tell him?

Before she could come up with anything else to say, he asked, "Why do you do that? Hurt yourself with the needle?"

Why indeed?

Because if she could focus on outside pain, she could ignore the inside pain. As though a curtain had been lifted with this child's innocent question, her actions of the past few years suddenly, undeniably, emerged crystal clear.

A choked sob caught in her throat. "Because I hurt inside." She dropped her knees to the floor so that she could talk to this lost little boy without looking down at him.

"Why do you hurt?" Another innocent question.

"Because I haven't always done the right thing." She would be honest with this child. "I haven't always *felt* the right thing."

This seemed to confuse him. He tilted his head, still watching her carefully. "So, you punish yourself?"

But it hadn't been a punishment. Had it? "At first. A little. I think."

"I've heard of men marking their bodies with ink. In far-off lands." Luke's eyes lit up for a moment at such a thought.

Ah, but such a boyish dream. Likely, Cameron had dreamed of worldly travels as a boy, away from his father's overbearing presence.

She shrugged. "I don't like that I've marked up my arms." She held one out for him to see the lines. "I suppose I didn't like myself very much."

But she'd done it for reasons other than to punish herself. It had made her feel *better.*

"But you did it today. Do you still not like yourself?"

At this, she finally could smile. She'd felt some of the euphoria at first but would have had to cut a great deal more to bring on the comfort she'd desired. "It wasn't the same today. I suppose I'm beginning to like myself more now."

He smiled back.

Since the day they'd taken him home from the funeral, this child had not smiled at her once. He'd looked at her suspiciously, angrily, defiantly. But *now* he would smile at her.

For my weakness.

"You are a duchess, after all." A sly little grin. He reached out and grabbed her arm. At first, she wanted to resist. His close scrutiny embarrassed her.

But this child.

Gripping her wrist with one hand, his other traced small fingers along the white lines she'd so carefully carved over the years. "You shouldn't hurt yourself. You're a nice lady." He lifted his gaze to hers. "You still want to keep us? All of us?"

She nodded, giving his question the seriousness it deserved. "I do. We do."

"Where did His Grace go?"

"London. Would you mind terribly if I went to London to fetch him?"

"You'll come back?"

"Of course, I will." Without hesitation, she opened her arms.

Studying her scars one more time, Luke squeezed her hand. "Then I suppose it's okay." And then he stepped into her embrace.

She needed to go to Cameron. She needed to find him and make him understand.

Because at that moment, she was beginning to understand herself.

* * *

Louella had never arranged a journey before. Her father had, and then her husband. And she needn't only make arrangements for herself. Several little people depended upon her who would need to be cared for in her absence.

And big people, apparently, who would share their opinions with her.

When she introduced the subject that evening, over the

dining room table, Martha and Cora jumped into the conversation immediately, insisting she not go alone. Even Lillian added her opinion. She thought Louella ought not to go at all.

"Crawford would much prefer you await his return here. What if highwaymen accosted you? Or your coach was to break down? Whatever has given you such urgency can wait." The eldest girl met her gaze earnestly.

"I cannot imagine anything that would send you gallivanting off at such a time as now. Especially with all of the children about." Estelle, as the dowager had requested Louella address her, had resisted the Smith orphans at first, but more recently showed appreciation of some of the twins' antics. She'd joined the maid on one of their walks. "Unless you have pertinent news for him." Her brows rose in question. "In which I think you ought not to risk your health by traveling at all."

Pertinent news? But... oh, no! "No. No! Nothing like that."

"Then it most certainly must wait." Estelle lifted her knife to carve a small bite of venison.

No. Louella could not wait for however long Cameron might be gone. Good heavens! He'd mentioned the possibility that he might travel north to inspect some of the dukedom's more distant estates. By then, he might set his heart completely against her, thinking she cared nothing for him or their future. Thinking she would forever torment him with her cuts.

Thinking that she found some sort of fault in *him*.

"We've fought," Louella admitted while gazing at her mostly untouched plate. "And I need to apologize."

At these words, she had their full attention.

More embarrassment. More exposure.

She'd not discussed anything so personal with any of them, these women who were her new family. How much would they wish to know? Had she offended them by saying this much?

"This fight. It was... serious?" her mother-in-law asked carefully.

"It was." Taking a deep breath, Louella dropped her fork, lifted her hands, and slowly untied and then unwound the ribbon around her wrist. For the moment, no servants were present. What she was going to do squeezed her heart tight.

She hated the idea of showing anyone, but somehow, it was important that she be honest.

The other ladies looked on curiously, a little confused at first, but then with widened eyes when Louella reached one arm into the candlelight.

She inhaled deeply, closed her eyes, and did her best to explain. "We fought over this. And before you ask, I do it, I did all of it, to myself. It's a horrid, horrid habit, much like biting one's nails." The worst part of it. "It scares people. I'm sorry if it scares you. Cameron hates it. I want to stop."

She'd expected to experience shame, but instead, her spine straightened, and her voice became stronger. "I know it doesn't make sense. Why anyone would do this. I am not happy about the scars. The wrist bows." She met Martha's gaze with an apologetic wince. "They are not about fashion at all. But I couldn't let anyone see them. I'm sorry to have misled you, all of you. I have many faults."

Martha leaned forward. "Do you use a knife? Some sort of blade? Doesn't it hurt?"

Louella shrugged. "I usually use a sewing needle. And it's always been a pain I've embraced. In the past, it released something inside of me. I wish I could explain it other than that I liked how it made me feel."

"You continue to do this?" Cora's words were more of a statement than a question, practically an accusation. For yes, the more recent cut stood out harshly, appearing to be almost black.

"I hadn't for a few weeks. And when I did today, when Cameron found me, it wasn't the same." This was oh, so very personal. But she was tired of hiding. She was done pretending she was anything *more* than any other girl—any other lady.

"And so, you and Cameron argued." Lillian's expression was serious but otherwise without judgment.

Louella nodded. "Yes."

"Well then." Estelle arranged her cutlery carefully upon her plate. "I imagine it's most imperative that you explain all of this to your husband. Sooner, yes, rather than waiting."

One look in the dowager's direction and Louella knew her mother-in-law was to be her friend and not somebody she would forever be challenged by. The woman offered her something she hadn't expected. Understanding, yes. But also, surprisingly enough, acceptance.

"I'm afraid that if matters remain, that we might not..." She couldn't even voice such a thought.

She loved him.

She loved her husband!

"And quite right for you to consider this." The elegant and rather formidable lady turned to her daughters. "Lillian and Cora, the two of you shall accompany Louella, as well as her maid. Four outriders, of course. That ought to deem the journey safe and respectable. If you leave early in the morning, you can arrive at Crawford House before dark tomorrow."

"But, Mama! What about me?" Martha was obviously not pleased to be left out.

"You, my dear," Estelle answered firmly, "shall assist me with all of these children."

* * *

With the dowager's support behind her, the plans for Louella's journey fell into place almost effortlessly. The next morning, as the sun crested the horizon in the east, Louella, Lillian, Cora, and Jane climbed into a most elegant carriage while the dowager and Martha watched from the door of the manor.

"Bring me a present!" Martha raised one hand and waved.

"This isn't a pleasure trip," Lillian groused.

"I'll see what I can find!" Cora called as the footman closed the carriage door securely.

Louella sat beside Jane, front-facing while her two sisters-in-law arranged themselves on the back-facing bench.

They'd been so busy the night before that Louella hadn't had any time to regret telling so many people her secret. She'd intentionally ignored the fears that arose whenever she imagined Cameron's reaction to their arrival.

He'd been none too happy with her when he'd left. What if he wasn't there?

Of course, he would be there. He'd been angry but he'd never lied to her.

But what if he didn't want to listen to her? Refused to hear her out?

She'd have to make him. He was her husband, after all. Not some stranger.

Louella bit her lip and stared out the window.

"Do you think you can stop doing it?' Cora broke the silence that had settled over the four women.

"Don't ask her that!" Lillian shushed her younger sister.

Jane covered her face with both hands and shook her head. Louella had told her maid, and Jane had been terrified for her. "What if your mother learns of this? What if they tell the vicar? Or worse Mrs. Fry? She'll tell everyone! You'll become an outcast. They'll send you off to Bedlam."

Louella hadn't considered any of this when she'd told them, but her new family had been raised as daughters of a duke. They would know the importance of discretion. She had no choice but to trust them.

Telling one's secret to close family was one matter. Sharing it with the entire village, quite another.

Glancing across the carriage, Louella was surprised to see that Cora wore a bow tied around her wrist.

"I hope so," Louella answered. "It... didn't feel the same last time. I don't want to do it anymore." She didn't know what else she could tell her. "Please. Don't ever try it," she added suddenly. Cora was young and impressionable. As was Martha. "It isn't worth it."

Cora looked horrified, but Lillian nodded in understanding. "I had a talk with Martha last night. She quite looks up to you, you know."

"I wish I'd never started it. I didn't realize what I was doing when I did."

"We know." Lillian turned her head, seeking agreement from Cora.

Cora nodded as well.

"Do you think you can patch things up with Cameron? Once he sets his mind against a person, he doesn't change it easily." Of course, Cora would be remembering the breach between Cameron and her stepfather, the late duke.

A chill passed through Louella. "I hope so."

After such an eventful evening, the night before, all four passengers seemed inclined to remain in their own thoughts, making conversation scarce for the remainder of the journey. Perhaps they sensed Louella's misgivings. Perhaps they were wary of her after all that she'd shared.

By the time the carriage rolled up to the familiar townhouse that night, Louella's nerves were tighter than the strings on a harpsichord. A stoic butler greeted them, showing no surprise despite their failure to send the household staff any notice.

"His Grace is out," he informed them, however.

The four ladies met one another's eyes. Was he at a club? Would he return that night?

She didn't think she could handle it if he'd found solace with another woman. She set her chin and refused to contemplate it.

Unwilling to invite further pity, or attention, for that matter, Louella forced her lips to smile calmly. "I'm ready to retire for the night, myself. Traveling oughtn't be so exhausting, should it? When all we do is sit and ride for most of the day?"

After an uncomfortable pause, Lillian agreed, and Cora shrugged. They bid one another good night and Jane led Louella to the mistress' chamber.

Louella had considered the chamber she'd shared before to be plush and luxurious, but this one was even more so. The walls were covered with tasteful gold and maroon wallpaper, set off by warm brown carpeting and a deeper colored maroon counterpane and canopy. Such elegance.

Fraught with fear, she wished she could appreciate all of it.

"Do you really think you'll stop this time?" Only Jane would dare to ask Louella such a question. But she had every right. She'd lived with it for as long as Louella had.

Could she? Would the thought of drawing blood always lure her? Fearful of the encounter to come, the sewing box tucked away at the bottom of her trunk taunted her.

But other thoughts crowded the urge. Thoughts of Luke, Cora, and Martha.

She did not want to carry this darkness into the future.

"I hope so, Jane." The words came out something of a whisper.

Jane studied her closely, as though searching for something. "I do believe you will."

Her maid's words nearly drew tears. If Jane could believe in her, perhaps Cameron would as well.

In quiet contemplation, Jane assisted Louella into her night rail, brushed out her long, dark hair, and with an encouraging embrace, bid her good night.

Long after her maid had disappeared into the adjoining dressing room, Louella watched out the window for a rider or coach to arrive.

And damn her, but the longer she waited, the more she thought about her needles.

She tried reading.

She paced the floor.

She considered doing embroidery but didn't want to access her needles. What if he came while she was attempting to thread a needle? What if she accidentally poked her finger and drew a few drops of blood?

She would not do it.

She wouldn't.

Where is he?

CHAPTER TWENTY-NINE

LOVE

"*Y*our wife and sisters arrived earlier this evening," reported Cameron's dedicated manservant, who'd awaited his arrival despite the lateness of the hour. He and Kingsley had spent the past several hours playing cards with Lord Haversham, doing their best to convince him that the new reform bill to be introduced that fall would benefit everyone, not just the poor, not just the children. Kingsley's bachelorhood had been extended once again. Apparently his fiancée wanted her wedding to take place at the height of the season, with all due fanfare of a lady who's had to wait nearly a decade.

But wait—

"*My wife?*" He could not have heard correctly. He'd left his wife, abandoned her practically a full day's journey away.

"Yes, Your Grace. And Ladies Lillian and Cora."

Cameron couldn't have been more surprised if he'd been informed that his father awaited him, back from the dead. "When did they arrive?"

"Earlier this evening, a quarter past ten, I do believe." Longley showed no reaction that his new master had had no knowledge that his duchess and sisters were to join him here in London.

Fear clutched his heart. So many tragedies recently. Had she come to inform him of another?

Not taking time to question the valet further, Cameron sprang to life and ran up the stairs, skipping every other one. At first, he looked for her in the suite they'd shared on their prior visit, but finding it empty, realized she'd be in the suite that adjoined his. Of course. Damned houses were too big. Too complicated.

He spun around and dashed to the front. Upon arriving at her chamber, the mistress' chamber, however, he checked himself from entering unannounced. He could have entered via his own suite, which adjoined hers unfettered, but instead, rapped twice on the solid mahogany door before him.

He'd promised once not to enter her chamber unannounced, hadn't he? He had, but he'd failed to keep such a simple pledge.

Why was she here? Why had she come?

The last time she'd been here had been their wedding trip. Nearly a fortnight of unadulterated bliss until word had arrived from Ashton Acres.

His heart dropped into his stomach as he imagined one of the children falling ill or being injured. But Louella wouldn't have left them. She'd have sent somebody else.

After what felt like a lifetime, the door pulled open, and she peeked out. Red rimmed her eyes, and tendrils of hair had escaped the braid Jane would have carefully knotted earlier.

"You're here." She bit her lip, tentative and nervous.

He'd done this to her. He swallowed hard. He'd hurt her.

"May I come in?" His voice sounded more gravelly than he expected. He'd only been away from her for two days, but God, how he'd missed her.

His bed had felt empty. Cold. He'd not slept well the night before.

She nodded and pulled the door wide for him to enter.

Her white cotton gown fell to her toes and covered her from wrists to neck. He would not demand to see her arms ever again.

He loved her, but he wanted his love to be enough. It would have to be, because he wanted her beside him.

The counterpane on the tall bed was ruffled, and only one candle had been lit. He turned around at the same time he heard the door click shut.

"I'm sorry—"

"I'm sorry—" They both began at the same time.

She clasped her hands in front of herself, primly, considering the intimacy they'd shared in the past.

"I missed you. I shouldn't have left like that." He would go first. She had come. He would make amends for how he'd treated her. He would no longer allow the cuts on her arm to come between them.

Before he could say another word, she jammed her sleeve up, almost to her shoulder, and shoved her arm toward him. "I haven't made any cuts since the children came to Ashton Acres, and I don't know why I did yesterday. But I only made a few. I didn't finish." She shook her head. "I didn't want to."

Cameron blinked. Staring at her arm, he required a moment to process her words before flicking his gaze back to her face.

Please understand, her eyes seemed to be begging.

"I stopped. It wasn't the same," she added.

Please understand.

God, how he loved those eyes. And her lips. Everything about this woman had come to command his soul.

"I doubt the urge has magically gone away, and I don't want to mislead you but—"

"You stopped that day? Before I entered the room." He lowered his brows. But he would not expect her to stop for him. Except a glimmer of something light began to fill his chest. "Why did you stop? Wait. You don't have to answer that—"

"I want to answer it." She licked her lips. "I want you to know. I want you to know everything. That is, if you want to."

Cameron hadn't expected any of this. He'd barely come to recognize the extent of his own imperfections. But—"I do." His eyes burned into hers fiercely. "I do, Louella."

She nodded at his assertion and then seemed to organize her thoughts. Cameron wanted to take her into his arms but held himself in check. All of these barriers needed breaking down. He wanted to make love to her without any of the doubt that had crept into him before.

"It didn't work the same. It didn't feel right. And I kept imagining if Cora, or Martha, or Luke, or even you were to do it. How it would make me feel. I had never imagined it hurting others before. I tried. But I never felt it." She lifted her fist to her breast. "In here. I don't want to hurt anyone. Using my needle isn't going to fix anything. Even the momentary relief didn't help. But it's never had anything to do with our marriage. I didn't expect I could ever be so happy with the husband chosen for me by my parents. You are more than I ever could have asked for. More than I knew I wanted." She shook her head, looking as though she couldn't find the exact words she needed. "I—"

Something broke inside of him and in one swift motion, he took her into his arms, pressing her cheek into the wool of his jacket. Could she hear how loud his heart was beating? Could she feel the pulse of it pounding beneath her ear?

He'd been such a fool. He'd not really listened to her. He'd never truly understood, so muddled had he been in his own opinion of himself.

She'd *never* rejected him in any way.

"Dear God, I love you, Louella," he said into her hair. "I haven't been able to stop thinking about the horrid way I spoke to you. You didn't deserve any of it. Will you forgive me?"

She nodded beneath his chin. He loved the feel of her soft curves beneath the flimsy night rail she wore. So vulnerable, so feminine. He'd make love to her. Every inch of her. She'd never have to hide from him again. He'd make damn sure of that.

"I'm sorry I got angry. I had no right. Can you ever trust me again?"

* * *

Could *she* ever trust *him* again? But she was the one who had lied!

"Can *you* ever trust *me* again? I hurt you! I lied about cutting my feet the night of our ball! I hid it from you. I lied!"

He took hold of her face and met her gaze. "You did. But I told you I would not try to stop you. And broke that promise. I expected that if I could give you things, if I could satisfy you, you'd be happy enough as my wife and then you would stop. And then I got angry with you when it didn't work. That wasn't fair of me."

Louella blinked away tears. He had given her so much since they'd married, even before. He'd shown her sensual delights and an intimacy she'd never imagined.

She had been happy.

Mostly.

They'd not truly known one another. It had been a beginning. And if the mine hadn't caved in, if his father hadn't been killed and then the Smith children needed a home... Well, perhaps they would have grown closer.

But all of what they'd found when they'd returned to Ashton Acres had been real. It had caused both of them to adapt to new roles they were unprepared for.

It had nearly broken them.

She bit her lips. Was she still sleeping? Was he really saying all these things? She'd come prepared to force him to hear her out. She'd lain awake for hours worrying that he would not want to see her.

And now... She watched his lips as he said all the words she'd dreamed of.

"I've realized what knowing you has done for my soul. I didn't think I needed anybody. I didn't think I needed to be needed or wanted to be needed. But having you, loving you, has somehow given me purpose. Allowed me to find meaning in life again. Real meaning."

What? Had he said that he loved her?

"It was as though I was simply passing through life before. But since you..."

"You love me?" She tilted her head back so that she could see the truth in his eyes. And it was there, shining, clearly, emphatically. So much love.

"I'm utterly filled with imperfections." Such a silly thing to remind him of. But she said it nonetheless.

He would know this more than anyone else.

He lifted his hand, the one he'd injured on the ship. "As am I. And I'm not talking about the outside. I'm a sorry bargain for certain. I have conflicted feelings about my position in life. I hated my father and yet see a great deal of him inside of myself. I drink too much. I forget to bring my wife flowers. I—"

She placed her finger over his mouth. "Shush." She smiled. "Together, we are perfectly imperfect." She could hardly believe that this charming, handsome, thoughtful man could love her, and yet he did.

Thank God he did.

"I love you." She grasped his other hand and kissed the place where each finger had been cut. As she did so, he dropped his face to the curve between her shoulder and neck and feathered his mouth along the sensitive skin there. "I especially love that you are not perfect. Heaven knows what I'd do if you were."

He chuckled at her words, but his mouth continued mapping a path down her shoulder. His lips journeyed past the curve of her upper arm, all along, tasting her, dropping kisses.

To her elbow, the tougher skin on the back and then to the softer, almost translucent skin at the crease.

And then he dropped to his knees, licking a trail along the inner skin of her forearm. He would feel the ridges of her scars with his tongue. Louella swallowed hard, unrecognizable emotions churning to the surface.

"I love all of you. Oh, my love." The heat of his breath made her heart flutter and her lips begin to tremble. He was kissing a particularly long ridge. Swirling his tongue over it. Worshiping it with his mouth.

"We have battle scars, my love. And they won't disappear merely because we want them to. We cannot will them away."

With a choked sob, she nodded. "I know." She knew she'd feel the lure of the needle again. Perhaps it wouldn't be so strong. Or perhaps it would be. She didn't know.

But she knew she loved this man, and not hurting him by hurting herself was reason enough to fight the lure.

He then seized her other arm and pushed up the sleeve; this one scarred more recently with the dark line of her blood neatly placed between the lighter pink and white lines. "They are a part of you." He gazed at them in awe as he drew a line along one of them with the tip of his finger.

Watching him study something so personal about herself, she felt vulnerable and yet utterly safe.

"They are you. They show me how you survived."

"My battles," she laughed at herself, "seem so petty compared to the very real battles you've waged."

But he was shaking his head. "Sometimes, the battles we cannot see are the most difficult of all." And then he lowered his lips again.

The feathering of his mouth sent tingles up her arm, into her chest, into her very soul. His touch on her arm was not relief. It was not escape. It was something she could hardly comprehend.

All those times they'd made love before – she'd never felt so close to him.

She'd never felt so close to anyone.

And then his face pressed into her abdomen, and his arms wrapped around her waist. "Louella."

Her breathing hitched and another fire lit inside of her. A fire that had her clenching her thighs together, anticipating an even more intimate touch from him.

"Cameron." She clasped her hands in his hair, heat at her core igniting the need to be closer.

She'd missed him. It was as though she'd missed him her entire life.

They would heal together.

He rose to his feet and in one effortless motion, lifted and carried her to the large bed, all the while his gaze caressing her face.

He'd told her he was not perfect. He'd admitted weaknesses he'd hidden from himself for most of his life. He'd thought he was like his father.

"You are not like him." She shook her head. "Perhaps you share a few insignificant characteristics, but in the qualities that matter most, you are your own person."

He made himself comfortable beside her and grimaced. "I find myself wanting to exploit the mine." The thought sent the slightest unease racing through her but then she glanced at his work-worn hands. She remembered how grim he'd been at every single funeral and how angry he'd been at his father's insistence upon accelerating production.

"But you care. You will be patient and you will make certain of the workers' safety. And of your own," she added at the terrifying thought that something could happen to him.

"Of course. Of course." He closed his eyes, almost as though he couldn't bear to look at her. "But as I've examined the estate books..." He shook his head in disgust. "I've discovered the monies are needed greatly. So many repairs are necessary for tenant conditions to improve up north. I—"

And again, Louella touched his lips, halting his speech. Challenges lay ahead of them. "Not so that you can gamble, nor for your own comfort. You do not wish to mine the gold out of pride or in order to boast. You see need." She swallowed hard. He was not like his father at all.

No wonder he'd been so overwhelmed when they'd returned. He'd been forced to cope with multiple deaths, his stepmother and sisters' grief, his own grief, and all the responsibilities that came with the title.

And she'd acted so foolishly, like an immature child.

"I'm sorry for adding to your burdens," she whispered, her voice failing her at what she'd done. "How can you ever forgive me?"

"You are not a burden, Louella. Never." And then his mouth was on hers again, the warmth of his tongue sliding easily past her lips, tasting, sliding along her teeth, stroking the roof of her mouth.

She arched her back, needing more. Needing him to fill more of her.

No more talking right now. No more hiding. No more barriers.

He drew her gown up, almost frantically now as she tugged

at the waist of his falls. They would join together, sealing new promises, consummating new vows of love.

And then he was in her, filling her, his lips never leaving hers, his hands clutching the sides of her head.

"Louella," he said into her mouth, their primitive motions engulfing her completely.

Nothing in life could have prepared her for this union. They'd made love but it had never been like this. He'd shown tenderness with lust. They'd experienced that together. But this was different.

Everything she had, her very essence, belonged to him. And in the sounds that he made, in the desperation of his touch, she knew he felt the same.

"I love you." He thrust deeply, his eyes glistening as he lost himself in her. Lightning exploded in her core and then spiraled throughout her.

"I love you." She gasped on the words as he buried himself deeper, pressed harder, and moved deeper still.

As the warmth of his seed seeped into her, she clung to him, knowing he would always be her anchor, her only love, her soulmate.

Perfect. Absolutely perfect.

EPILOGUE

HOSTING A BALL

"Estelle has assured me everything has been taken care of but what if the musicians are late? What if we've forgotten to invite somebody important? You did give Kingsley his invitation, didn't you?" Louella fidgeted with the ribbons on her arm.

Tonight was the first ball she and Cameron would be hosting as the Duke and Duchess of Crawford. Earlier that day, she'd made her bow to the queen in that ridiculously uncomfortable dress, and they were to celebrate the occasion in the magnificent Crawford Ballroom. Along with a taffeta and velvet gown, and the heavy train, Louella had worn lace ribbons on her arms – not because she needed them to cover new cuts but because the bows had become a fashion statement, even in London.

Beneath the lace, white lines remained and would require years to fade, but she'd gone thirteen and a half weeks without cutting, and before that, she'd gone ten.

"The musicians arrived an hour ago, we haven't forgotten anyone, and yes, Kingsley will most certainly be making an appearance. Now hush. Have I told you yet how imperfectly beautiful you looked this afternoon? I was almost afraid to touch you in that gown." Her husband of nearly ten months nuzzled the skin behind her ear.

"I'm glad you don't feel that way now," she whispered.

Nobody comforted her the way that Cameron could. Acceptance, encouragement, support, and, of course, that heightened sensual awareness that sparked between them.

His hand dropped to her abdomen and covered it protectively. "Are you certain this isn't too much excitement for you? I've always thought a woman in your condition required rest."

Butterflies danced in her heart. She'd only realized she was expecting two weeks ago, and her husband had become unusually attentive. He'd even suggested they forgo the Season, which she'd adamantly refused. They'd done that last year.

Excitement buzzed through her at the knowledge that a future little Captain Lord Cameron Samuel Benjamin Denning, Marquess of Stanton, was growing inside of her.

"It may just as well be a little Louella Rose." How did he do that?

"Either way, I'm so happy!" She'd thought it would happen sooner, only to be disappointed month after month.

Cameron had worried as well. She'd known that. But each time her monthlies had arrived, he'd only reassured her. And often, made love to her, evil man that he was. A wicked smile played upon her lips at the thought.

"As much as I'm game, we haven't time for that." But then his tongue did something absolutely amazing along the line of her jaw. She never could have imagined the intimacies they shared.

Louella moaned. Would it be so horrible to be a few minutes late?

The answer came with a loud knock on her chamber door. "Louella?"

Louella enjoyed her husband's embrace for one second

more before he stepped away and adjusted his perfectly tied cravat. Given a few minutes more and poor Longley would have had to spend ten or twenty minutes tying another knot.

"Come in!" Louella bid her sister.

Mary had swept Olivia's golden hair into an elaborate knot of tiny braids. Her dress had been made especially for the occasion. This would be Olivia's first ever London ball. She'd refused to allow Louella to make her a guest of honor, insisting that she would be far happier to sit inconspicuously with all the other wallflowers.

"You shall not be a wallflower for long, Livvy. You're looking lovely this evening." Cameron stepped across the room and placed a kiss on Olivia's cheek. He then turned back to Louella with a teasing glint in his eyes. "I'll double check all those details and then return to escort you downstairs."

Oh, how she loved this man. He, more than anyone in the world, understood how she felt about her sister. "Thank you, my love."

He winked and then closed the door softly behind him.

When she turned again, to view her sister wringing her hands nervously, she frowned.

"Louella, what if Mama was right? I have no wish to ruin your ball." She stared into Louella's vanity mirror. "I could wait until later in the Season, or better yet, next year."

Louella bit her lip. "Do you not *want* to have a Season, Olivia?"

Olivia closed her eyes tightly. "I do. Oh, I do. It's just–"

"Mama and Papa have exaggerated your wandering eye for far too long. I don't even notice it anymore. You must give the rest of the world the opportunity to see beyond it as well." Louella would like to wring her parents' necks sometimes. "If you want a Season, it is yours to take."

Olivia inhaled deeply and then met her gaze and nodded. "You are correct. How did my younger sister become so wise?"

"From her older sister, of course." Louella grinned in satisfaction.

She couldn't help thinking her sister's ensemble required something else, however. And she knew exactly what it was. In fact, she'd spied it earlier that week when Cameron had taken her shopping to celebrate the continued success at the mine. "I have a gift for you."

As she withdrew the velvet box from her bureau drawer and then opened it to reveal the amethyst pendant necklace and earbobs, Olivia gasped. "I cannot. Oh, Louella, I cannot."

Louella withdrew the necklace first and lifted it over Olivia's head so that it rested just above the décolletage of her sister's gold-trimmed lavender gown. "It reminded me of your eyes. As soon as I saw them, I knew they'd been made for you."

Olivia's hand fluttered up to touch the cool stone. "I feel like a princess."

Which was exactly how Louella wanted her to feel.

After donning the earbobs and repinning a few stray hairs, Olivia seemed far more self-assured than she had when she'd first stepped into her chamber. And as much as Louella hated to admit it, there were times when wearing expensive jewelry was far more effective at bolstering a girl's confidence than the most lavish of praise.

Cameron returned just as the ladies finished. "Everything is going exactly as planned," he told her before she could ask after the musicians, or the flowers, or the... "Are you ladies ready to greet our guests?"

Olivia smiled.

"Oh, yes." Louella slipped her hand in Cameron's arm to be led downstairs.

"The two of you look far too happy," Olivia teased.

Louella grazed her hand across her belly for the barest of moments and leaned into her husband. "That's because we are, Olivia." She grinned. "Imperfectly so."

***

Did you enjoy reading Louella and Cameron's awesome love story? DON'T MISS **Olivia's Story: THE PERFECT SPINSTER,** now available!

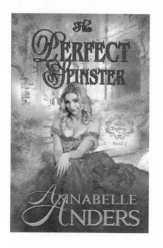

FIRMLY UPON THE SHELF... Miss Olivia Redfield labors under no misapprehension that anything other than spinsterhood lies in her future. Not for lack of dowry, or breeding, or education, but because of one tiny flaw.... one might even call it... a curse. Removed from society for this ill-fated defect, she's resigned herself to caring for others in a somewhat dreary existence. Until, that is, she falls for the charming but unattainable, Lord Kingsley.

Book 2
Olivia's Story: THE PERFECT SPINSTER

THE PERFECT REGENCY SERIES

The Perfect Debutante

Louella and Cameron

The Perfect Spinster

Olivia and Gabriel

The Perfect Christmas

Eliza and Henry

The Perfect Arrangement

Lillian and Christian

ABOUT THE AUTHOR

Married to the same man for over 25 years, I am a mother to three children and two Miniature Wiener dogs.

After owning a business and experiencing considerable success, my husband and I got caught in the financial crisis and lost everything in 2008; our business, our home, even our car.

At this point, I put my B.A. in Poly Sci to use and took work as a waitress and bartender (Insert irony). Unwilling to give up on a professional life, I simultaneously went back to college and obtained a degree in EnergyManagement.

And then the energy market dropped off.

And then my dog died.

I can only be grateful for this series of unfortunate events, for, with nothing to lose and completely demoralized, I sat down and began to write the romance novels which had until then, existed only my imagination. After publishing over thirty novels now, with one having been nominated for RWA's Distinguished ™RITA Award in 2019, I am happy to tell you that I have finally found my place in life.

Thank you so much for being a part of my journey!

To find out more about my books, and also to download a free book, get all the info at my website!

www.annabelleanders.com